The Inheritance

Howard Linskey is the author of a series of crime novels set in the North-East, featuring detective Ian Bradshaw and journalists Tom Carney and Helen Norton. Most recently, he has written standalone thrillers including *Alice Teale is Missing* and *Don't Let Him In*. Originally from Ferryhill in County Durham, Howard now lives in Hertfordshire with his wife and daughter.

By the same author

The Drop
The Damage
The Dead
Hunting the Hangman
Ungentlemanly Warfare
No Name Lane
Behind Dead Eyes
The Search
The Chosen Ones
Alice Teale is Missing
Don't Let Him In

The Inheritance

HOWARD LINSKEY

PENGUIN BOOKS

PENGUIN BOOKS

UK | USA | Canada | Ireland | Australia
India | New Zealand | South Africa

Penguin Books is part of the Penguin Random House group of companies
whose addresses can be found at global.penguinrandomhouse.com.

First published 2022
001

Copyright © Howard Linskey, 2022

The moral right of the author has been asserted

Set in 12.5/14.75pt Garamond MT Std
Typeset by Jouve (UK), Milton Keynes
Printed and bound in Great Britain by Clays Ltd, Elcograf S.p.A.

The authorized representative in the EEA is Penguin Random House Ireland,
Morrison Chambers, 32 Nassau Street, Dublin D02 YH68

A CIP catalogue record for this book is available from the British Library

ISBN: 978-1-405-94511-0

For Erin and Alison

Chapter One

'Did you bring it?' the old woman asked, with the urgency of an addict needing a fix.

'Yes.' He showed her the canvas bag he was carrying and took his seat opposite her, setting the bag down on the floor next to him. 'But this isn't strictly necessary, Evelyn, not if there is going to be a will.'

She snorted. 'Wills can be contested, Dickie. This one probably will be. I want to be sure I'm taken seriously. Then no one can say, "The batty old girl obviously lost her mind at the end."'

'I'm sure no one would . . .'

She cut him off. 'Money brings out the worst in people. Distant relatives come crawling out of the woodwork and start grasping for everything. I will not have it, you hear?'

'As you wish.'

'Set it up then.' She was getting impatient. Evelyn hated to waste time on pleasantries and loathed small talk. Heaven help anyone inane enough to remark upon the changeability of the weather. She would give them what he always called her 'death-stare'.

He began to rummage in the bag for the equipment.

'Time is the one thing I do still value,' she told him.

Evelyn watched as her solicitor took the video camera out of the bag then placed it on the tripod, turning the camera so that the lens was pointing straight at her. He checked the framing and decided it would do.

'Ready?' she asked.

'I just have to press this red button.'

'Good,' and she gave him a questioning look as to why he wasn't doing just that.

'Okay,' he said, 'on three.' Then he counted, 'One . . . two . . . three,' and pressed the button. Evelyn sat up straight, her face serious, her voice clear.

'I, Evelyn Moore, being absolutely of sound mind, do hereby leave everything I own to my niece, Sarah Hollis . . .' then she paused for a second, perhaps for emphasis, and leaned a little closer to the camera, before adding, '. . . on one condition.'

Chapter Two

A few minutes later, she was done. Evelyn didn't mess around. Every moment had to be used. Dickie thought of Kipling then. 'If you can fill the unforgiving minute with sixty seconds' worth of distance run.' That was Evelyn Moore all right.

'Why now?' he'd asked her, when she had insisted on him coming to see her today. 'I've been on at you for years to get your estate in order.'

'It wasn't urgent before,' she said quietly.

'And it *is* urgent now?' he asked her gently.

'I'll be gone by the end of the year,' she told him matter-of-factly, and he was shocked. What was she? Seventy? How could this whirlwind be dying?

Dickie sat silently through the whole recording, while Evelyn outlined her wishes. When it was over, he turned off the camera and she waited for his response. Her solicitor had handled every legal transaction Evelyn had been involved in since he had helped her agent with the finer points of a publishing contract years earlier. 'You did a decent job on that,' she had told him then. 'Now, I want you to buy me a house and not just any house. I want Cragsmoor and no one can know it's me, not even the seller. *Especially* the seller.'

That was thirty years ago, when Dickie was still a relatively young man. Somehow, he had managed to purchase the house and its entire contents for her, though they were quite possibly the most fraught months of his life.

Now, he felt he had to summon the courage to tell it to her straight. 'Have you lost your mind, Evelyn?'

He braced himself for the storm that would surely follow, but in true contrarian fashion Evelyn burst out laughing. It was almost a cackle. 'Maybe I have.' She nodded slowly, before repeating quietly, 'Maybe I have.' And then, 'But it's my money, Dickie, and I have no brats to leave it to.'

'But you do have family,' he reminded her, 'apart from this niece?'

'Distant family,' she retorted. 'I haven't seen any of them in years and you know why, Dickie. Sarah is the only one worth a damn. The rest can whistle. I'm not leaving them a penny.'

'You can do what you want with your money. It's just the . . .' he faltered, '. . . unusual nature of your bequest to Sarah. It is conditional and the condition, if you don't mind me saying so . . . or even, in fact, if you do . . . is . . .'

'Stop waffling, man,' she interrupted. 'I know it's not normal, but what part of my life has ever been normal? I'm not doing this out of eccentricity or ego. I am in full control of all my faculties. I'll get my doctor to write you a note confirming this, if you wish?'

'That might be wise.' He was sure someone was bound to challenge a will containing such strange conditions.

'I'm expecting you to defend me, Dickie, once I am gone. Tell them what I want and why I want it.'

'Why *do* you want this?'

'Justice,' she told him, 'plain and simple. People read

4

my books then talk about what I meant by this or that and the themes I explore in my writing.' Evelyn didn't enjoy anyone trying to analyse her. 'Love, hate, revenge, betrayal – but they all miss the most obvious one. Justice! For the victims of murder and those left behind to mourn them.'

'Of course.' It seemed obvious now.

'But *I* never got it,' she explained. 'I never cheat my readers, there are no loose ends in my books, but real life isn't like that. I spent thirty-six years with a very dark cloud hanging over mine. My dear friend was taken from me. She disappeared one day and not a trace of her was ever found. There was no body for burial, no funeral service; she was never even officially declared dead. There was no end to her story.

'The grief was made worse by my inability to explain her disappearance. It became my obsession. It's why I asked you to buy me that house and everything in it. I thought I'd find the answer somewhere in her family home because that was the place she was last seen in, but no.' She looked so sad then. 'I'll be in my grave soon. I don't believe in the afterlife. I think you have one go at this and if you mess it up, well, tough. I doubt Lucy will be waiting for me on a cloud, with the name of her killer on her lips, because make no mistake, she was murdered, Dickie. I just don't know who it was or why, though I have my suspicions.

'I have to accept that I will die never knowing the truth, but that doesn't mean I have to give up. Let someone else pick up the baton, go over it all again with a fresh pair of eyes. I've come to the belated conclusion that I was too close to Lucy to ever see this one clearly. Perhaps my niece will finally solve this mystery for me and get justice for Lucy.'

'But the police couldn't find the answer,' he said. 'What makes you think Sarah might be the one to solve it?'

'Because she has a very sharp mind, Dickie. You'll see.'

'All right then,' he acquiesced.

'If she can do this within six months of my passing, then she will inherit everything,' Evelyn told him firmly. 'If not, then it goes elsewhere.'

'So, she gets the lot,' he concluded, 'but she has to catch a killer first?'

'Exactly.'

Chapter Three

Eight Months Later

Sarah was an idiot. She had caught the mug with her arm as she reached for the milk and had upended the tea, spilling it over the countertop and down her dress. She grabbed the hem to avoid getting burned but the dress would no longer do. Now she would be late for possibly the most important appointment of her life.

Idiot, idiot, idiot!

She had to root around in her wardrobe to find a suitable skirt and top, wondering if there was even a point to this. They were going to fire her, she knew it. Her career was over before it had begun. Why else had she been summoned to lunch by her publisher and was simultaneously unable to get hold of her literary agent? Sarah was an author not an employee, so it wouldn't be a case of getting her P45 and a nice little redundancy cheque to tide her over. They just wouldn't bother to renew her contract, but it would amount to the same thing. Sales of the last book had been 'underwhelming', the one before that 'disappointing'. 'Not your fault, of course', though 'we probably need a bit of a reset.'

Oh God.

It was the lunch invitation that really sealed it. That normally only happened to celebrate the completion of a book and she had barely even started the new one. Perhaps they would tell her not to bother. She was out of contract anyway. Sarah felt as if she was barely getting started, but three books in three years had come and gone so quickly. Now it was probably all over and she was still only thirty-two.

Three years since she had pitched up in London as a young author with a book deal and hope in her heart. Let's not forget the two failed relationships during that period and no fewer than four different day jobs, because writing wasn't that lucrative, for her at any rate. Sarah had to double up with a career, if you could call it that, freelancing at anything vaguely matching her 'skill set' and experience. Editing, copywriting, proofreading, even writing occasional articles that sold for little money because so many amateurs were happy to write for free these days. 'They're not as good as you, of course,' she was told by one website editor, 'but they cost nothing, so . . .' He meant it was no contest, obviously.

Each of Sarah's jobs had ended due to economic conditions beyond her control. The start-ups and even the medium-sized companies that used her went to the wall, swept away by the perfect storm caused by Covid and Brexit. All of them were insolvent now and Sarah knew how they felt. She didn't even have a family home to run back to any more. Both parents were gone. That was the price of being the only child of a late, second marriage. You were barely an adult when you became an orphan.

Sarah would have been grateful for a good lunch in a nice restaurant under normal circumstances. She hadn't been able to afford to eat out in months, but this was different. She could feel it. She had re-read her editor's message several times and tried to read between the lines, but emails don't have a tone of voice. 'Come to lunch, for a catch-up.' Why? Because we love you, or because we are about to hold your wake?

She had emailed her literary agent three times and received no reply. In an effort to rouse Victoria from her torpor she messaged, 'I'm a big girl. I'd far rather get bad news than no news.' Yet still her pleas went unanswered.

Sarah's imagination ran riot. That's what happens when you sit at home on your own all day, she concluded. You become increasingly paranoid. She tried calling Victoria, as she walked briskly through the West End streets on her way to the lunch. When her agent finally picked up her phone, Sarah demanded why she hadn't responded to her emails. 'Not seen them, doll. I'm on holiday, remember? . . . Didn't I mention it? Don't tell me I didn't put my out-of-office on?'

Sarah confirmed she hadn't, through gritted teeth.

Then she told her about Andrew's invitation. Victoria pondered this. 'I've not heard anything, but that *is* a little strange.'

'He's firing me, isn't he?'

'Over lunch? I doubt it, Sarah.'

'I'm out of contract and they've been dithering about making me an offer for the next book for ages.'

'They do seem a bit reticent,' Victoria conceded, 'but let's not panic yet, shall we?'

Easy for you to say. You don't have to find the rent money. It was worse now that she lived on her own. Chris had been a shit boyfriend, but at least he was usually good for half of the rent before she finally kicked him out. Victoria always gave the impression that money was just something other people worried about. Christ, Sarah would be evicted if she couldn't get a deal for the new book.

'When are you meeting him?'

'In fifteen minutes.'

'Probably not much point in me trying to track him down at this late stage, then?' Sarah did think there might be a point. It could prevent her from bursting into tears in front of everyone during her main course. 'Why don't you just go along and see what he has to say?'

Sarah managed to arrive on time, only to get an apologetic text from her editor. *He* was running late now and couldn't get a cab. She drank a large glass of wine in the bar to calm her nerves and ordered another when he still hadn't turned up. He finally arrived thirty minutes later looking flustered, and immediately ordered a bottle to take to their table by way of apology, before insisting on giving her every detail of what had caused his delay, including an overrunning meeting and 'horrendous' traffic, then picking up the menu to peruse it. Perhaps it was the wine she had already consumed that led Sarah to abandon caution and manners, but she suddenly blurted, 'I'm sorry, Andrew, but could we cut to the chase, because this is killing me.'

'How do you mean?' He lowered the menu.

'I'm talking about the reason for this lunch. I'm out of contract, no offer has been forthcoming, my agent seems . . .' *Disinterested?* Sarah settled on, '. . . out of the loop. I just want to know what's going on.'

'Ah, I see.'

'It's over, isn't it?'

'In a manner of speaking.'

'You're letting me go.' She picked up her glass and took a very large swig of wine to fortify herself against the pain of rejection.

'Letting you go?' he repeated, confirming her worst fears.

'Knew it.' But he was frowning at her and she realized it had been a question, not a statement.

'It's really more a case of handing you over to someone else,' he clarified.

Another publisher? There was no guarantee she would ever get one. Sarah had to face it. She was toast.

'I suppose I could change my name,' she said reflectively. 'Be a sexy debut. A virgin all over again.' She would have to write something on spec, get her agent to send it to all the publishers under a nom de plume and pray someone liked it.

'No, no,' he said quickly. 'I meant another editor. I'm leaving, Sarah; retiring, actually, so I won't be able to take on your next one. By the time you've finished it, I will be gone.'

'Oh, thank God,' she clasped her hand to her chest in relief.

'I didn't expect you to be that pleased,' he said dryly.

'I'm so sorry. I didn't mean it like that, Andrew, but I've just spent a week panicking. I thought you were throwing me on the scrap heap.'

It was his turn to apologize. 'I didn't think that's how you'd take it. It was just an invitation to lunch.' And he was right, it was. Sarah felt incredibly foolish all of a sudden.

'Yes, I can see that now.'

'I know sales of the last two have been . . .'

'Shit.'

'Below par,' he corrected her. 'But that's common enough in any writing career. Peaks and troughs and all that. You'll come good in the end. Too good not to,' he reassured her with a warm smile.

'Thanks, Andrew.' But did he really mean that?

'Your new editor will make you an offer,' he said vaguely, and she guessed he meant the same money or possibly less. 'We've hit a few economic headwinds this year.' Definitely less, then. Bugger. But at least she was *getting* an offer. She took another stress-sip of wine and realized she wanted to get absolutely wankered out of sheer relief. Crisis averted, for another year at least, but what then? Park that thought for now.

Sarah felt emotionally drained. She felt warm, light-headed and already quite drunk.

'She's joining us shortly,' said Andrew.

'Who is?'

'Poppy,' he said. 'Your new editor.'

Oh, no.

That afternoon, the inner voice that liked to point out Sarah's shortcomings would not leave her alone.

The poor bloody woman must think I'm a psycho.

Did I say anything that made any sense? Anything at all?

Was I actually slurring at one point or was that just my imagination?

What a wonderful first impression to make on my young and incredibly bright new editor. Half-pissed at lunchtime and she probably thinks I'm like this every day.

Those bloody wine glasses in the restaurant were enormous, she recalled, but then no one forced her to drink so many of them. In truth, there was nothing Sarah could recall saying or doing that was too embarrassing, apart from at the end, when she gave Andrew a farewell hug of such intensity that it probably shortened his life, because she was pathetically grateful that he had actually published her at all, let alone three times.

Yep, she will definitely think I'm a psycho.

But that still wasn't the worst bit. Oh no. The worst bit was when her new editor had asked her how she was getting on with her new book. 'Very well, I think,' Sarah had lied. She'd hardly written a word, or rather, she had actually written quite a lot of words but most of them would have to be discarded because they were so awful.

Her new editor seemed strangely uninterested in this reply. She had something else on her mind.

'Actually, I came up with a bloody good idea to max the hell out of your next book.' The editor's supreme confidence in her own idea was already off-putting. Sarah knew this wasn't going to end well.

Chapter Four

Sarah avoided the underground, turning the journey home into a sizeable walk so the fresh air would sober her up. She had been under considerable pressure to agree to her new editor's big idea but she knew it wasn't right for her. Not right now. Not ever, in fact.

Poppy failed to mask her disappointment or her surprise. 'Why not? Everyone knows you have a famous aunt and Andrew tells me you were close. What could be a more fitting tribute than a sequel to her greatest work, *The Gallows Tree*, written by her talented niece? Think of the exposure,' she urged. 'Think of the sales! This could be the answer to all our problems.'

Viewed coldly through the prism of her ambitious editor's young eyes, there was a business logic to Poppy's suggestion. But Sarah had always sworn that if she was going to make it as an author, she would do it without cashing in on her aunt's name or trying to copy her.

The discussion had been polite but lengthy, finishing with an uncertain 'Well, if you're sure?' from Poppy, who regarded her as if she was hell-bent on career suicide. I've made an enemy of her already, thought Sarah.

Worse than that, Poppy had told Sarah that, due to financial restrictions, she wouldn't be in a position to make an offer for Sarah's new book until it was complete. Sarah wouldn't earn a penny until then. If she hadn't been under enough pressure to deliver an amazing book already, her refusal to play ball with the publisher had just ramped up her stress levels. 'You'll have it by the end of the year,' she assured her new editor, setting herself a deadline in the process.

Sarah dug into her handbag but couldn't find her front door keys. By the time she located them, a strange man was standing by the door to her apartment block, staring at her intently.

'Sarah Hollis?' She recognized the man but couldn't quite place him. He was short, portly and dressed in a grey raincoat too tight for him and carrying a laptop case. He looked to be in his late fifties. 'I'm here about your aunt Evelyn.'

'Are you a journalist?' She was about to decline an interview on her doorstep.

'Solicitor,' he corrected her. 'Your aunt's solicitor.'

'The funeral,' she blurted, 'I saw you there.' Along with precious few others, nearly all of them from Evie's publishing house. The service had been short and the wake sparse, in line with her aunt's long-held view. 'Why should I pay for a party I can't attend?'

The solicitor explained he had been sitting in a café across the street waiting for Sarah to return. Why hadn't he just called or emailed her?

'Your aunt preferred to do things face to face,' he explained.

She invited him into her tiny flat, which was a strange place for a meeting about legal matters, but she assumed whatever he wanted to discuss with her wouldn't take long.

It was still hard to accept that Aunt Evie was dead. She had been a much-loved but eccentric presence in Sarah's life since her earliest childhood memories. No one lives forever, but Sarah always had the suspicion that, if anyone could, Aunt Evie might have managed it. Now she was gone and Sarah would never be able to call on her again, to hear Evie's opinions on books (a necessity), writing (a shared passion as well as profession), life (still a mystery), men (largely untrustworthy), politicians (wholly untrustworthy) and the cost of everything these days (increasingly exorbitant). In the end, it was cancer that took her.

'Thank you for coming, Mr . . . erm . . .' He had told her his full name but, as usual, Sarah had forgotten it within seconds. Why did she always do that?

'Your aunt used to call me Dickie.' He seemed to be inviting her to do the same. 'I'm here because Evelyn asked me to follow her detailed instructions, in person. Your aunt had a substantial estate.'

'She told me she had just enough money to pay the rent,' said Sarah. 'Aunt Evie lost a lot of money in the financial crisis. She said the rest went to the taxman.'

'That was a white lie to protect her from grasping relatives and fair-weather friends. Evelyn knew that this way if someone took the time to visit her, it wasn't in the hope of an inheritance.'

'Oh, I see.' Except she didn't really.

'She owned the apartment with no mortgage. She also owned a sizeable manor house in Northumbria, and there's money too.'

Sarah opened her mouth to say something but no words

came out. She was in complete shock. Her almost penni-less aunt turned out to be anything but.

'She has named you as her sole beneficiary,' he said and before she could digest this, he added, 'but not without conditions.'

'Me?' She was stunned. It wasn't as if there was anyone else, aside from a few of Evie's cousins that Sarah had never met, but it was still a surprise to learn there was any-thing to bequeath. Evie always said she preferred dogs to humans and that whatever remained at the end of her life would go to Battersea Dogs Home. Then the second half of his sentence belatedly registered with Sarah. 'But there are conditions?' Were they typically eccentric, like swear-ing off marriage for life or agreeing never to have children? That would be classic Evie. It might even be worth it, to move from a state of severe financial insecurity to a level of comfort.

'There is *one* condition, chiefly.'

'And that is?'

'To use her own words, she wants you to catch a killer.'

Sarah stared at Dickie, half expecting him to explain this was a joke. 'Did you just say ... a *killer*? Are you serious?'

He sighed. 'This would have been so much easier if she had explained it to you before she passed, but I'm afraid Evelyn insisted you weren't to know until she was gone. She told me she trusted you to do the right thing.'

'The right thing? You mean she wants me to turn into some sort of bounty hunter to catch a murderer?' she asked in disbelief. 'They *are* dangerous, presumably – if they've already killed someone, I mean?'

'The authorities were unable to identify the killer at the time,' he explained, 'or even to prove that a murder had in fact been committed.'

'You don't actually know that a crime took place?' She was starting to feel utterly bewildered now.

The solicitor looked apologetic. 'Evelyn was convinced it did take place. A body has never been found but a woman did go missing years ago and she was never seen again.'

'What woman?'

'Lucy Woodfell,' he told her, 'your aunt Evelyn's dearest friend.'

'And Aunt Evie was convinced she was murdered?' He nodded. 'And now she wants me to identify a killer who has eluded the authorities since . . . how long ago, exactly?'

'Thirty-six years,' he said.

'Thirty-six! Should be a doddle! And then what? Bring him or her to justice?'

'Exactly.'

'But they might not even be living.'

'Most of the persons of interest identified by the police are still alive and in the region. The family members live in cottages that were held in trust for them after the estate was purchased.'

'There are *persons* of interest?' she asked. 'Plural? Not just one?'

'Your aunt has written all of this down for you,' he said a little helplessly.

'How kind of her, and where did this not-officially-a-crime take place?'

'At Cragsmoor Manor,' he said, 'the Woodfell family home.'

Her aunt had never even mentioned the Woodfells or her supposedly dearest friend to her. 'So that's the crime scene. How do I get access to it? Can I even do that?'

'That's the easy part,' he explained. 'It's the manor house in Northumbria I mentioned. It was formerly the victim's home.'

Sarah considered the implications of this. 'You're saying that Aunt Evie bought the place?'

'Along with its entire contents,' he added, 'following the collapse of the estate into near bankruptcy.'

'And she did this when? After this person disappeared from there?'

'Some six years later.'

'Why did she do that?'

'I believe it was so she could look into the case herself. The police had wound down their own investigation by then. Evelyn told me she searched every inch of the house and gardens looking for clues, though she never found any.' He thought for a moment. 'She visited the estate often over the years, did a lot of her writing there as a matter of fact, even though I think she always felt a little haunted by her memories of Lucy. Evelyn said she felt drained when she returned to London after one of her stays there.'

Not morbid at all, thought Sarah. 'But why ask me to do this?'

'She said you have a very sharp mind.'

Sarah blinked at him. 'She wasn't starting to lose it towards the end, was she?'

He shook his head. 'Evelyn told me you wrote intricate, complex mysteries that were impossible to second-guess until the very end and that she ought to know.'

'Yes, but that was fiction!' Sarah was pleased to learn that her illustrious aunt thought so highly of her work, but the feeling of pride was offset by a rising sense of panic. She couldn't possibly live up to Evie's expectations. 'I'm no good in real life. I can solve *my* mysteries because I write them, but I can't investigate cold cases.'

'Your aunt rather thought you could,' he said, as if that was the end of the matter.

'If I find the guilty party, I inherit, but if I don't, what happens then?'

'Then you will not become the beneficiary of Evelyn Moore's estate.'

'So where does it go?'

He gave her a thin smile. 'To the Conservative Party.'

'You're joking, right?' And when he said nothing, 'You're not joking. Is that intended to wind me up?'

'Your aunt was fully aware of your more left-of-centre leanings politically and felt this might concentrate your mind.'

'It does,' she admitted. Sarah was hardly an activist but she did take a keen interest in politics. She always considered herself to be soft-left in her political views, whereas Aunt Evie tended towards a more Thatcherite ethos of self-reliance, causing occasional arguments between them. The thought that this inheritance might end up going to a political party instead of a worthier cause definitely increased her motivation. 'But it might take ages. How much time did she expect me to devote to this?'

'Evelyn didn't want you to waste years on it or to live in false hope. There is a time limit. You have six months.'

'From when?'

'Today.' Then he added, 'It's May the thirty-first, which means your deadline is November the thirtieth.'

'I have to come up with the name of Lucy Woodfell's killer by the end of November?'

He nodded. 'And I will need proof. Something that could lead to an arrest and a conviction in a court of law. You can't just point at someone and say, "It was him."'

This already seemed like an impossible task. 'But what am I supposed to live on in the meantime?' she asked. 'I can't play amateur detective for months. I have to finish a book and make some actual money from it, not pin my hopes on the vague promise of a possible inheritance, if I solve a mystery no one else could.'

'Evelyn suggested you relocate to Cragsmoor Manor for that period, saving months of London rent. You can write your book there, while also undertaking the investigation into Lucy Woodfell's disappearance. A living allowance will be provided from the estate. I am permitted to advance you up to twenty thousand pounds for your time spent looking into the matter.'

'*Up to* twenty thousand? What does that mean, in reality?'

'It means, we can discuss a suitable sum for this work.'

'But the maximum I am permitted to receive at this point is twenty thousand?'

'Correct.'

'Then I want the twenty grand,' she told him firmly.

'You are expected to justify the amount,' he protested. 'Do you really need that much?'

'It's not about *need*, it's compensation for uprooting myself and spending months investigating something with little guarantee of anything at the end of it. It's not worth it otherwise and you will have failed to grant my aunt's dying wishes.'

He held up his hands in a gesture of surrender. 'Give me your bank details and I will send the money to your account.' He couldn't resist adding, 'You do rather remind me of her. She didn't like to negotiate either.'

'That *was* a negotiation,' she told him. 'You just didn't notice.'

Chapter Five

The rest of the meeting included a viewing on Dickie's laptop of the recording Aunt Evelyn had made outlining her final wishes, followed by a personal message to her niece. It felt strange to be sitting there watching a woman who had been a big part of her life since she was a child, speaking to Sarah as if from beyond the grave.

'Hello, Sarah.' Evie half smiled. 'I expect you think I have gone quite mad, but I simply want to finish the one story I have been unable to complete. Like the books we both write, this one involves a mystery and, I am almost certain, a murder. My dearest friend, Lucy, went missing and stayed that way for thirty-six years. I wonder if you can imagine the distress that caused me?

'I want justice for Lucy. She deserves it and so does the perpetrator of what must have been a truly terrible crime. We tend to forget the victims. Have you noticed that? In the newspapers and most of the books, they are always two-dimensional. You get a name and an age, a physical description and perhaps a few words on what their loss meant to their family, but most of the coverage focuses on the details of the crime and the killer. Lucy was real, dammit! I think we knew each other about as well as it is possible to know another person. I have mourned her loss for so long and I want a resolution, even if it comes after I have gone.

'Are you wondering about the police? They were no bloody good. Too stubborn and unwilling to delve deeply into the Woodfell family secrets. Too in thrall to their ancient name and influential friends. There were other suspects too, and their stories didn't stack up. One of them got a life sentence for another murder but was never charged with anything concerning Lucy.

'I admit I could never see this one clearly. My grief prevented it. That's where you come in, Sarah. With a keen mind like yours and a fresh pair of eyes, I feel sure you will find something. Even if you fail, I know you will do your utmost, and that is all I can ask of you.

'I have tried to help you, by writing everything down; about Lucy and me and her family, and how they became such a large part of my life, almost by accident. I started this process a while ago, before my diagnosis. It began as a memoir, written for my own satisfaction, and still reads like one, I suppose, because I have no idea what information will prove useful to you. I have never written so many words in such a short space of time. Impending death is the ultimate deadline. It certainly concentrates the mind. Why did I do it, instead of lying here waiting for the end? Because I had to. You need to read this before even attempting to speak to anyone in that family. Be warned; they are a slippery bunch and will only give you their time if forced to.'

Evelyn grimaced then as if in pain or discomfort. 'I'm going to stop now because I am so very tired. I don't fear death, Sarah, but I do dread the prospect of leaving this life with unfinished business. Maybe you will have better luck than I did. I do hope so.'

And with that the old woman fell silent and the recording ended. Sarah felt emotionally drained from seeing Evie again like that. It made her realize how much she missed her.

Dickie snapped her back into the present. 'I expect you are wondering about the value of the estate? Your aunt didn't wish you to know exactly how much it was worth, in case it distracted you. She wanted you to focus on the disappearance of Lucy Woodfell. The reward comes afterwards, if at all. In any case, it's quite hard to put an amount on it because of the manor house.'

'Why? Is something wrong with it?'

'It's five hundred years old, Sarah. There's almost always something wrong with it. Evelyn spent an average of thirty thousand pounds a year just to keep it in good nick, the heating bill alone is colossal and there are also the staff.'

'She has staff?'

'Part-time employees who tend to the house and gardens.'

'Bloody hell, I've inherited staff,' she mused but he was quick to put her right.

'Not yet, you haven't.'

'Not until I've found a killer. Yes, I get it, but what if I do find him . . . or her . . . and they try to kill me too?'

There was quite a long pause then until he admitted, 'We never really discussed that possibility.'

'What did my dear departed aunt expect? That I would solve this like a crossword puzzle and the killer would immediately confess then come quietly?'

'She was convinced you would know the best course of action,' he reassured her.

'Was she?' Evie clearly had far more faith in her than she had in herself. It would have been touching in less unusual circumstances.

'If you are going to speak to people about the case, you'll need to get around. There is a car at the manor house and I'll add you to the insurance. Take the train there and I'll expense the ticket.' Then he added, 'That's if you want to do it, of course. It's your choice, Sarah.'

The temptation to take this case on, however difficult it might prove to be, was high. There was nothing really keeping her in London any more, though she would still miss the place. Living in the capital always made her feel as if she was at the heart of everything. Twenty grand was quite a lot of money, even for someone who was not worried about making ends meet, like she was. Throw in the additional prospect of living rent- and bills-free for months and it would make a massive difference to Sarah financially.

'And if I find nothing, I get nothing?' she asked. 'Nothing more, I mean.'

'Correct. Evelyn gave me two sealed letters: one to be opened if you succeed and the other if you do not. They will confirm everything, apparently.'

Sarah found she was almost getting used to Evie's idea, however eccentric. There was a certain cold logic to it and the case sounded intriguing.

'All right,' she said, 'I'll do it.'

'Excellent.' Dickie seemed relieved he'd managed to persuade her.

Sarah thought for a while and eventually said, 'I don't have the faintest idea how to begin this.'

'Getting started is the hardest part.'

'I'm pretty sure the hardest part will be proving someone murdered Lucy Woodfell.'

He reached into his bag and took out a wire-bound book. It looked like the proof copies publishers produce for reviewers, in advance of publication. 'I thought it best to get her handwritten version typed up for you.'

The manuscript had no title, except for three block capital letters printed on the cover.

NFP.

'What does NFP stand for?'

'Not For Publication. This is Evelyn Moore's own story,' he told her with some ceremony, 'her last work, in fact, written just for you.'

It took Sarah some time to process everything Dickie had told her and far longer to accept it all. The fact that her aunt had never confided in her about any of this made it doubly shocking. They were close, but Evie had never mentioned the prospect of an inheritance – had even lied to Sarah about her finances, when it turned out she was a woman of considerable means. Sarah had been unaware of the manor house in Northumbria and had never heard of this Lucy Woodfell. Why had Evelyn never mentioned her closest friend, let alone the fact that she had gone missing? Why was she so determined for Sarah to investigate the woman's disappearance and not a private detective or retired policeman? It was madness.

It could also be the answer to all of Sarah's problems. She had descended on London filled with hope, but time and money were both running out. She did not want to get mixed up in a possible murder, however intriguing, but she could certainly use the inheritance, if by some miracle she could actually crack the case. For weeks now, Sarah had tried to tell herself that something would turn up and now, bizarrely, it had. Aunt Evie had seemingly ridden to the rescue, but only if Sarah could solve a problem that had baffled everyone else for more than three decades. I'm not greedy, she thought. If Evie had just left me a few grand it would have been nice. Instead, she's trying to leave me a small fortune, but how the hell am I going to earn it? I'm no detective. Where would I even start?

Chapter Six

Sarah half expected to find that Lucy Woodfell wasn't real, but information on her wasn't hard to find online. She was real all right, and had gone missing just like Dickie said.

Lucy disappeared back in 1986, at the age of thirty-four. She was spotted walking away from Cragsmoor Manor by four witnesses, heading towards a track that led to the beach. She was never seen again.

Archived newspaper footage online shed some light on why the case had fascinated reporters. Lucy was from an eccentric, aristocratic family, which made her doubly interesting to a tabloid's voracious readers. She was described as 'a beautiful and kind-hearted socialite with a job in publishing'. Perhaps that was how she had met Sarah's Aunt Evie. Others wrote that she was a debutante whose family had fallen on hard times, so there had been no coming-out party for Lucy. If they were broke, it would explain why Evie had ended up owning their ancestral home, if they were forced to sell it. There was blue blood in the family and reporters hinted vaguely at links to royalty, but these appeared to be distant.

There were a few pictures of Lucy on the web. In one, she was riding a horse, in hard hat and jodhpurs, and in another she sipped champagne at a wedding. One of the red-tops had managed to get hold of a photo of Lucy in a bikini on a foreign beach somewhere. One photograph in particular caught Sarah's eye. The police had used it in their appeal for information on Lucy's whereabouts. She was standing slightly in profile but her face was turned towards the camera. She was outdoors and Sarah got the impression the photo might have been taken by a close friend, possibly even a lover, as Lucy's eyes were staring intently back at the camera and there was the faint trace of an enigmatic smile on her lips. She was certainly an attractive woman. The photograph was taken a year before Lucy disappeared and there was something about the way she looked in it, so poised and confident, which made Sarah feel her disappearance more keenly somehow.

There had been several members of Lucy's own family in the manor house that day and Sarah noted down their names. Her oldest brother was called Oliver and there was another brother by the name of Freddie. Lucy had an older sister too. Persephone Woodfell was there that day with her young son. Along with the child's nanny, they were the last people to see their sister alive. If only one of them had witnessed her departure, then Sarah might have been suspicious of that account, but it was unlikely they all lied about it or that they somehow conspired together, to abduct or murder Lucy, so who else could have been responsible?

Lucy had said she was going to the beach and hinted she might not be back for a while. Because of this, the police speculated she might have been secretly meeting someone. But who? Was she killed by a secret boyfriend or married lover, perhaps? Sarah realized she was already becoming intrigued and wanted to know more.

She read further and discovered there were two main suspects who were identified early on, neither of them family members. An eighteen-year-old man called Warren Evans was taken in for questioning. He had been sitting alone on the beach for most of that afternoon. Warren had argued with his girlfriend and she had described him as the jealous type. She had walked off and left him there. Warren had been seen at different times during that day, by occasional passers-by, who confirmed he was sitting right at the end of the path that led from Cragsmoor Manor down to the relatively secluded stretch of beach there. He did not deny this but said he never saw Lucy, a claim the police evidently thought preposterous, judging by their reaction to it, which was to keep on questioning him for hours. Warren never changed his story and they were eventually forced to let him go due to lack of evidence, though they made it clear to journalists that the young man remained a 'person of interest'.

David Young was the next to attract the attention of the police because the local man was already a self-confessed killer. A fortnight before Lucy Woodfell had disappeared, he had beaten Megan Smith to death. David considered her to be his girlfriend but she was less committed to their relationship. This was not a premeditated killing but one carried out in a rage, caused by jealousy or criminal insanity, depending on which expert you believed.

Crucially, David Young had gone on the run after killing Megan and was still at large when Lucy vanished a few miles from his town. He would have known the area; he had been roaming around a wide stretch of Northumbrian coastline and had been spotted more than once but had slipped away again before the police could apprehend him. David had been sleeping rough not that far from Cragsmoor. He might have seen or even stalked Lucy before she disappeared.

When he grew tired of living rough, David Young handed himself in. He immediately admitted the killing of Megan Smith but firmly denied he had developed a taste for murder or had ever seen Lucy Woodfell, let alone attacked her. He was eventually convicted of Megan's murder and given life, but when Sarah keyed his name into a new search, she discovered he was out on licence after serving a long prison sentence. David Young was back in the same area, living at a secret address, only a few miles from his former home, a fact that had caused consternation within the community when he was first released some years earlier. No charges were ever brought against him in relation to Lucy.

Sarah read more and discovered quite damning portraits of Woodfell family members in the media. Oliver and Freddie Woodfell were variously involved in drugs, alcohol and gambling, and Sephy's marriage was described as troubled.

It was at the foot of one of these reports that Sarah discovered an interesting fact about Lucy Woodfell. Her brothers and sister were only her half-siblings. They all shared a father but Lucy was the only child of her mother, Robert Woodfell's second wife, his first having drowned in the Mediterranean while on holiday, in what was described by a tabloid journalist as *mysterious circumstances*, presumably because the word *suspicious* was considered too libellous. It didn't matter. The reporter had made his point.

Sarah stumbled upon the next piece of information about the Woodfell family almost by accident, but that only increased the sense of shock she felt on reading it. The thirteen-year-old child that had been casually mentioned in one of the old archived reports as being present on the day Lucy disappeared grew up to be the man widely tipped to be the country's next prime minister. Toby Ramsay was the son of Lucy's half-sister, Persephone Woodfell, and her husband, the late Captain Alex Ramsay. These days it was hard to turn on the television without seeing Toby Ramsay's distinctive face beaming out from it, a semi-permanent hundred-watt smile in place, often accompanied by his trademark thumbs-up, as if to assure voters that the world was about to become a much better place with him leading their country.

Why hadn't Dickie told her about this connection? Except she knew why. He was trying to persuade Sarah to investigate Lucy's disappearance. The presence of a soon-to-be very powerful man in the missing girl's family would surely complicate matters for her. What if the next prime minister didn't want her poking around in a cold case that might draw unwelcome press attention when he was about to ascend to the highest office in the land, once he had secured the leadership of his party? If that was the case, Sarah knew she would have to tread carefully.

What a family, she thought. However did Aunt Evie get mixed up with them?

Those were the facts. Sarah was able to glean more of the story from a short magazine profile of the 'cursed' Woodfell family and their many misfortunes. There was more recent discussion about the case on true crime blog pages, inspired in part by the unstoppable political rise of Lucy's nephew. Contributors speculated freely on what they thought had occurred at Cragsmoor Manor on that fateful day. Lucy had run away; she had been murdered by a serial killer or by a family member with a grudge; a guy took her from the beach; another attacked her in the woods; she was buried somewhere secluded; she had drowned while swimming and the body was never washed ashore; she was secretly buried in the grounds of her family home or was still alive and had been seen in America and Europe. The only thing these theories all had in common was that none of them could be proven. Lucy Woodfell had vanished and, though the police maintained the case was not officially closed, there were 'no leads being actively explored, currently'. In other words, they'd hit a dead-end years ago. She marvelled at Evie's notion that, somehow, her niece would be able to do any better than they could. What in God's name had her aunt been thinking?

Chapter Seven

Thinking about Evie made Sarah feel guilty for insisting on the twenty thousand and threatening to turn the job down if she didn't get it. Then she imagined her aunt applauding that. 'Always know your worth, dear,' Evie used to tell her, and that was something Sarah still struggled with, particularly once she'd realized she might always live and write in her aunt's shadow. If Sarah had been under any illusion that anyone cared about her first book, apart from the fact that it was written by Evelyn Moore's niece, then she was soon corrected. The invitation to host a Murder Mystery weekend, with a very decent fee for an unknown author, had provided her with a clue.

'Tell us all about your wonderfully wicked aunt,' the host had demanded, almost as soon as she was through the door. She had spent the rest of the weekend fielding questions from men and women of a certain age, who would clearly have preferred it if the real Evelyn Moore, famous author of *The Gallows Tree* and a dozen other almost-as-successful books, had been their guest, not her anonymous relative.

Later, once wine had been consumed, the questions became more personal. 'She *is* a lesbian, right? They proved that, didn't they?' The questioner made it sound as if someone had made Evelyn undergo a series of tests to confirm her sexual leanings.

'It never came up in conversation.' And it really hadn't. Aunt Evie never discussed such matters and Sarah certainly never asked her about them. She could tell her audience was disappointed but she was too protective of her aunt's private life to fuel their gossip.

Now she was about to go and live in Evie's secret manor house. It could be fun and maybe even turn out to be the perfect spot for writing. Her imagination might be stimulated by the location, as Evie's had been all those years ago, and she quite liked the idea of at least pretending to be the lady of the manor for a while. For a moment, Sarah imagined herself in one of those classic gothic novels her aunt was justly famous for writing. She was the heroine of *Rebecca*, heading to Manderley, she was Jane Eyre about to arrive at Thornfield Hall, to meet Mr Rochester for the first time. Then she decided that no, she was actually just plain Sarah Hollis, about to visit a crumbling sixteenth-century manor house, most probably on a wild goose chase, but what exactly did she have to lose?

Sarah picked up the bound copy of her aunt's memoir then and began to read.

Sephy called me when it happened. 'Lucy's gone missing,' she told me, and I wasted no time in getting up to the house. They were all there, even Oliver who had been in the process of attempting to forge a reconciliation between himself, Freddie and Sephy when Lucy vanished. Sephy's husband, known as the captain, seemed to be the only one capable of taking charge at that point and he was the initial liaison with the police when they arrived the next morning.

Me? I was in pieces and feeling so helpless. Aside from wandering the grounds searching for traces of Lucy, I contributed nothing.

In fairness to Freddie, he kept the search for Lucy going long after the police had given up hope of finding her. He was convinced she had fled the house to escape the family's constant in-fighting and possibly gone abroad. He went on the radio and TV, appealing for information about his lost sister. He even offered a reward of fifty thousand pounds, a great deal of money back in those days, for the safe return of his sister, and twenty thousand to anyone who could pass on information that might lead the police to her whereabouts.

For a while, virtually every private investigator, adventurer, retired sleuth or amateur detective in the UK seemed to be in on the act, and word about Lucy flooded in from all corners of the globe. She had been spotted in Thailand and photographed in Cairo, though the picture was too blurred to say conclusively that it was her. There was a sighting in Buenos Aires and another in the Philippines, and an old school chum of Freddie's swore he had seen her sitting at the bar at Raffles in Singapore, drinking Singapore Slings, but before he could cross the room to challenge her, she managed to slip away.

I still believe she was murdered and that there were no fewer than six possible suspects. Perhaps I could have narrowed it down further if I'd had an inkling as to why anyone would ever want to kill Lucy.

1. Oliver
2. Freddie
3. Sephy
4. Sephy's husband – Captain Ramsay
5. Warren Evans – the man on the beach
6. David Young – the convicted killer

Assuming I am right and she is indeed dead, then Oliver was one of the last people to see Lucy alive. He was the passed-over elder brother who had been disinherited by his father because of his addictions; first to drugs then to alcohol. Oliver watched from an upstairs window, drink in hand, as she walked away from the house. He described what she was wearing and those items were indeed missing from her wardrobe. He said she carried no bag. If she really was of a mind to run away, would she have travelled so lightly? But if Oliver was lying and he killed her, then why? What did he have to gain from it or what did he have to lose if he let her live? I can think of nothing.

What can I say about Freddie? The self-confidence I so lacked seemed to have been handed to him at birth, because he always exuded it. Perhaps if he'd had a modicum of self-doubt then he might not have made such a mess of his life, but he was trained from an early age, by his family and school, to believe he was part of an elite; born to govern and destined to effortlessly succeed.

Lucy might have found something out about Freddie, but what could it have been that was damning enough by now for any of us to care? That he did drugs? We all knew. That, like his elder brother, he was incapable of running the estate or protecting the family fortune? Pretty much everyone could see that. He quarrelled with Lucy, but then all siblings bicker, don't they? And Freddie was the kind of man who could start an argument in an empty room. It might have been different if she could have inherited the estate, but Lucy was fourth in line behind her brothers and Sephy, and always maintained that she never wanted any of it. Obviously, she worried about the estate being run into the ground until they lost it all, but she still had a decent income from her trust fund. I was never able to link the future of the estate to Lucy's disappearance.

Who else then? Her older sister? If I could take a step back and be cold about it, which I am of course incapable of doing, then I would say Sephy was a more likely suspect. Lucy was a dutiful aunt to young Toby and Godmother at his christening, but I did detect friction between them, as far back as Sephy's wedding. Did she imagine Sephy had sold herself short and was taking the safe option, marrying more for appearance than love? Possibly, but the landed upper classes rarely married outside of their circles and I wondered if there was more to it than that.

Ironically, Lucy then developed a close friendship with the captain and I think she could see just how miserable his wife made him, for theirs was an unequal partnership. He was devoted, she indifferent. Lucy always maintained there was nothing going on between them and Sephy was never jealous of the apparently platonic relationship her sister developed with her husband, but who knows what really goes on inside someone's mind and what might finally make them snap?

As for the captain, personally, I found him quite impenetrable, but he had a history of violence in wartime and may have become too close to Lucy for her own good. Would rejection be a sufficient motive? Murder is a big and almost unfathomable step for most people, but someone killed Lucy. Work out the reason and you are close to identifying the killer.

In one of the last letters I received from her, Lucy told me Oliver was irredeemable, Sephy disgusting and Freddie worse than she had ever imagined, but that was the kind of overblown language we always used. We were quite deliberate in our exaggeration, the hyperbole of our letters designed to amuse each other. We didn't have mishaps, we had disasters, there were no dull days, only twenty-four hours spent in purgatory out of sheer, unadulterated boredom. I had to take that into account when I re-read Lucy's letters and I suggest you adjust for it too. God, we were still so young and full of life. How cruel that hers was cut short.

Chapter Eight

June

First the train was late, then it became absurdly late. Apologetic announcements were made on the tannoy as the train limped along at far below its normal speed and occasionally stopped completely. A signal failure had caused the entire line to grind almost to a halt and cancellations meant Sarah's train was packed, so she had to stand for most of the journey and couldn't read more of Evelyn's story.

Any idle notions Sarah might have had about being welcomed to her new, temporary home by an attentive housekeeper evaporated. The train was three hours late by the time it limped into Newcastle. She contemplated staying there for the night, but a member of the station staff said there was a Metro service leaving soon for the closest town to the estate, which she had been told was a short hop away by taxi. Sarah decided to risk it, partly because Dickie had failed to include a phone number for the estate, so she had no way of contacting its housekeeper to tell her she might not make it after all. She didn't want the poor woman to worry or be kept late at the house, waiting for a guest that did not arrive.

The Metro rattled down a narrow stretch of track and seemed to call at every small town in the county before it eventually arrived at her destination. The station there was tiny and there were no cabs parked outside. She had to walk further into the town, which had a handful of shops, all closed at this hour, and there was no cab firm operating from the high street. In desperation, she walked into a pub and asked the guy behind the bar if he had a number for one. He disappeared and came back with a crumpled business card and the not very reassuring words, 'He might do it for you.'

The name on the card was Aardvark Cabs. *Guess who wanted to be first in the phone book*, she thought, *when phone books still existed*.

She dialled the number. It rang for a long time, and Sarah would have hung up if the owner of the card hadn't been her last chance of a lift to the estate before the pub eventually closed and she was stranded for the night. The pub didn't look as if it offered accommodation. Would she end up sleeping on a park bench?

'Yeah?' The reply that eventually interrupted her increasingly gloomy thoughts was a low growl.

'Aardvark Cabs?'

'Yeah.'

'I need a taxi from the Red Lion to Cragsmoor Manor.'

'Yeah.' Was *yeah* the only word he knew?

'So, you'll do it?' He seemed to take a while to think this over.

'You want it now?' Had she not made that clear?

'As soon as possible, yes.' Sarah was tired, she was hungry and she really wanted to get there.

'Can't do it now.'

Oh God.

'Thirty minutes?' he offered.

'Yes, that's fine.' Thirty minutes was not fine, but it was much better than no taxi at all.

'Right.' And he hung up.

'Wait . . .' but he was already gone. 'Don't you want my name?' she said, pointlessly. There probably wasn't anyone else in need of a cab in the almost empty pub, so perhaps he didn't need her name.

She ordered a glass of wine and sat down but could not relax. The previous days had been a whirlwind, what with giving notice on her flat and emptying it of her belongings. The flat was furnished and Sarah had few actual possessions, but even these had to be ruthlessly whittled down for her journey north. Anything that wasn't needed was let go. The process was a surprisingly liberating one. As she boarded the train to leave London, Sarah had felt remarkably free.

With thirty minutes to kill before her taxi, she decided to read more of her aunt's memoir. The extract focused on Evie's childhood and the first time she met Lucy Woodfell.

I was born in 1952, presumably out of a sense of duty on my mother's part. She rather gave up on life afterwards and retreated from it, to the bafflement of my father, who regarded her with concern then bemusement and, eventually, outright hostility. When I tried to engage with her as a child, more often than not she would say, 'not now, darling,' or 'Mummy has one of her heads.' I later understood this to mean a migraine, but at the time I wondered if she had other heads that were interchangeable, depending on her mood. Looking back, Mother was probably bipolar, but young people are self-centred and I did not notice her anguish, merely the fact that I appeared to be of no interest to her.

I was a solitary child without friends. I read a lot and invented imaginary worlds, peopled with characters who kept me company. I don't recall a single thing of any real interest that happened to me until I was fourteen, when my father encouraged me to enter an essay-writing competition to earn a two-year scholarship to a private school. St Hilda's was trying to modernize by occasionally admitting bright children of lesser means who could not afford their eye-watering fees – but how they stood out amongst the children of the wealthy or landed.

It was only after I won the scholarship that my father told me St Hilda's was a boarding school. I arrived there in a state of trepidation bordering on terror and was regarded as a curiosity by the other girls, who called me a 'plebeian', thereafter shortened to 'Plebby', a nickname that stuck.

I was placed in a dorm with a group of other girls who were all part of 'Lucy's set' and was either picked on mercilessly or completely ignored. When girls don't like someone, they exclude them, from everything, until they slowly die from it.

The teachers were stern and unforgiving, the girls mean and hard and the school the coldest place I have ever known, even in summer. The only remotely pleasant part of the day was just before bed when we were permitted a cup of cocoa and a sugary biscuit.

I doubt I would have plucked up the courage to ever speak to Lucy from 'Lucy's set', if the girl sitting next to me had not been moved to accommodate her as a punishment for talking in class. Lucy never made me feel welcome, but I didn't feel she was under any obligation to do so, and nor was she a bully.

Our teacher was in vengeful mood that day and decided to humiliate Lucy by getting her to conjugate Latin verbs aloud in front of the class, which she failed to do. Lucy turned quite red, a fact the teacher gleefully pointed out to everyone, noting her humiliation, 'which comes from the Latin *humus*, and what does *humus* mean?'

I knew what humiliation felt like and did not enjoy witnessing someone else's. I wrote the answer in pencil and turned my exercise book so that Lucy's eye would catch it.

'Dirt,' she answered confidently.

Surprise delayed the teacher's response. 'More often soil. So, you occasionally understand something.' She hadn't finished with Lucy yet. 'What is the word for understand?'

I quickly repeated the process, while Lucy pretended to think.

'*Intellegere*,' she answered.

'Yes, well, let us hope that you do.'

Lucy was finally off the hook. When the lesson ended and twenty girls scraped back their chairs, she looked at me and said, 'Thanks, Plebby.' That sounds cruel, but I got a smile and a wink, and it was the first time I felt the tiniest glimmer of acceptance.

Later in the dorm, Lucy's acolytes were appalled by the cow of a Latin teacher and I warranted a mention.

'Plebby?' I heard one girl ask in consternation, as if a simple-minded person had helped Lucy with her Latin.

'She's all right,' said Lucy, loud enough for me to hear.

*

45

A few weeks later, when some cigarettes and a bottle of wine were consumed in a corner of the school grounds that was out of bounds, our headmistress deemed it a hanging offence; the empty bottle and cigarette packet were evidence of depravity that had to be nipped in the bud.

When there was no admission of guilt, all Christmas-related events were cancelled, including the heavily chaperoned Christmas dance, which was the social highlight of the year, since it involved that most mysterious of commodities: boys. We were meant to be bussed to the neighbouring boys' school for an event that was full of exotic possibilities, but I did not much care for either boys or dances. The rest of the school body, however, was plunged into despair.

After days of complaining and crying from my dorm mates, I decided to confess and take the blame so their bloody dance could go ahead, but this wasn't an unselfish act. I had begun to dream of being expelled so I could leave St Hilda's and never come back.

It was not to be.

Instead, I got the ruler, slapped against both palms with enough force to make the pain last well into the evening. I was not to be expelled after all, just beaten, humiliated and starved. I was ordered to go to the dorm room straight after class, with no dinner, so I could think about my degeneracy.

The school dance was now back on, causing a murmur of excitement which was quickly shushed by our teacher. Lucy risked speaking to me in a whisper. 'Did you do it?' I could tell she was sceptical.

At first, I didn't mind missing dinner because the food was never any good, but as the evening wore on, I started to feel hungry. When the girls finally came back into the dorm room, I turned my face away so I would not have to look any of them in the eye. They all filed wordlessly past my bed, each one pausing just long enough to place something on my bedside cabinet. I looked up from my pillow as one of them put her evening biscuit there. The next girl did the same thing. One by one, my dorm mates placed their biscuits on my bedside table until they formed a neat stack. It looked like a little sugary shrine and my heart almost melted in gratitude.

'I stole a glass of milk,' explained Lucy, who was the last one to leave her biscuit and clearly the instigator of all this. She had somehow managed to hide the glass under her blazer, even though the teachers could usually detect an undone top button from a thousand paces. 'Well done, Moore,' she said.

The next day I was accepted.

If I had known all it would take was a beating and a single missed dinner, I would have engineered that weeks ago.

By the time I returned from the Christmas holidays, I had become a sort-of-member of the set. Lucy was nice to me, so the other girls tolerated me. I helped them with homework, as some of them were not all that bright, and could make them laugh by poking fun at myself. I had learned that people were less cruel towards me if I got in there first.

As the school year drew to a close, Lucy approached me. 'I'm allowed a friend during the summer. I wondered if you might like to come and stay?'

When the other girls found out, they couldn't let me simply bask in the moment. 'You know she's asked everyone, don't you?' Marjorie Gallagher told me. 'None of us can come. We're all wanted at home.'

It was classic Marjorie. Not only did she make me feel like a ninth-choice option but she also managed to twist the knife in deeper. Their parents would not release any of them because they were wanted, whereas I clearly was not. 'I know,' I said brightly, 'but I don't have any plans.'

'Evidently.'

Even Marjorie was not going to ruin this for me. My position as a junior member of the set had been hard won. So what if I wasn't first, second or even third choice? Lucy still thought enough of me to extend the invitation.

Father wasted no time in writing back to grant his permission. He was busy with work and Mother's health was 'mixed'. I was too thrilled to even think about Mother's health, which had always been erratic.

We were picked up at the station by one of the estate workers. I was excited but apprehensive as we sped towards the manor house. When we approached the estate, I spotted a huge, ancient, gnarled tree on the corner, set back from a bend in the road, behind a stone wall. Its many branches were so thick they seemed to shut out the light.

'That's a Dule tree,' Lucy told me.

'I thought it was an oak.' I had never heard of a Dule tree.

'It's a tree of lamentation,' she explained patiently. 'They used to hang criminals from it.'

48

'It's a gallows tree?'

'Yes,' she said.

'So close to the house?'

'My ancestors were involved in the law,' she said vaguely. 'They made sure peasants like you behaved themselves.'

'Oh dear, I'm not sure I'll ever learn how to behave.' And we joked about how strict Lucy's family were and that I would end up hanging from a gallows tree, because I used the wrong knife at dinner or cut the nose off the brie.

I'll never forget my first sight of the manor house, which was every bit as grand and imposing as I had imagined it to be. Lucy's home seemed huge to me and every inch of it imbued with a sense of history. It was made of a grey stone, turned darker by centuries of harsh Northumbrian weather. It looked like something out of a Gothic novel, and I was simultaneously excited and a little scared at the prospect of actually sleeping within its walls. If ghosts lurked anywhere in England, then surely Cragsmoor Manor was the ideal place for them to do their haunting.

Above the door, a motto had been carved into the stone. *Dona Nobis Pacem.*

I knew that this was Latin for 'Grant Us Peace', which I can only assume was wishful thinking on their part, for – as I was about to find out – there was hardly a family in England that led a less peaceful existence.

Chapter Nine

Almost forty-five minutes after Sarah called him, a man walked into the bar, saw her sitting there on her own with her bags and asked, 'Cab?'

Christ, he was a man of few words.

'Yes,' she said eagerly, 'I thought you weren't coming.'

'Said I would.' He sounded affronted.

The car had no markings to indicate it actually was a cab. Once inside, he confirmed the destination and fare with Sarah then drove out of town. They spent another twenty minutes travelling along a winding road that passed through a rural area, lined by fields and dark woods. He didn't say another word to her.

Sarah had been told the house was just up the road from the town, but it clearly wasn't, and she was glad she had not been foolish enough to try and walk there. Another thought struck her then. What if it *was* just up the road and this guy, whose name she did not even know and who drove a cab that did not look like a cab, wasn't a cab driver at all? No one else saw him arrive in the bar to meet her, not even the barman who was out back somewhere. Perhaps she would never be seen again.

Stop thinking like a bloody author, she told herself. Why did she always view perfectly normal situations then ask herself '*what if?*' all the time? What if a man jumped out of a car and grabbed that child playing on the swings?

What if that woman suddenly hurled herself in front of the bus and no one knew why? What if a man in an unmarked car pretended to be a taxi driver so he could take women out into the countryside and kill them?

Sarah was seriously beginning to entertain the notion that she had in fact been kidnapped by a monosyllabic serial killer when the car lurched quite severely to the left and pulled over on to a gravel road by the side of the main one. He indicated a large metal gate blocking the car's progress. 'You'll have to walk,' he told her.

Sarah paid him with cash and before she even reached the gate he was gone, turning the car in a tight arc that scrunched the gravel underfoot, before speeding off back the way he had come.

Now Sarah was left standing in the dark entirely on her own. She confirmed the gate was indeed locked against vehicles but was mightily relieved to see there was a gap to one side that allowed pedestrian access to the house, which she still couldn't see at this point. Reaching for her phone, she jabbed at the torch button and that at least gave her some light to show her the way.

Sarah passed through the gap easily enough, but the wheels of her suitcase kept getting stuck in the gravel on the other side and, dog tired now as well as frustrated, she pushed the handle down into the case and lifted the heavy bag to carry it all the way along the drive. She had to carry the other bag on her wrist with the phone in her hand while pointing the torch ahead of her.

The gravel road seemed to go on forever. The house had to be in a different postcode to the gate. There was, at least, some light from the moon and the torch on her phone lit the ground immediately ahead of her, but it failed to illuminate much else of her new surroundings. She tried not to think of the possibility that someone could easily jump out at her from the trees that lined her way.

At last, the house came into view and she was relieved to see there was a light on inside. A sign of life.

As she drew closer to the house, it seemed to rear up at her, looming even larger than its three stories. Its walls were opaque in the darkness, with the moonlight causing deep shadows at its corners. The place looked like something from an old horror film, but Sarah told herself it would seem far less imposing in the morning.

She had a key in her pocket somewhere but didn't want to startle the housekeeper by using it, so she put down her bags and rang the bell. No one came. The housekeeper must have left the light on for her then gone home – and who could blame her?

Sarah heard a loud crack from behind her then, as if a stick had suddenly been broken by someone's footfall. Alarmed, she turned but saw no one, just the outline of trees in the darkness. She quickly wrestled the keys from her pocket, telling herself it was obviously an animal – a fox, an owl, a fucking big mouse – definitely *not* a serial killer or the monosyllabic cab driver who had come back to grab her.

She pushed the key in the lock and tried to turn it, but nothing happened. No! She would be stuck out here all night in the cold and dark.

Sarah instinctively pushed against the door with one hand and turned the key with the other. The key was old, the door incredibly ancient and the mechanism stiff and unyielding but eventually it gave. Gloriously, the key turned and the door slid open. Sarah almost flung herself through it in relief, grabbing her bags as she did so and closing and locking the door quickly behind her.

The light was on in the large open hallway, which faced a huge staircase that went up to the next level, before splitting then going off even higher to both left and right. There were four doors nearby on the ground floor: one on her right, one on the left and the other two directly ahead of her, either side of the staircase. None of them looked welcoming.

There was a large open fireplace here and above it hung an impressive wooden carving of the words '*Respice ut ante videas*'. She recognized it as Latin but did not have any idea what it meant.

'Hello!' she called, in case there was still someone in the house who had failed to hear the doorbell. Sarah realized that, till now, she hadn't really given her arrival much thought. She had vaguely anticipated a welcome from the housekeeper, before being shown around and allocated a bedroom. Instead, the place was empty and she had no idea where any of these doors led.

The door to the right took Sarah into what she assumed was the dining room, where she got a brief glimpse of a long table with several chairs as she turned on the light, but there was an immediate pinging sound as the bulb went and the room instantly fell dark again. She went to the door on the left instead, which opened into a corridor that led to a number of rooms in varying states of readiness and comfort. She peered inside them all. Some had shabby furniture that looked as if it had been there since the

1950s. Others had more modern-looking sofas and chairs as well as a TV set or a radio, instead of an ancient wireless. She could only guess which rooms Evelyn liked to sit in, but none of them appeared too welcoming, especially at this hour.

This place was bigger than Sarah had imagined, and she decided to explore the rest of it in daylight when the place might feel less eerie. The more immediate need for food sent her back to the door to the right of the staircase, and behind it she found the kitchen. There was a plain wooden table and chairs here. There wasn't much in the fridge, just some milk and butter and a large bottle of water. She went to the cupboards and opened them. As well as an assortment of crockery and pans, she discovered some tinned food. There was soup and she found a fresh loaf in the bread bin. Success. She warmed the soup, toasted the bread and ate lots of it with generous amounts of the butter, washed down with a mug of hot tea.

Her next priority was to find somewhere to sleep. Sarah noticed more Latin phrases on the wall by the stairs. They couldn't all be family mottos, surely, but it was obvious they had been here for a very long time.

As she climbed the stairs, she passed a series of portraits on the walls. They became more recent as she ascended. First, there was a Woodfell ancestor dressed in First World War-era military uniform. She glanced at the engraving on the bottom of the frame which told her this was Major Wilfred Woodfell. He must have been the grandfather of Lucy and her siblings. Next to him was a portrait of their father, Robert, that had to have been painted when he was in his forties. There was a painting of his second wife, too, and Lucy's mother was definitely a beauty. As she reached the first landing, she was met by the gaze of four more figures looking down upon her from the second staircase above. Sarah had seen enough photographs of the Woodfells by now to instantly recognize them as Oliver, Freddie, Sephy and finally Lucy, whose portrait was positioned almost at the top of that second staircase. Sarah paused for a moment to take in their likenesses. The portraits must have been painted when they were in their twenties or early thirties at most. They all seemed so youthful and full of promise. The two boys were handsome and both women attractive, with Sephy in particular so striking that she resembled a young Hollywood starlet from a bygone era.

Sarah turned away from the portraits and opened the nearest door, switched on the light and peered inside. There was a decent-sized bed already made up, as well as a wardrobe, chest of drawers and a bedside cabinet. The room was cleaner than some hotel rooms she had stayed in. This would definitely do.

She went to bed gratefully but with her nerves still frazzled by the journey and more so by the size of the house and its atmosphere. One night here on her own would be something of an ordeal, let alone six months. What had she signed up for?

According to her memoir, Evie had a far more positive experience on her first night at Cragsmoor.

I slept like a log and woke refreshed the next morning. The Woodfells actually had servants and they were coming and going downstairs, but I needn't have worried about being accepted by the family. Lucy's parents were still in London and her three older siblings away at schools or college. Lucy and I were free to roam around the manor house. It seemed so big and full of mystery.

'The house is supposed to be haunted,' Lucy told me, 'but I've never actually seen a ghost.' She went on to explain some of the legends behind those hauntings. 'Our family clung to the old religion,' she said, 'and still does, obviously.' That explained her place at St Hilda's. My father was a lapsed Catholic who only pretended to be otherwise when it suited him.

'One of my ancient forebears was executed,' she said with some pride, 'for disputing the legality of Henry the Eighth's marriage to Anne Boleyn. He denounced her as a whore and proclaimed her daughter a bastard, which was possibly not the wisest move, since she became Elizabeth the first and cut off his head.'

'How gruesome.'

'The entire family could have been executed or imprisoned, but they swore fealty to the Queen,' she grinned, 'while plotting against her in secret.'

'So, they were traitors?'

She didn't like that. 'Not to their consciences. They didn't recognize Elizabeth as their true Queen.' And I wondered what would happen if everyone took that attitude. 'They used to take illegal Mass in the house,' Lucy explained. 'It was very dangerous for the priests. If they were caught, they would be tortured and killed by Francis Walsingham's secret service. That's why we have priest holes.'

'There is a priest hole in the house?'

'More than one,' she told me, 'I'll show you them.'

Chapter Ten

Sarah woke with a start the next morning, thanks to a loud bang from downstairs. Her room was light, so it had to be morning, but she felt groggy and had to think for a moment to remind herself where she was. She did identify the sound, though, and realized that it was the heavy front door being pushed closed. She then heard another door being opened and closed. Someone was in the house – but who? The housekeeper? She hoped so.

Hurriedly she got out of bed, pulled on yesterday's clothes and grabbed her phone. It was only seven o'clock. Did the housekeeper start this early every day?

Sarah went downstairs and cautiously approached the kitchen, keen not to scare anyone. 'Hello?' she called.

No answer. Surely they'd heard her? Gingerly, she opened the kitchen door and walked in to find the room empty, but she could hear a scraping sound coming from beyond the far door. A woman in late middle age walked in carrying a metal bucket. Sarah's relief must have been palpable.

'You're here then?' the woman said calmly. So much for Sarah worrying about scaring her.

'Yes,' she said. 'Mrs Jenkins? I'm Sarah.'

'Of course.' Who else could she be?

'I'm so sorry I missed you. The train was hours late and I couldn't get a cab for ages.' Then Sarah realized the housekeeper had spotted the washing-up she had left in the sink the night before because she hadn't had the energy to do it. Mrs Jenkins put down her bucket and went to the sink, retrieved the bowl and side plate, then ran some fresh hot water.

'Oh, let me,' said Sarah.

The woman shook her head as if that was an absurd idea, but she didn't look particularly happy about it either. Sarah stood feeling a little helpless.

'I'm sorry I left it. It was very late. I had some soup and then crashed.'

The housekeeper turned towards her, seeming put out. 'But I made you dinner.'

'Did you? I didn't see it.' She even looked around the room now to see if there was a plate left somewhere. How could she have missed it?

'I left you a note,' Mrs Jenkins said sternly.

'Where?'

'In the dining room.'

'I didn't go in . . .' and she was about to explain about the bulb going but was interrupted by the housekeeper.

'I left your dinner there with a bowl over it. I set you a place. All you had to do was microwave it.'

Exasperated now, Sarah wanted to ask why the food hadn't been left somewhere more sensible, such as on the kitchen table or inside the fridge, but it was clear that the housekeeper had wanted things to be done properly by setting a place at the table, so instead she just said, 'I'm so sorry. I didn't realize.' Then she offered, 'I'll have it for lunch.'

The housekeeper sighed audibly, as if Sarah was a very

dim specimen indeed. 'It'll be spoiled now.' And she trudged off in the direction of the dining room, presumably to retrieve the ruined meal and tut to herself while scraping it into the bin.

Why do I feel like I work for her and not the other way around? Sarah wondered.

There wasn't much by way of introduction to the house either. The older woman merely asked where she had slept the night before and tutted again when Sarah revealed it was the nearest room on the first floor. 'We keep that as a guest room. I'd made your bed up on the second floor. I'd given you your aunt's room.'

'I'm sorry,' said Sarah, again. 'I didn't know.' Presumably this had been written on the note that had been placed in the blacked-out dining room, along with the meal that was now in the pedal bin. Mrs Jenkins did not reply, except to indicate that Sarah should follow her to the room that was actually intended to be hers. It was larger and seemed lighter somehow, even though it was directly above the room Sarah had slept in.

'I'll change the bedding downstairs,' said Mrs Jenkins and she shuffled off, having made her point that this was another job that had been foisted on her by Sarah's inability to locate her precious note. Sarah resolved to stop apologizing for that. Her welcome could hardly have been more frosty.

She managed to keep out of Mrs Jenkins' way for the rest of the morning and instead explored the house. It wasn't quite as intimidating in daylight but not all of the rooms were welcoming. Some of them held little furniture and what they did have was covered with dust cloths.

Doubtless, Aunt Evie had only partially used the place when she came to stay.

There were good spots for reading, though, and an antique desk that fitted into a bay window in one of the downstairs rooms that would be ideal for Sarah's writing. She wondered if her aunt had written her own books there. At the end of the house, there was even a quite beautiful library. The walls were entirely taken up with rows of books on dark wooden fitted shelves, filling all four sides of the room, and there were two sofas, an armchair and several lamps. Sarah could have happily spent hours sitting there just reading but she wanted to see more of the house.

The two floors above housed numerous bedrooms and bathrooms, and Sarah marvelled at how much furniture they contained between them. It was no wonder Cragsmoor needed a housekeeper. It would be a full-time job just to clean the place.

The third floor had smaller rooms which had probably once been servants' quarters. Opening the door to a larger room, Sarah was shocked by what she found. A pair of eyes stared back at her.

Instinctively, she brought her hand up to her chest and had to hold on to the door to regain her balance. A jolt of fear had gone through her but now she felt foolish. The eyes that were staring at her might have been at head height but they were not human. An ancient china doll was staring lifelessly from a shelf, as if it was about to ask Sarah what she thought she was doing entering the room without an invitation. What little light penetrated the nursery windows seemed to have picked out the glass eyes of the doll, which surveyed Sarah critically. 'Christ,' she said aloud and turned on the light.

This made the doll seem marginally less creepy, but Sarah still wondered why anyone would have wanted to give this ugly thing to a child. Its deathly pale face and thin lips were contrasted by a pair of dark eyebrows that failed to match two wisps of blond hair protruding from beneath a white bonnet. The dark, staring eyes completed the picture, making it the stuff of nightmares.

Was the doll Persephone's, or even Lucy's? Next to it on the shelf were a series of well-worn teddy bears, a rather bedraggled rabbit and a wooden duck with wheels and a string, so you could pull it along. There were toy boxes filled with board games and jigsaw puzzles, as well as child-sized chairs and a table. A forlorn-looking rocking horse completed the scene, his sadness seeming to reflect his lack of purpose since the Woodfell children had all grown up and left the house. Evie had bought the house with all of its contents and clearly nothing had changed in this room for decades.

On the landing, a narrow set of steps was built into one of the walls. Sarah climbed them into an enormous attic. She turned on the light and realized it stretched the entire length of the third floor it was built above. Sarah entered it gingerly, testing the ancient wooden floorboards to be sure they could hold her weight, then she surveyed the room, which was full of tea chests, wooden boxes, paintings and old ornaments. She walked further into the room, being careful to avoid items that had been placed on the floor, and as she went past an old single wardrobe she got another shock. This time it was an animal that was staring back at her. The old stag was real. Its enormous head had been severed from its body then stuffed and mounted so it could be hung on a wall somewhere as a trophy. One of its antlers had broken off at some point and now it occupied a place on a similarly battered dressing table, its position designed to startle anyone who came upon it unexpectedly.

Nerves frayed by one unsettling experience after another, Sarah decided to return to ground level. She had intended to spend the rest of the day walking the grounds, but as she came down the stairs from the attic, she heard the unmistakeable sound of raindrops hitting the windows, which quickly became intense enough for her to abandon her plan to explore the rest of the estate.

She gazed down on to the courtyard just as Mrs Jenkins emerged from the front door at the end of her morning shift.

'I've got six months of you,' she said to herself. 'Great.'

The rain was coming down hard now and Sarah wanted to think about her next moves and come up with some kind of strategy. She had not been exaggerating when she'd told Dickie that she had no idea where to begin. There were at least half a dozen suspects to investigate, and somehow she would have to uncover new information that no one – not the police or Evelyn – had been able to find for more than thirty years.

How would actual detectives go about investigating something as mysterious as this? Sarah's knowledge of that world was restricted to research for her novels, but she could try to track down and interview all the suspects and question them about their whereabouts on the day Lucy Woodfell had disappeared. She could quiz them about their relationship with the missing woman too, to see if they might have any reason to kill her. Theoretically that was possible, as long as those suspects agreed to speak to her, and there was of course no guarantee of that.

It was starting to feel like the semblance of a plan. Sarah would approach each of the suspects and probe them with questions to try to . . . what was it the police used to say? Eliminate them from her enquiries. One by one, she would discount them, until she had whittled their numbers down to just a single prime suspect whose guilt she would then have to prove. That was the theory; all she had to do was put it into practice somehow – which wasn't going to be easy.

Where to begin? Perhaps by talking to the police who'd investigated Lucy's disappearance in the first place to see what they knew, before she then tried to trace the suspects. Would they be willing to share information with her though? Police officers might not want to assist a member of the public who was undertaking a personal investigation into an unsolved murder, but she could at least try to contact them and see if anything came from it.

Sarah turned on her laptop and started searching for information about the detectives on the original case. Eventually she found an article by an investigative journalist who had spent time looking back into Lucy Woodfell's disappearance. The reporter bemoaned the fact that police officers involved in the case had refused to speak about it to him, even decades after the event. Detectives at the time had been left bruised by negative newspaper coverage, but the reporter claimed that wasn't the only reason they remained silent. According to the journalist's sources, they had been ordered from on high never to talk about the case. This was supposedly to spare the feelings of a humbled but still influential family: the establishment had closed ranks to protect them. The official line was that there were no 'active lines of enquiry' or any 'solid evidence of wrongdoing', and that was that. There was a 'veil of silence' surrounding this cold case even now, which the journalist claimed he had never encountered before, despite having reported on many important and contentious cold cases during his career.

Great, thought Sarah. Would getting in touch with the local force as a private individual work, if they wouldn't even give a comment to a respected journalist? But she really wanted to talk to someone who had worked the case. That way she could work out the difference between the facts and some of the myths surrounding it that had built up over the years.

This was going to prove difficult, especially as everybody involved would have retired or died by now. There might be no one left who could tell her what actually happened, even if they would speak to her. She found the names of two of the police officers assigned to the case and quickly learned that Detective Inspector Mountjoy was dead, but she eventually found a Facebook profile for his Detective Sergeant, Edward Crozier, after going down a list of Edward Croziers from all over the world. She scrutinized his profile photo then compared it to the old black-and-white images of him standing with his DI which had been taken from newspapers and posted on a blog page. She was sure this was the same man, and his page confirmed he was a retired police officer still living in the area. It also showed her a possible way in.

Edward Crozier was helping to raise funds for a local community centre but they were still well short of the total needed. Sarah sent a £50 donation to the fund he had set up, along with a direct message to Crozier, promising more if he got in touch with her with further information about the project and leaving her mobile number.

Next, she turned her attention to members of the family. Evie had warned her niece not to contact the Woodfells until she had a reason to compel them to speak to her. Clearly, Sarah lacked that, but she wanted to meet Lucy's siblings face to face so she could form her own impression of them. Perhaps her aunt would be wrong and they would cooperate, if only to deny their own involvement in her disappearance. If they were innocent, then why wouldn't they?

Dickie had provided her with addresses for Oliver, Freddie and Sephy because they all still lived in separate cottages that had once belonged to the estate. Sarah sat down at her aunt's writing desk and wrote three letters to the Woodfell siblings. In each, she explained that she was Evelyn Moore's heir, leaving out all references to the conditional nature of that inheritance. Sarah claimed to be fascinated by their family history and the manor house. She told them she would love to come and see them or possibly invite them to return to their family home, so she could gain an insight into Cragsmoor Manor from them. She hoped that approach might appeal to one or perhaps all of the siblings. She would post her letters that morning and wait for their response.

Sephy's husband, Captain Ramsay, was one of the other three suspects Evelyn had identified but he had died within a couple of years of Lucy's disappearance. Neither of the other two suspects were family members, so tracking them down might not be easy. She had no idea where Warren Evans – the teenage boy spotted on the beach that day – might be now or how to contact him. She spent some time trying to find any trace of Warren online but there was none. Tracking down David Young, the convicted murderer, might prove easier. He was back in the community, but would it be possible to speak to him? More importantly, was it safe to try?

Chapter Eleven

When Sarah returned to Evelyn's memoir, she expected to pick up the story where it left off, talking about hidden priest holes, but it took a decidedly unexpected turn.

As the man emerged from the lake in the grounds of Cragsmoor Manor, I expected to see his lower half clothed in a bathing suit, but no. He was completely naked and thoroughly unabashed by it. After the initial shock, I had to make a conscious effort to look away for fear of making my fascination obvious to him and my friend.

'For God's sake, Freddie, cover up!' Lucy implored. 'We have guests!'

So, this was her older brother, back from school, but we had not seen him up at the house. It was an unusual first meeting.

'Don't be such a prude, Squirt.' It sounded like a well-worn family nickname. 'Why don't you join me?'

Lucy was appalled. 'Because we don't have costumes.'

'Don't need 'em. Come on, the water is wonderful this morning. You'll love it.'

Lucy didn't answer immediately and I experienced a sense of absolute panic, in case she agreed and started stripping off in front of him and I might be expected to follow her example.

'We are not as Bohemian as you,' said Lucy.

'If you didn't have a guest, you would be peeling off your dress now.' He reached for her hem with a damp hand and pulled it upwards, exposing her legs.

'Freddie!' Lucy squealed in chastisement as she tugged it down again, but there was another emotion there too, a kind of shocked amusement that her brother could be so outrageous, standing there naked and trying to pull her dress up. She stepped away from him as he let go of it and he turned towards me.

'I'm sure she's seen it all before.' Of course I hadn't, but I tried to act as if I had.

'No, Freddie, she hasn't,' said Lucy.

'Then I am happy to advance her education.' He scooped a towel from the grass but instead of wrapping it around himself, he used it to wipe the water from his face then dab at his hair. He was completely on show and stayed that way even as he drew nearer, water still dripping from an impressive torso, a mop of blond, very damp hair above an obviously handsome face, sporting a grin the girls back at St Hilda's would have described as 'rakish'. He was confident to the point of arrogance and I was confused as to whether I found this attractive or not. The spectacle he presented was distracting enough as it was, without taking his personality into consideration too.

He thrust out a hand and said, 'Freddie Woodfell. You must be the Squirt's latest project.' As if I was a painting or an unweeded garden.

'Evie,' I managed and he clasped my hand with his still damp one and shook it firmly.

'Oh, do stop showing off.' Lucy was exasperated by his insouciance but he just laughed and strolled past us. We watched as he walked away, still using the towel to dry his hair, leaving me with an uninterrupted view of a pale but muscular posterior which made me feel quite giddy.

We continued our walk around the lake. 'Does your brother always swim . . .' I was going to say 'in the nuddy', but I realized how prudish it would make me sound.

'Like that?' she finished my sentence. 'He is a complete exhibitionist. Oliver's the same. My sister used to do it too, would you believe? Freddie thinks he is being very modern . . .' then she frowned, '. . . or classical, or something,' she couldn't make up her mind, '. . . you know, like the Greeks.'

I had heard that the Greeks wrestled naked at the ancient Olympics but had assumed they did it without ladies present. Stepping from the lake like that, without caring that there were two young women present, one of whom was his own sister (cringe) appeared to me to be the oddest behaviour imaginable. To learn that Lucy's older sister had also done this seemed even stranger to me.

'Don't they mind people seeing them?' It was a foolish question. I had already learned that Freddie didn't mind at all.

'The lake is far enough from the house so the help can't see, and it's only really family that comes down here. I don't approve of it and I'd rather the girls,' she meant the ones at school, 'didn't get the wrong idea about me.'

'Oh, I shan't breathe a word.'

'Thank you, Evie,' she said earnestly.

69

'We all have eccentric family members. My mother is barking,' I confessed.

'Is she really?'

'Absolutely, so my father says.'

At that we both fell into a silence that was only broken when I said, 'He doesn't look like you – your brother, I mean.'

'He's a half-brother. Our father remarried two years after Freddie's mother died. I am of the second marriage,' she said quite formally, and I wondered why she had never mentioned this at St Hilda's. 'She drowned, actually, in the Mediterranean while on holiday.' Perhaps that was my answer. I reasoned that it must have been a strange feeling to know that you only existed at all because someone else had died in a tragic accident.

'Freddie, Sephy and Oliver are all my half-siblings.'

There were four of them and that seemed like a lot to me, but then I was an only child, which was rarer in those days. I couldn't help feeling that my mother had taken one look at me and immediately decided against having any other children because I was deficient in some way.

'Do you get on?' I asked.

'Usually, when we see one another. Freddie and Oliver can be a bit beastly, but then they are boys.'

My personal experience of boys was confined to brief glimpses of the delivery boy at school or the young man who helped the gardener. I had never had a proper conversation with one, let alone held hands or actually kissed one, though I had practised on the back of my hand, because the other girls assured me that one had to, in order to do it properly when the time finally came.

> Now I had seen a man completely naked and felt as if
> I had somehow leapt forward, bypassing several stages
> along the way, thanks to Lucy's entirely shameless brother.

Sarah realized she was smiling to herself. She had always known her aunt as an older woman. Sarah's mother and Evelyn were also half-sisters, Sarah's grandfather having married suspiciously quickly following his divorce from Evelyn's mother, so she expected her grandparents had already been having an affair. Sarah's mother then arrived and when she in turn grew up, married and had a child of her own, Sarah was blessed with an aunt; a somewhat distant but glamorous figure from a different era, who Sarah found herself irresistibly drawn to from an early age. She kept in contact with Evie and, as she got older, their shared love of books and writing kept them connected. When Sarah eventually became a published author too, no one was prouder or more supportive than her aunt.

She had never imagined what Evie was like as a young girl, had not even considered the possibility that she had once been one. It's as if we think the world starts when we are born into it, thought Sarah, and everything that came before is merely unknowable history. Now that she was reading Evie's own story, it felt as if the young girl she had once been was speaking to Sarah directly.

> It was raining and our plan for a long walk had been
> foiled by the weather. We read books in the library instead
> but eventually tired of that and grew restless. For the first
> time since my arrival at Cragsmoor, I was in danger of
> becoming bored.

71

'How would you like to see a secret room?' Lucy asked me abruptly.

'The priest hole? Yes, please.' I'd been worried she had forgotten about her promise to show it to me.

Lucy led me out of the library, along the corridor and up the grand staircase almost to the very top. She sat down on the penultimate stair and turned back to face me. 'Can't you see it?' Her mischievous tone made me realize that I wasn't meant to.

'No.' I couldn't see much of the top floor from here but the walls seemed normal; the floor, the ceiling, its wooden supporting beams all looked as I assumed they should. 'Where is it?'

'You're very warm,' she said, so I took a step closer, advancing up the stairs towards her. 'Warmer,' she told me, then 'warmer still' as I reached the step she was sitting on. I walked past her to the landing then took a couple of paces down the corridor. 'Cold,' she told me, so I turned around and walked back the way I had come. I was about to go along the other end of the corridor when she said 'colder . . . colder still.' So I stopped. I was getting a bit tired of the game. I just wanted her to show me this secret room.

'I can't see it, Lucy. I give up. Where is it?'

'Here,' and she knocked on the step below, then the stair she was sitting on and finally the top step. The sound this one made was very different to the solid wood she had knocked on before. It was hollow.

Excited again now, I urged her to show me, and she lifted up the top stair as if it were the lid on a wooden box.

There was a good-sized space behind it. I later learned that it was six feet in length and five feet across.

'It's quite roomy,' I said.

'A priest might have to stay in it for days. Some houses have tiny rooms, but this one was big enough to stand up in. They could put food and drink in there too.'

'It's amazing that you have one.'

'One? We have three. There's rumoured to be a fourth but we've never found it.'

'Can I see the others?'

'When everyone is out.' Lucy's parents were back by now but they more or less ignored the two of us, except at mealtimes, which were formal affairs where hardly anyone ever spoke at all. Lucy's father was quite fierce and none of his children dared break the silence his presence warranted at mealtimes. It was all very strange. 'They are smaller and I don't go in them when Father is around because he doesn't like it. He thinks I'll get stuck. I only showed you this one because it's bigger and at the top of the house. No one ever comes up here.'

'Did you just say you can go in them?'

'Do you want to?'

I could have passed out with excitement. This was like something out of the Famous Five or Secret Seven mysteries. They always had secret passageways, hidden caves or smugglers' coves, but this was the real thing.

Lucy slid over the step and lowered herself down. She was now standing in the hole, her eyes level with the step. She moved to let me do the same but I was much less graceful and, as I was coming down, she grabbed my hips to slow me then lowered me more gently. I turned and was face to face with her for a moment. 'Thanks,' I managed.

'Don't close it yet,' Lucy warned, 'or we'll be in darkness.' She bent lower and reached behind her then brought up a box of matches and two metal candlesticks containing half-burned candles. Once she had lit them both, she beckoned me to sit on the cold stone floor with my back to one of the walls, placed the candles between us and closed the hatch over our heads. I experienced the contrasting emotions of excitement and claustrophobia in such a confined space. What if the catch stuck and we couldn't get out again? Would anyone hear us from the top of the house, even if we screamed? Lucy seemed completely relaxed, however, and had obviously been doing this for years.

'This is my sacred place,' she explained. 'I come here whenever I have to get away.'

'What from?'

'Anything. Everything,' she said vaguely then became more specific. 'Father,' she said, without explaining what it was about him that she was forced to escape from. Then she added brightly, 'Next time we'll bring cushions and sandwiches and cake. I'll pinch a bottle of wine from the cellar.'

I could not even imagine her doing that but I smiled at the illicit notion. 'Did you come up here with Freddie when you were little?' I asked.

She frowned at me then and I wondered if I had been too clumsy in mentioning her brother, betraying my interest in him. 'Years ago, but we don't come in here

74

together any more. Freddie can be . . .' she thought for a moment, '. . . unpleasant, and Oliver too.'

'Well, they are boys,' I said, 'and they are all unpleasant.'

'And how would you know, Evie? What experience of boys have you had?' She was teasing me now.

'Absolutely none, but I have read about them in books,' I intoned solemnly, 'and they seem full of mischief.'

'They are. I wouldn't advise going into a priest hole with Freddie. Who knows what he would do to you?' Then she laughed, 'Though by the look on your face you might not be fully against the idea.'

'I have no wish to be trapped in a confined space with a young man who has no sense of shame,' I retorted, trying to make light of it.

'Yes, you've already seen far too much of Freddie,' she agreed.

'I'm surprised it doesn't get in the way,' I said, 'you know, when they walk around, sit down or ride a bike.'

She laughed at that notion before saying, 'Well, I don't think he has to wrap it around the handlebars.'

Chapter Twelve

This wasn't like reading one of Aunt Evelyn's novels. They usually started with a bang, sometimes quite literally, and there would be a body, often on the first page, then an investigation and, at the end, a terrible reckoning, with justice for the victims and harsh punishment for the offenders. This was different and Sarah knew why. *You're easing me into this. You want me to know Lucy. You need me to care about her, because then I might just go the extra mile for you both.*

There were several parts of Evie's account of her early days at Cragsmoor Manor that had intrigued Sarah, including the exact location of the priest hole, but none more so than the casual reference to a wine cellar. Was it still there and, more importantly, did it contain a few bottles that might still be drinkable?

Sarah tried three doors before she found the right one, which had a short but steep staircase going straight down into a pitch-dark and possibly empty cellar. Locating a switch that turned on a single bare bulb to light the stairs, she walked down them but could barely see into the room, though there was another switch here. When she pressed it, several overhead lights blinked on, illuminating the whole cellar. It was a large open space with a curved stone roof and tall racks filled with old bottles of fine wine.

'Jackpot,' she said.

*

Sarah brought two bottles of impressive-looking wine up to the kitchen with her. Then she got cold feet. What if the solicitor had an inventory of every bottle of wine here then billed her for each one she consumed in six months? It could cost a fortune. Best to clear it with him first.

She called Dickie and they talked about her journey and how to process future expenses such as petrol for the car, and then she said, as casually as possible, 'While I'm here, am I allowed to consume items of food and drink I find on the premises?'

'Of course,' he said.

'Including the wine?'

He seemed perfectly relaxed about that, 'I don't see why any of that should go to the Tory party, do you?'

'Absolutely not.' Since Sarah could see no way in which she would ever end up owning the manor house, she figured she might as well enjoy its wine while she was here, if only to keep it out of the Conservative Party's clutches.

Sarah cooked and ate dinner. She was on her third glass of wine when she decided she could put off the priest hole no longer. It was quiet with no one else in the manor house, and the only sound was her own footsteps and the creak of the stairs beneath them. It felt decidedly eerie being the manor house's sole occupant. Even the presence of Mrs Jenkins would have been preferable.

Sarah stopped just below the final stair. Just like Evie all those years ago, she could see no sign of an opening. She took hold of the top step and pulled it upwards. It opened surprisingly easily and now Sarah was staring into a sizeable dark space.

She decided not to climb in, in case she became trapped somehow and would be stuck in there until morning at the very least. Instead, Sarah turned on the torch from her phone and held it at an angle till it was shining into the priest hole. There wasn't much to see but it was still an exciting discovery, a glimpse into a secret world from five hundred years earlier. What would it be like to hide in there for hours, possibly even days, knowing that at any moment you might be discovered, tortured and executed? As she swept her arm around, two small, dark, metal objects were caught in the beam of her torch. Lucy's candlesticks. They were still there. Sarah thought of her hiding here whenever she felt the need to escape from her siblings and domineering father. Seeing the candles like this made it feel as if she was making a connection with that young girl, decades later.

Sarah stayed up late that night, reading more of Evelyn's book, but she didn't learn anything that could help her to solve the riddle of Lucy's disappearance. Evelyn had admitted she did not know what had happened to Lucy Woodfell and found it impossible to narrow the story down, in case a small part of the memoir became a vital clue. Even so, it was almost as if her aunt had become lost in a nostalgic reverie of past, precious times with her friend.

Evie was dying as she completed this memoir, and she knew it. Who would begrudge her reminiscences of what must have been one of the happiest periods of her life? The two girls spent almost all their time together, on long walks or squirrelled away in the priest hole, the library or their bedrooms. There were no other members of the set to divide them or exclude Evie and little in the way of parental supervision. For a young girl who looked up to her friend, it must have been idyllic.

They saw Freddie at mealtimes and occasionally listened to LPs with him if they all felt in the mood. It was the time of the early Beatles and Rolling Stones, and that must have added to Evie's excitement. She always did have a soft spot for Mick Jagger.

Sarah found herself thinking about the priest holes again. Lucy had said there were three and might even be a fourth somewhere, but no one had ever found it. She herself had no way of locating the other priest holes. Considering that Lucy Woodfell had disappeared and her body had never been found, would it be unreasonable to think that her remains could have been hidden in one of them? No, that didn't make sense. The one below the staircase wasn't deep enough to be a grave without the smell of a rotting body filling the air. Presumably, the other two were of a similar type and the family knew of their whereabouts, so someone would have searched them for Lucy. The idea of a fourth priest hole was still intriguing. Someone might have known of its existence. If they did, would it have been a good place to hide a body, at least for a little while, before moving it again?

It struck her then that she knew nothing about the architecture of the manor house and had no plans of the building. Dickie probably wouldn't be much help since he hadn't realized there was a cellar full of wine. What she needed was an expert.

*

Thanks to the internet, it didn't take Sarah long to compile a short list of local historians with expertise in the Tudors and Stuarts. Up popped a number of names, some old and some part of a new breed who were social media-savvy and had YouTube channels and Instagram pages, as well as jobs as university lecturers. The older guys looked stuffy or severe, so she chose three of the younger breed and did further research. One turned out to be entirely self-taught but made a living writing books containing contrary opinions. Richard the Third didn't order the deaths of the Princes in the Tower, Elizabeth the first married her lover in secret and Hitler never intended to start a world war. That kind of reasoning might get you a book deal but it didn't exactly engender trust. The next candidate travelled the length of Britain uncovering historical secrets for a documentary, but his delivery was so monotonous she became bored before she had finished watching the trailer.

Maybe this wasn't going to be as easy as she'd first hoped.

That was when she found Marcus. It absolutely wasn't just his good looks that drew her to him or the fact that she recognized that noble, seemingly sculptured face, having once caught a late-night re-run of one of his populist history documentaries. Handsome, yes, but knowledgeable too, she told herself several times, after viewing him on his YouTube channel. Here you could see clips of Marcus Fernsby's 'greatest hits', as one female admirer had dubbed them. There were other, equally direct comments from women beneath each video, including, 'He can besiege me any time!' In one of the clips, Marcus strode manfully along a castle's ramparts. In another, he wore an old-fashioned white cotton nightshirt in a dimly lit Tudor bedroom as he talked breathlessly of Henry the Eighth's all-powerful lust for Anne Boleyn. It was all a little bit distracting, but he knew his stuff.

The clincher was the clip in which he declared his fascination for priest holes. 'The craftsmen who built these hidden rooms were driven men,' he explained, 'who had to mask the noise of their labours or hide them behind the cloak of normal renovations. They were the secret agents of their time, operating behind enemy lines, placing their very lives at risk!'

Sarah decided she could listen to this bloke all day. On his website she learned that he was a scholar of Latin, which would be useful, since she was limited to online translation tools that failed to fully explain the meaning of the Latin mottos inside the house. He was still based in the north-east, guest-lectured to college students between filming engagements and could be contacted via an email address or through his television agent.

Sarah decided to cut out the middle man and write to Marcus directly. She then spent far too long on an email to him. She wanted it to sound like an invitation rather than a plea for help. Would he perhaps like to come and look around the house, as she was sure he would find it interesting? She dangled the mystery of the fourth priest hole as a tantalizing incentive.

She read and re-read the email, hesitated, then hit send.

Sarah told herself it would be fine. He probably wouldn't even bother to reply, so where was the harm?

Chapter Thirteen

It wasn't the most ethical thing she had ever done, but her ploy with the retired detective, Edward Crozier, worked. He finally called Sarah back, hoping to solicit a further donation to the community centre he was raising funds for. He was friendly at first until he learned the true motive behind her donation and sounded far from happy about it. She feared he might immediately hang up on her. 'Hear me out,' she urged. 'I'm a friend of the family, sort of.' This at least kept him on the line, while she explained her connection to Evelyn Moore and her aunt's friendship with Lucy Woodfell, leading to her own, more recent interest in the case.

'You should have just asked me about it then,' he chastised her. 'Not pretended to be a donor.'

'I know,' she admitted, 'but I thought you might not have responded to that approach and I was more than happy to donate to such a worthy cause.'

'It's to stop all the anti-social behaviour,' he said then. 'Give the kids something to do.'

'That's commendable,' she said. 'And since I did give you a donation, I was hoping you might be able to spare just a few moments of your time, to discuss the Lucy Woodfell case.'

'Not interested,' he growled at her and hung up.

Great, she thought. I can't even get the police to speak to me, let alone the suspects.

That night, Sarah heard what sounded like whispering. She had been lying in bed, entirely alone in the house, and had reached the point where she was struggling to keep her eyes open, when she heard the voices and sat up in a panic.

At first, she couldn't work out what it was. Had that really been whispering? Who was in the house with her? Had somebody broken in? Were they looking for something or did they want to hurt her? And what, if anything, could she do about it?

Or perhaps she was simply hearing things. She was quite still, straining her ears to listen, but there was nothing now. No sound, no voices and no whispers, no one moving around.

Just when she thought she must have imagined the whole thing or that it was simply an unfamiliar sound from outside carried on a breeze, the sounds came again. Whispers that somehow reached her from the floors below.

What should she do? Call the police? She wanted to, but what if it was a false alarm? She'd never dare call them again. Sarah's instincts were telling her someone was downstairs but her brain was saying this couldn't be. She had locked every door then checked them all again before going to bed.

Maybe she should investigate the sound on her own. It would put her mind at rest if she found no one downstairs, but it was a terrifying prospect.

Sarah climbed out of bed and went to her door, then

pressed her head against it to listen. Was someone on the landing? Perhaps they were already outside her door, about to turn the handle and burst in? Why was there no lock on this bloody door anyway? She resolved to get one fitted. For now, though, despite telling herself that there really was no one there, she couldn't bring herself to open it and go down the stairs to check for intruders.

She didn't want to go back to bed either, with only a door that couldn't be secured between herself and any threat. How could she sleep like that? Sarah scanned the room for a suitable object. The bedside cabinet was a solid piece of furniture. She removed a lamp from it and found the cabinet was heavy, but she managed to drag it along the floor until it was right up against the door. Crucially, it was the right height to fit snugly below the door handle. If anyone turned it from the outside, they would meet resistance when the handle caught against the top of the cabinet and Sarah would hear them. She wished she had brought a knife from the kitchen but wasn't about to go downstairs and get one now.

She went back to her bed and lay there for a while. There was no sound at first, then that bloody whispering started up again, or was it actually a crackling sound, like an electrical item that had been left on somewhere? A radio perhaps? Maybe it was the water tank bubbling away or a breeze whistling through the roof tiles. They were all more rational explanations than whispering burglars? She felt a little calmer now that she had secured the room, but still couldn't sleep. Instead, she lay there listening, her mind restlessly turning over every sound she heard. A creak was a foot pressing on a stair; the north-east wind that battered the house and seemed to shake it, was really the sound of someone up on the roof, trying to find a way in.

And then there was that damn whispering, which absolutely could not be human voices, surely? It continued for so long that it could only have been caused by something else from within the house – but what? In the end, she was so exhausted she finally fell asleep until she was woken by what sounded like another sound from downstairs. Light was pouring into the room from outside and she realized it was morning.

Sarah kept perfectly still in order to hear the sound more clearly if it came again. There was no repeat and she put it down to one of the many natural noises the ancient manor house made, as it expanded and contracted when the plumbing system forced hot water through cold pipes.

Satisfied that there was no one there and knowing that Mrs Jenkins was not due in again for a couple of days, Sarah got up and took a shower. As she was drying off, she heard a light thud from downstairs that sounded as if the mail had been delivered. She hadn't thought to bring a dressing gown with her, so she wrapped the towel around herself and went down the stairs, planning to make a cup of tea then return to her bedroom with it.

But not only was there no post on the mat by the door, there was no letter box. This confused Sarah. If the noise had not been the post landing on the mat, what was it? A worrying thought hit her then. What if it was a door closing with a thud – which meant it had to have been opened by someone?

Just as that thought struck her, Sarah heard another

sound and the kitchen door opened behind her. She spun round to find a startled-looking man staring right at her.

'What the hell?' she cried out in alarm. 'Who are you?'

Christ, was this man an intruder or more 'staff' she wasn't aware of? He seemed at least as surprised to walk in on her as she was to see him. He continued to gaze at her as she clutched the towel tightly to herself but gave no immediate answer. He didn't look threatening, but why wasn't he explaining himself? The towel was short. She hunched forward slightly, the better to fully cover herself.

'Gardener,' was all he managed in answer to her question.

'Niece,' she told him in reply, losing all eloquence now. 'Evie's niece. I . . .' how to explain her presence? '. . . live here now,' she settled on.

'I'm sorry,' he said. 'No one told me.'

'No one told me about you either.' It was good to know he hadn't just broken into the place, but she did feel vulnerable standing there wearing only a towel, in front of an admittedly good-looking man around her own age. She wondered when he would notice her discomfort and go back out to the garden.

'I thought I'd seen a ghost.' And when she frowned at this over-reaction, he said, 'You look just like her.'

He clearly meant Evie. 'Do I?' This can't have been a compliment. Evie was seventy when she died.

'In her old photos,' he explained, '. . . for a second there I thought she'd come back from the grave.' He shook his head. 'I didn't mean to scare you. I'm sorry for your loss. Your aunt was a lovely lady.'

She almost blurted out, 'Was she?' but managed not to.

I liked her, she thought, but I was never sure if anyone else did. Sarah was relieved to hear that her aunt's rather combative personality did not prevent others from appreciating her in the way that Sarah had.

'I'll leave you to it, then.'

He turned to go and she said, 'Er . . .'

He turned back to face her. 'What's your name?' she asked.

'Sorry, Patrick,' he said.

'I'm Sarah. And how many days a week do you work here, Patrick?'

'Two in the gardens.'

'Which ones?'

'Tuesday and Thursday.'

'Right, thank you.' And she made a mental note to ensure she was properly dressed on the days when he was due to be gardening.

'But I do other days around the house,' he explained. 'That's if you still want me to?' He had assumed she'd inherited the manor and was now probably worried about his job here.

'Absolutely,' she said. 'No changes.' She could have added, 'As long as you don't burst in on me again when I'm almost naked.' But she knew it wasn't his fault Mrs Jenkins hadn't bothered to tell him she was moving in.

He smiled at her, nodded in agreement and she watched him go before padding back up the stairs to get dressed. It seemed you got a lot less privacy when you were the lady of the manor.

Chapter Fourteen

After spending several hours trying and largely failing to write her own book, Sarah gave up. Months before, a lifetime ago now, she had considered the idea behind this novel to be the best she had ever come up with and couldn't wait to get started on it. Now, she was genuinely worried it might possibly be the most ludicrous plot anyone had ever dreamed up. It was slim consolation to Sarah that, at some point in the writing process, in every novel she'd ever written, she always felt like this.

It was about a man who had suddenly gone missing and how he may or may not be a killer. Even Sarah wasn't very sure about that at this point but she hoped to work it out eventually. A woman was trying to find him, because they had been in a relationship when he disappeared and she had become obsessed with discovering the truth about him. There was a police officer who was also looking for him. The detective thought he was a guilty man and the woman still clung to the belief that he was innocent, despite everything she had learned about him since he vanished and . . . that was about it so far. Currently it was a book with no ending, just a beginning and what was turning out to be an interminably long middle section that, at this rate, might never reach a conclusion. Not for the first time, Sarah was seriously contemplating abandoning it and writing an entirely different story instead. The only thing preventing her was an extreme reluctance to scrap the thirty thousand words she'd amassed so far, when writing each one had felt like pulling teeth.

She closed the file on her laptop and distracted herself by reading more about the day that Lucy Woodfell went missing, in order to get a timeline of events. It took a while but eventually she had a chronology of sorts.

Lucy was last seen in the afternoon. Oliver said he had looked out of an upstairs window and watched her crossing the courtyard on her way to the rear of the house, but he wasn't sure what time that had been. He never saw her again. Possibly around the same time, Lucy's half-siblings Sephy and Freddie looked out of the kitchen window and saw her walk away down the path that led to the beach, which was several hundred yards away from the manor house. The family's nanny was there too, supervising Sephy's young son, the likely future prime minister, Toby Ramsay, and she saw Lucy leave too.

No one reported that Lucy was in any way upset, distressed or appeared to be anything other than her ordinary self that afternoon. Someone in such a normal frame of mind wouldn't simply wander off or disappear or commit suicide without ever being found. It seemed far more likely that someone else had taken her.

The weather brightened that afternoon and Sarah took her first opportunity to explore the grounds, to familiarize herself with Lucy Woodfell's home and walk in her footsteps. She wanted to find the locations mentioned in her aunt's memoir, including the lake and the path Lucy took that went down to the beach. It was good to be out of the house, after a fruitless morning's writing, and research that hadn't revealed much that was new. She hadn't realized how much land lay around the house, until she walked all the way down to the lake where Evie had chanced upon a naked Freddie. The lake was larger than she had expected and there was a little island in the middle covered with bushes and trees. She walked the lake's edge, using an old path that was partly overgrown, then went beyond it and crossed a couple of fields that had been left fallow and taken over by wildflowers. Dots of bright red, yellow and violet appeared here on a tapestry of green.

When she reached an old, dry-stone wall that marked the end of the estate, Sarah headed back to the house via a longer, circuitous route that took her round its perimeter. She walked past a dozen strange, roofless grey buildings. They looked like compounds designed to house animals but were all empty now, with weeds growing through cracks in their concrete floors.

When Sarah reached the back of the house, she saw what a good job Patrick had done with the gardens. Were those brightly coloured bushes hydrangeas? She wasn't sure. Nor could she name any of the many other flowers or shrubs here. But she could at least appreciate the beauty of the place. There was even a walled garden, set apart from the rest of the land, which contained an orchard, with rows of pear and apple trees, as well as a herb garden that smelt wonderful.

She passed through the walled garden and out the other side, then found herself at the start of the path that Lucy Woodfell must have taken that day. Sarah could see the sea some distance away, her view dominated by tall, jagged cliffs which rose above the beach and jutted out into the water. This appeared to be the only path that led down to the coast and Sarah started to walk the same route her aunt's best friend had done all those years ago. Just as then, it was a warm day. The path was still distinct enough for her to follow it easily, though wild grasses and bushes threatened to overwhelm it in parts and there were tall trees beyond on both sides. It seemed isolated and, even though she could have turned and run back to the house in minutes, that made Sarah feel uneasy. If someone did step out from the bushes intent on harming her, there wouldn't be much she could do about it. If she called out, no one would hear her. Was that what happened to Lucy?

Sarah increased her pace to reach the beach sooner. She found herself glancing from left to right as she did this and, even though she told herself it was unlikely, she couldn't quite shake the feeling that she was being watched.

Sarah emerged on to a beach of fine sand with pebbles, driftwood and large dark clumps of seaweed scattered on it. There was no one else here. She was looking for other paths that led down to the beach to see where they went and whether Lucy could have followed one of them. There must have been at least one somewhere as it was not a private beach and other people were able to reach the sand without trespassing on the estate. At either end of the beach, she could see those imposing cliff faces, which jutted outwards before narrowing into sharp edges as they pointed into the sea, creating a large, natural but inaccessible cove. It made this stretch of beach feel like a separate world.

It wasn't a tourist spot but it was lovely in its own wild way. Lucy might have had it almost to herself on the day she disappeared except for occasional passers-by, some of whom witnessed Warren Evans, the man on the beach, sitting there, and he swore he had not seen her. Sarah was standing in almost the exact spot where Lucy would have emerged, near where Warren had been lying on the sand, and she couldn't understand how he could have missed her.

She walked along the beach for two hundred yards or more before she found what she was looking for. Another track, which led her away from the sand, between some dunes and on into more tall grass. She followed this because it had to lead somewhere, but she felt very alone here. Sarah reasoned that it was not a beach you would know about unless you grew up around here. It wasn't until she was almost at the end of the path that she finally saw another soul; a middle-aged woman coming the other way, with a Labrador on a lead. She passed Sarah without a word.

It was another half a mile before the path led her to the village, which could only have been a couple of miles from the manor house by road. It looked quite small but there were a good number of homes set back from the street. There was only one shop here, which appeared to serve as post office, newsagent and general store combined. There was a solitary pub, a junior school, a village hall and some common land in the middle that was the village green. A parish church lay at one end of the village and the pub at the other, as if to highlight their contrasting but important roles as the twin hubs of village life. The street was quiet now with no one else around.

Sarah decided she might as well pick up a few things, so she entered the shop and found herself alone there, apart from an older woman standing behind the counter, who regarded the new arrival with undisguised interest.

'Hello,' said Sarah brightly.

No response. Had the woman not heard her, or was she so captivated by the presence of a stranger she'd temporarily forgotten her manners? The village was a little isolated but surely it had some visitors.

'You're from the house,' the woman behind the counter said belatedly and Sarah wasn't sure if she was asking a question or stating a fact. 'You're the niece.'

'That's right.' Sarah was used to London, where no one ever enquired about or even cared who you were.

'Sorry to hear about your aunt. Been coming in here for years. Always paid her bills on time.' This seemed to be a compliment and it was followed by, 'Not like the family.'

'You mean *the* family, who owned the hall before she did?' It was not intended to be a rhetorical question but it was treated as such by the shopkeeper. 'Weren't they very nice?'

'If I was looking for someone to model my life on, I wouldn't have picked them.'

Sarah feigned innocence then, hoping to hear more. 'I hardly know anything about them.'

'It was all a long while ago.'

But you are old enough to remember them, thought

Sarah. 'Arrogant, I should imagine? Upper class people often are, aren't they?'

The woman behind the counter muttered something that might have been agreement. 'They were into all sorts,' she explained. 'Drugs, for one thing, and . . .' she seemed to check herself then, as if she might be about to confide something too juicy.

Sarah gave her warmest fake smile and said, 'Oh, do go on. I love a good gossip.'

This proved to be the wrong tactic. 'It's not gossip. It's all true. I don't gossip.'

'No, sorry, of course.'

'What are you wanting?' It took Sarah a second or two to realize she meant groceries, not a wider purpose for being in the area.

'The basics: some bread, butter, milk, eggs,' and she looked at the shelves around her. She was underwhelmed by the contents and reminded herself she was no longer in London, land of the over-priced deli. There were no olives or charcuterie here. 'And some of that lovely ham, I think.'

The woman filled a carrier bag for Sarah but when she went to pay, she was waved away. 'I told you. It's on account.' That was not actually what the woman had said, only something about her aunt paying her own bills on time.

'It might be better if I do pay for this lot now. I'm not sure when I'll be in next.'

The woman sighed. 'Suit yourself.' And Sarah wondered if she had offended her or if she was as brusque as this with all her customers.

She paid in cash. The whole transaction felt awkward now and Sarah decided to be direct about it. 'I'm sorry if I offended you. I didn't mean to imply you were a gossip. I'm new to the manor and interested in the family that lived there before my aunt. That's all.'

'I wouldn't bother looking into them,' said the woman, but her tone softened a little following Sarah's apology. 'A bunch of wrong 'uns if you ask me, even before the murder.'

'There was a murder?' Again Sarah decided to play dumb and see what the woman might tell her about Lucy in an unguarded moment.

'That fella, what's-his-name?' She was trying to remember. 'The captain, Captain Ramsay.'

Sarah was thoroughly confused now. She had read that the soon-to-be prime minister had lost his father in a car crash when he was still a teenager but that wasn't murder, surely?

'How was he killed?'

'Car ploughed into a wall not two miles from here.'

'But you don't think it was an accident?'

The woman shook her head. 'He used to tear round here in his car right enough, but he never crashed before. They'd messed with his brakes. Everyone said so.'

'Who had?'

'That wife of his,' she said confidently. And she let that soak in before adding, 'This was all more than thirty years ago now but I still remember it.'

Sarah would have pressed her further, but just then the bell above the door rang to signal the arrival of another customer, and the atmosphere was transformed. It was as

95

if a shutter had come down between them. 'Excuse me,' said the shopkeeper, all business now as she turned to the other woman to see what she wanted. Sarah realized this was her cue to leave.

'Thank you,' she called on her way out. 'I'm Sarah, by the way.'

'I know,' said the woman but she did not offer her own name in return.

The north-east of England was meant to be a warm and friendly place but it seemed the shopkeeper had attended the same charm school as Mrs Jenkins. Perhaps they were sisters. It had been worth persisting with her, though. Sarah now knew that she considered Persephone Woodfell, Lucy's older sister, to be a murderer, and if she really had killed one person, Sarah reasoned, then why not two?

Chapter Fifteen

That night Sarah went back into Evelyn's memoir to read a section of it again. It concerned Persephone Woodfell, the oldest Woodfell girl: socialite, widow and murderer, perhaps?

'Sephy's home,' Lucy told me.

'Why is she called Sephy?' I asked. It was an unusual name, even in their aristocratic circles.

'It's Persephone actually, you know, after the Greek goddess of . . .' she thought for a moment, '. . . nature or something. I don't know. Anyway, she hates it, thinks it's cursed for some reason and will not respond to anything but its abbreviated form.'

I wondered why Persephone might think her name was cursed but thought no more of it. 'Do you like her?' This was a more pressing concern, particularly if I was about to meet the girl.

'Most of the time,' she offered cautiously.

Sarah reasoned that only a very posh girl would be saddled with a name like Persephone, but why would she think it cursed and refuse to answer to it? She stopped reading Evie's story to do a quick search on the internet until she found what she was looking for.

Persephone was a queen, though not of anywhere you

would want to visit. Her mother was Demeter and her father, Zeus, the king of the Greek gods. The unfortunate Persephone was abducted by Hades and forced to become Queen of the Underworld. When her mother found out and demanded her return, Hades tricked Persephone into eating the food of the dead before she was freed, which meant she was forced to spend the winter months in Hades from then on. Persephone was only allowed to return during the spring and summer months, bringing life back to the world in the process and creating the seasons. She was worshipped as the goddess of spring, flowers and vegetation but also of death and destruction. Even her name meant bringer-of-death. That must have been why Sephy thought her own name was cursed. Did she have an ominous feeling all those years ago and was somehow able to predict her own future? Sarah knew that was nonsense, of course, but did Sephy?

Evie described meeting Sephy for the first time later that day. She was a beautiful and glamorous figure, who seemed far more worldly and sophisticated than Evie and Lucy, though she wasn't that much older than them. She was kind enough, reserving her occasional flashes of temper for her older, male siblings. Evie would occasionally hear them shouting at each other from the floor below hers and it was clear that Sephy gave as good as she got.

Evie's interactions with Persephone were not all that frequent but one moment stood out and clearly had an effect on the younger girl.

I accidentally walked into her room because I was on the wrong floor. What I took to be Lucy's bedroom was actually Sephy's.

'Sorry,' I mumbled. I was embarrassed because she was still in her dressing gown. It was silk and there hardly seemed to be enough material to keep her in.

'Don't be,' she said easily. 'My door was open.'

I would have left then but I suddenly got a whiff of the most wonderful perfume. 'That smells lovely,' I told her.

'Like it? It's from Grasse.' And when she noticed my confusion, she added, 'Grasse, as in France, not grass, as in lawn. It's in the Côte d'Azur. They make it there from orange blossoms and pomegranates or something. It's called Diva.' Then she walked towards me and I swear that silk dressing gown swished. 'Have a dab,' she offered, her voice deep and husky, and she inverted the bottle to let the perfume touch the stopper. I held out my hands with the wrists exposed and she leaned in close to press the glass stopper against my skin. As well as her perfume, I could smell the sweet scent of her hair, which was almost as powerful. Sephy was taller than I was and she had to bend low to apply the perfume. Her ample figure almost spilled out of the gown. She was everything I wanted to become but knew I never would.

I raised my wrist to my nose and inhaled. I had never smelt anything quite like it.

It was intoxicating.

She was intoxicating.

I can remember the strong but subtle aroma of that perfume even now. I bought bottles of it when my book took off, but somehow, being able to put as much of it on as I wanted never felt quite as satisfying as those first dabs.

Of course, being me, I managed to turn the episode into an embarrassing event. Later, I stood in front of the mirror in my room trying to recreate it, only this time I was Sephy and it was me being watched and adored by someone from my door, which I deliberately left open. I stood there, with my far tattier dressing gown daringly opened at the front and barely a hint of cleavage on display, but I tried my best to pose in the same way that she had, with such effortless chic. Then I said the words she had used. 'It's from Grasse,' and I made my voice as deep and husky as I could. 'Have a dab.'

'What on earth are you doing?'

I was so shocked I almost shrieked. It was Lucy, looking in on me from the open door.

'Just . . . being silly,' I stammered. 'Like the woman in that film.'

'Which one?'

'I can't remember,' I said. 'Have you had cocoa?'

'No. Want some?'

'Yes.' Anything to stop her from questioning me further. Mortified as I was, at least it was Lucy who had caught me impersonating her half-sister in my unguarded moment. If it had been Sephy, I would have died of embarrassment.

Sarah's attempt to read more of Evelyn's memoir ended in confusion when she realized that she had seen the next section before. These were the pages she'd read at the start of the book, now repeated halfway through the bound copy. She flicked further through the pages and discovered she had in fact been given two versions of the opening half of Evelyn's memoir which had been pasted together and the second half was missing. Someone had messed up.

First thing the next morning she called Evelyn's solicitor.

'It's not all here, Dickie,' she told him. 'The book that Evelyn wrote. The second half is missing. There are two copies of the first half bound together. I was halfway through the manuscript and it started all over again on page one.'

'I don't understand. It should all be there. I got someone to go through it all and type it up for you on a Word doc.'

'They didn't do a very good job. Can you get them to sort it out?'

'Er . . . that's a bit tricky.'

'Why?'

'He's away.'

'On holiday?'

'No.' Dickie sounded very sheepish. 'Gone travelling actually, for a year.'

'He's left the firm?'

'Well, he wasn't actually a permanent employee.'

Sarah took a deep breath, 'Dickie, did you entrust Evelyn Moore's final manuscript to an intern?'

'I'm afraid so, yes.'

'An *unpaid* intern?'

'We paid his travel expenses.'

'He must have been highly motivated by that. Why don't you save us all a lot of time and just send me the original handwritten manuscript, but please use a proper courier.' Sarah was not thrilled at the prospect of having to decipher her aunt's spidery scrawl but it was better than waiting for someone to respond from a distant corner of the world.

'I would normally do that,' he began, 'but I'm afraid it appears to have gone missing.'

Chapter Sixteen

'You've lost it?' Sarah was horrified.

'Sean, our intern, was supposed to have put it back in a desk drawer but I looked for it the other day and it isn't there.'

'Has someone taken it?'

The pause before he answered seemed to indicate he may have been worried about that too, but he said, 'I'm sure it will turn up.'

'Can you get hold of this Sean, to ask him where he put it?'

'I'll ring round, speak to his family, check his last known address, all of that. Leave it with me, Sarah. There'll be no stone unturned. I promise.'

'There had better not be. The clock is ticking, as you're fond of reminding me.'

'I know.'

'Unless . . . ?' She was going to ask him for more time and he must have realized that.

'I have no power to halt that clock, I'm afraid.'

'Even though you have cocked this up?'

'Even then,' he admitted. 'I know it's an inconvenience, but it shouldn't hamper your investigation too much. And I am not allowed to give you any extra time.'

'Then please find it, Dickie, and soon.'

*

The sounds that reached Sarah in the night could not possibly have been whispers but, whatever the cause, they certainly sounded like them and they made it very difficult to drift off to sleep. When she finally managed it, Sarah's sleep was disturbed by vivid dreams involving the house. In her nightmare, she was searching for something but did not quite know what it was. She wandered the upper floors of the house, opening doors and walking into rooms that were full of the same items of furniture. Once she had gone into several rooms that all looked identical, she realized she was trapped in a recurring loop, in which the landing never ended and doors only ever opened on to the same scene. Every time, the forlorn-looking rocking horse was in the centre of the room, just as it had been in the nursery when she had explored it, only this time it rocked back and forth by itself. Behind it lay the shelf with the assortment of stuffed toys and the terrible white-faced china doll with its sightless eyes staring straight back at her.

To escape the recurring rooms, she tried to outrun them, haring past a series of doors without opening them, until she finally reached the steps on the third floor that led up to the attic, which looked just as it had when she explored it in daylight. Even the stag was still there, its antlers magically restored somehow, and its eyes seemed to follow her as she walked past. The door closed behind her with a slam but Sarah kept walking until she was half-way across the room and the bulb went with a ping, just as it had done in the dining room on her first evening there. Immediately, Sarah was plunged into complete darkness. She could not see the floor or even her hand out in front of her and she groped wildly, trying not to panic but doing just that as she flailed around, hoping to find her way back to the door and the steps that would take her down and out of this place.

She took a few fast and frightened steps back towards what she hoped was the attic door but, instead of touching floorboards, her foot came down on to nothing and she pitched backwards. She fell into the darkness with a terrified scream.

Sarah immediately woke with a start and felt her whole body twitch as she waited for the impact from her fall, but none came. She was covered in a cold sweat, her nightclothes sticking to her. It was morning but she still felt exhausted after another terrible night's sleep. She heard a sound from downstairs and assumed it was Patrick or Mrs Jenkins, so she got up, dressed and padded along the landing.

She was on her way down the stairs when she noticed that the portrait of Lucy Woodfell had been turned completely around, so that it now faced the wall. The painting was slightly askew and whoever had turned it around had hung it loosely from the top of its frame.

Who could have done it, and when did it happen? Lucy's portrait had been the right way round when Sarah had gone to bed but it had been flipped before she got up in the morning. Mrs Jenkins didn't seem like the kind of person who would try to prank Sarah. She supposed Patrick could have done it, but why would he? She almost wanted it to be him because it was less disturbing than the alternative: that someone else had slipped into the house in the middle of the night while Sarah was still asleep, crept up the stairs and turned Lucy's portrait around to obscure the missing woman's features before Sarah came down in the morning. If that's what had happened, it was an obvious warning, and it showed Sarah that whoever had done this could get into the house whenever they wanted. The only portrait that had been tampered with was Lucy's and that was a clear signal. Sarah was being told to stay out of this. The notion of a faceless, nameless intruder so close to her in the middle of the night, when she was alone and at her most vulnerable, was chilling. The thought of what they might have done, instead of merely flipping a portrait, was enough to leave her feeling truly terrified.

Sarah heard voices coming from the kitchen. They were falsely cheerful words, delivered in a singsong manner, and she realized it was the inane prattle from a radio DJ.

Cautiously, she approached the door, opened it and looked in. It was Mrs Jenkins, and Sarah was actually pleased to see her for once.

The older woman turned and frowned slightly at Sarah's presence, or perhaps it was her slightly dishevelled hair. 'You're up,' she said, without adding the word *finally*, but that was clearly what she meant.

'I didn't realize it was one of your days,' Sarah told her.

'It isn't, but I thought you could use the help.' Did she mean there was a lot to do or that Sarah clearly wasn't capable of looking after herself? She almost took issue with that but decided it might be sensible to avoid falling out with the housekeeper so early in her stay there.

'Thank you,' she managed, then she asked, 'The painting at the top of the staircase, the one of Lucy Woodfell?'

'What about it?'

'Did you turn it around?'

'Why would I do that?'

'I don't know. But someone did,' said Sarah hopelessly. 'Is Patrick in today?'

Mrs Jenkins shook her head. 'He *was* in but he went straight outside. He didn't turn any paintings around.' She was regarding Sarah doubtfully, as if she must have imagined the whole thing. Then the housekeeper said, 'I see you bought some groceries.' Was this a good or bad thing in Mrs Jenkins' eyes? Sarah couldn't tell.

'I called in at the local shop.'

'They've always delivered.'

'Well, I didn't know that,' said Sarah. Her tone was sharper than she had intended but she was getting pretty sick of the housekeeper's attitude. If the older woman detected this, she didn't let on.

'There's some post,' she said, handing Sarah three envelopes which she took eagerly, but none were handwritten. They all looked like bills to be paid, which meant she had yet to receive a reply from any of the Woodfell siblings.

There was the usual look of disapproval from Mrs Jenkins and Sarah realized the post was something else the older woman must have thought she had been neglecting.

'I didn't see them,' said Sarah.

'They're not posted through the door.'

'I gathered that.' There was no letter box, after all. 'But where does the mail go?'

'The postbox is outside.' The housekeeper indicated with a slight jerk of her head but she did not narrow down the location any further. Helpful as ever, thought Sarah.

'You'll be wanting to crack on,' said Mrs Jenkins and there was definitely judgement in her voice. Bloody hell, it's not that late, surely? Then Sarah glanced at the clock on the kitchen wall which showed her it was much later than she'd thought. Oh God, how long had the woman been here, cleaning the house and fussing round the kitchen before she had even emerged?

'I'll make a cup of coffee first. Would you like one?'

'No, thank you.' Her tone made it sound as if Sarah had just invited her to shirk her duties.

'Well, I need the caffeine. I've barely slept at all for the last few nights. I keep hearing sounds. Thought someone was breaking in.'

She expected more frowns or mocking words, but instead the woman regarded her curiously. 'What kind of sounds?'

'It was probably the wind or the old boiler or something.' The woman was still staring at her intently. 'It's stupid, but in the middle of the night I keep hearing what sounds like whispers, so it freaked me out a little, being on my own.'

She really expected to be mocked for that. A silly little city girl who was hearing things in the night. Instead, the older woman locked eyes with her. 'The lady's lament,' she said.

'The what?'

'You heard it.' She seemed almost impressed, as if this was an honour the house reserved for good people, then she repeated the words. 'The lady's lament.'

Chapter Seventeen

'It's a sad tale,' the housekeeper began. 'Dates back to the seventeenth century and Lady Alice Woodfell. Her father promised her in marriage to a landowner from the next county but Lady Alice was in love with a different boy and refused to wed another. Her father locked her in her room and said he would only let her out when she agreed to the marriage. She refused to eat and wasted away. The servants begged their master to free her but he was as stubborn as she was and Alice died in that room. Her father never uttered her name again, but she tormented him and everyone else in the household who heard her lament from beyond the grave. They say she cursed this house and everyone in it,' she concluded. 'And that would explain a lot.'

'I didn't hear any laments, just whispers.'

'Lady Alice still haunts this house,' maintained the housekeeper. 'Other guests have heard her whispering. I haven't made it up.'

'I'm sure you haven't.'

'You just think I'm daft for believing it.'

'No.'

'It's easy to be rational in the daylight,' said Mrs Jenkins, 'but not so simple when you're lying in bed on your own.'

'I think we can agree on that,' conceded Sarah, who was keen to change the subject now and not dwell on the disturbing possibility of a supernatural explanation for the sounds she was hearing in the night.

Mrs Jenkins was about to start mopping the floor. 'The solicitor said there was a car I could use while I am staying here?' Sarah asked before she was shooed from the kitchen.

'In the garage,' the housekeeper answered.

'Which is where?' Sarah hadn't seen one on her walk around the perimeter but it was a very big estate.

'Head for the paddock and it's just past the stables.'

She hadn't seen stables either. Was the woman being deliberately awkward? 'Which direction is that?' The housekeeper pointed in a vaguely southerly direction. 'And is it locked?'

Mrs Jenkins did not reply. Instead, she walked over to a large wooden board on the wall festooned with keys. There were no markings on the board to indicate what each key was for but Mrs Jenkins seemed to know them from memory. She handed a large, slightly rusty key to Sarah.

'What about the car keys? Are they in the glove box?'

Again, the housekeeper made no comment. Instead, she turned back to the wooden board and took a second key from a nail then handed it to her.

'Christ,' Sarah hissed audibly, but only once she was out of earshot. She was glad to be out of the house and leaving Mrs Jenkins behind.

Sarah decided to check out the postbox first, and when she peered across the wide gravel courtyard, she noticed something at the far end. It appeared to be a grey metal box mounted on a short pole close to the wall. There was a considerable distance between the house and the

postbox, which would not be too much of an inconvenience when the weather was mild but far less fun during a
cold winter. She supposed it would have been a servant's
job to bring in the post each morning.

Sarah walked over and examined the simple metal box,
which was very old. It had two slots: a smaller one for the
mail and a larger one that was presumably for newspapers.
She lifted the lid and looked inside the empty box while
making a mental note to beat Mrs Jenkins there every
morning to prove she wasn't naturally lazy.

Next, Sarah walked in the direction Mrs Jenkins had indicated and soon found the paddock. Behind it was a stable
block without horses. Just beyond this, an old garage with
two large wooden doors that were firmly closed. Sarah
unlocked it and dragged open one of the doors, which
scraped along the ground. She opened the second door to
allow enough light in to see clearly.

Wow.

It was a car all right, but not one Sarah was at all familiar
with. It looked like something sporty from as far back as
the mid-sixties but it seemed in excellent condition and had
obviously been cherished and restored at some point. The
bodywork was in great shape and it gleamed when the sun
caught it. It was as if the car knew it was about to be let out
for an airing and was waiting proudly in anticipation.

'Jenny said you were looking for the car,' called a voice.
She turned to find Patrick, the gardener or handyman, or
whatever he was, standing there.

'Jenny? Jenny Jenkins? Surely not?'

'Apparently so.'

'That's vindictive parenting,' she said.

'Lazy parenting, I reckon. They can't have spent long thinking about it. "Fuck it, call her Jenny." Job done.'

She laughed at this, glad of an ally in her mocking of the stern-faced housekeeper's name. She put her new, more positive opinion of Patrick to one side for a moment while she quizzed him about the portrait that was turned around but he seemed as genuinely bemused by the question as Jenny Jenkins, so she waved it away.

'You ever driven this?' she asked him.

'Often, with your aunt's blessing. I did some work on it for her and she liked me to drive her on an errand or two.'

'Gardens, houses *and* cars? You're a useful person to know, Patrick.'

'I mostly got other people to work on the car. Your aunt wanted to make sure no one ripped her off.'

'I have never seen a car like this before.'

'As soon as I opened the garage doors, I knew that this was a 1961 Triumph Sunbeam Rapier convertible.'

'Really?'

'No,' he laughed, 'I didn't have a clue, except it did have a Triumph badge on it. I tracked down an expert to get the bodywork restored. The rear wings were corroded and it needed two new driving lamps. The hood was rotten so that's been replaced. I don't think it liked the Northumbrian air. It's got a lovely walnut dash,' he said, almost to himself, 'and it purrs.'

She laughed at that.

'It does. Don't believe me? Hop in.'

'I will.'

'It's a weekend ride,' he explained, once she was sitting

in the car. 'It used to belong to Persephone Woodfell. Her son is Toby Ramsay.'

'Our next prime minister, according to just about everyone.'

'Evelyn bought the car when she purchased the house,' he explained. 'Got it for a song, along with everything else.'

Sarah turned the key in the ignition and the car started immediately. 'It's more of a growl than a purr,' she said, 'but I love it!'

'It's yours now,' he told her and she decided against disillusioning him about that. What could she say? *It's mine for a few months, probably, unless I catch a killer.*

He made to leave and she asked, 'Where are you going?'

'I thought you wanted to take her for a spin.'

'It's a she, is it?'

He knew she was mocking him but he played along. 'Definitely.'

'I do want to take her for a spin but I've never driven a car as old as this one. I was hoping you could show me.' This was true, but she also wanted to get Patrick alone and away from the house. He seemed to know a bit about the Woodfell family and she was eager to know how much. Then she added, 'If you're not too busy, that is?'

'Okay.'

She got out of the car and walked round to the passenger side. Patrick climbed into the driver's seat.

'Where do you want to go?'

She thought for a moment. 'Why don't you just see where the road takes us?'

Chapter Eighteen

They drove for around five miles before joining the coastal route. Here, they caught occasional glimpses of the sea until they were turned back inland by the curves of the road. They passed through more villages but mostly it was fields and woodlands. The Triumph was noisier than modern cars but they could still talk above the sound of the engine and it seemed a good time to quiz Patrick about the Woodfells.

'Did you know the family?' she asked him.

'No, but my mother cleaned for them. I used to go there in the summer holidays with her at the back end of the eighties, if the family were away. I was only about five or six years old then.'

That must have been a couple of years before Evie bought the house, Sarah reasoned, and it put Patrick in his late thirties now. 'Have you lived in the village all your life?'

'No, I left,' he said, 'and then I came back.'

Sarah was expecting to hear more but this was all she got. Maybe Patrick thought his life wasn't that interesting, or he didn't want to tell her anything about it.

'Did your mother like them?'

'She was the help,' he said simply. 'Hired to clean, so she got on with it. I doubt they spoke to her or ever gave her a thought. She didn't really talk about them. I used to think it wasn't fair that they had so much and she used to have to work so hard for what we had, which wasn't a lot, but she said that's just the way it is. She didn't seem to resent the fact that they were born into money. That was before they lost it all, of course.'

'How *did* they lose it all?'

'Slowly, I think, over time, and then very suddenly, at the end. They didn't really know how to adapt to a modern world. It used to be enough to be a landowner. You could sit back and do nothing. But that was a long time ago and you need to make money to keep an estate going. They tried a few things over the years,' he smiled. 'They invested in a gold mine in South Africa and lost money. At one point, I think it must have been around 1980 or so, they were going to build a golf course but it never happened. There was even a zoo before that, would you believe?'

That might explain the strange buildings she had seen. 'When was this?'

'Mid-seventies. Hardly anyone came to see it and when they did, people complained about the wild animals.'

'What didn't they like about the animals?'

'I can't remember which one of the sons decided to invest in the zoo, but he had no experience of wild animals and was pretty much terrified of them, according to my mam, so he drugged them all to keep them passive. Trouble was, they just lay there all day, so it was the most boring zoo in the world. He was reported to the animal welfare people and the place was closed down not that long after it opened.'

'How long have you worked for my aunt?'

'Eight years. I came back when my mother died.'

'Oh, I'm sorry.'

If Patrick was in his late thirties, as he appeared to be, and had left his village as a young man, which was likely, then he had to have been away for a while, but he still shed no light on where he had been in the interim.

She decided to use the story of the zoo to steer the conversation in the direction she wanted. 'It sounds as if the family weren't very lucky. Aside from their business failures, I mean. Didn't one of them die in a car crash and another was disinherited?' She hoped this sounded like natural curiosity.

'Yes, Persephone's husband was killed in a crash back in the eighties, not far from the house, actually.'

'That's awful.'

'It was a strange one. He was going really fast down a road he knew, which had a sharp bend at the end. Some said it was an accident, others that he had taken his own life.'

He didn't seem to share the shopkeeper's theory about murder, even though he was from the same village. 'Why would he have taken his own life?'

'He was twenty years older than Persephone, had fought in the Second World War and been in the thick of it. He lost men and killed men. He struggled after that.'

'PTSD?'

'They called it shell shock at the time, but yes, I think so.'

'Poor man.'

'It was less well understood in those days.'

'Do you really think he waited forty years to commit suicide? That's a very long time after the war.'

'I don't know. No one does. There were various theories.'

She stayed silent for a moment, while he took a sharp bend at speed. The car went smoothly around it and they were back on a straight road again, with the sea once more in sight.

'You said there were theories?' she reminded him.

'It was just village talk.'

'Tell me anyway.'

'My mother told me about his much younger wife possibly having other . . . I think she used the word *paramours*.'

'Illicit lovers?'

'That might have given the poor bloke another reason to kill himself,' he said. 'Or maybe it was more sinister than that. I was very young at the time, so what do I know?'

'Go on,' she urged him.

'The guy from the local scrapyard took the wrecked car after the police were done with it. He used to tell people it had been tampered with.'

'That *is* interesting.' And it tallied with what she had been told in the shop, so more than one villager suspected the captain had been murdered. 'Did he report it?'

'I think so, but for whatever reason the police didn't take it seriously. They reckoned it was an accident, so that was that,' he concluded.

They drove on for a while until Sarah spotted a pub and suggested they stop for a drink.

'If you're sure?' he asked. 'Technically I'm on duty.'

'You're a gardener, Patrick, not a police officer. I won't tell the fierce Jenny Jenkins if you don't.'

'She's not too bad, once you get to know her.'

'Why would I want to get to know her?'

He laughed at that and she realized she enjoyed amusing him.

They ordered drinks and took them to a quiet table by a window. Sarah started to relax for the first time since she had arrived at Cragsmoor Manor, even while she continued quizzing Patrick about the family.

'Since we're having a gossip, tell me about the disinherited son.'

'Oliver. He was the oldest son, so he should have inherited it all, but his father passed him over for his younger brother, Freddie.'

Or Freddie the nudist, as Sarah tended to think of him, thanks to her aunt's story.

'Why? What did he do?'

'Drugs,' he said. 'A lot of them. His father paid for Oliver to go to a clinic in Switzerland and get clean, which he did. He was out there for quite a while. It must have cost a fortune. Then he came back to the house and a day or two later he took a massive overdose. He almost died, and when they brought him round, his father kicked him out and changed the will to leave everything to his younger brother.'

'What a family,' she exclaimed.

As well as an enjoyable trip it had been a fruitful one. Sarah had learned more about Lucy's older siblings from Patrick. Persephone's husband had been traumatized by the war and died in a car crash that was almost as suspicious as Lucy's disappearance. Meanwhile, Oliver was a drug addict who nearly killed himself and Freddie had benefitted from that overdose, at least initially, until the estate eventually went bankrupt, under his management.

When they had finished their drinks, Sarah suggested she drive back and he handed her the keys.

She spent the first few miles getting used to the car, which was harder to manoeuvre than any of the modern vehicles she had previously driven. Patrick had warned her about the lack of power steering in vintage cars, which meant her reactions would feel delayed. It wasn't easy at first, but Sarah started to get the hang of it and was eventually relaxed enough to continue their conversation about the family.

'What about that girl?' she asked him. 'The one that disappeared? Lucy, was it?'

'Your aunt's best friend, you mean? I wondered when you were going to ask me about her.' He sounded suspicious of her light probing.

'I'd never heard of her until my aunt's passing,' she replied truthfully.

'You probably know the story. She went for a walk one day and didn't come back. They never found her.'

'What do people round here think happened to Lucy?'

'Honestly, I don't think anyone knows. There were a couple of suspects but no one was ever charged.'

'Who was in the frame for it?' She had read about those suspects but wanted to know what he thought.

'There was that guy who killed his girlfriend not long before Lucy disappeared then went on the run. David something? He was still free and roaming the area when she went missing so the police focused on him for a while. Then there was another bloke who was on the beach that day but denied ever seeing Lucy. The police had their suspicions about him too.'

'I walked the beach and I don't know how he couldn't have seen her if he was there,' Sarah said.

He turned slightly to look at her and she realized he was definitely suspicious of her interest. 'I'm an author,' she said, making light of it. 'We love a good story and we're all terrible procrastinators. I should be writing my book.'

He seemed to accept this. 'There was also speculation about the family.'

'What kind of speculation?' she asked.

'It was always a drama with them. There were four siblings from two marriages growing up together and getting into squabbles about the running of the estate and their trust fund. I'm not saying that people outright accused her brothers and sister of killing Lucy, but they fought like cats and dogs. It was always possible it went too far or there was an accident.'

'What do you think?'

'I really have no idea. I assumed that a stranger took her and somehow managed to dispose of the body without anyone ever finding it.'

'I doubt we'll ever know the truth now,' she said, and meant it.

Sarah drove the car back to the estate and parked it in the courtyard outside the house. Before they got out, she asked him, 'What have you got on today?'

'Missing roof tiles,' he said. 'Two of them came down in the last storm. Then next, I'm supposed to be painting the windows in the bedrooms.'

She could easily believe that storms were strong enough

to dislodge roof tiles here. 'The wind really whistles once it gets going,' she said. 'It can keep you awake.' Then she admitted, 'It *does* keep me awake, actually. Jenny Jenkins thinks I'm hearing the ghost of Alice Woodfell, whispering to me in the night. She calls it the Lady's Lament.'

'I've heard of that. It's what your late aunt would have described as a load of old bollocks.'

'But what do you think?'

He seemed to give this some thought. 'I think the dead stay dead. I don't think they rise from the grave to come and haunt us, but I do think they stay in our minds, which can feel like the same thing sometimes.'

'That's deep.'

'Is it?'

When they reached the front door of the house, she said, 'Thanks for taking me for a drive.'

'You got the hang of it pretty quickly,' he said. 'You didn't need me.'

'Well, I enjoyed your company.' And when it looked like this might be the beginning of an awkward silence she added, 'Be careful on that roof. Don't let the ghost of Lady Alice push you off.'

'I'll try not to.'

Chapter Nineteen

Sarah had thought long and hard about whether it was worth having another attempt to speak to the retired detective, even though he had been quite insistent that he wasn't interested in talking to her about Lucy Woodfell. It seemed an obvious way to cut through a lot of the myth and gossip that surrounded the case by talking to someone who was actually there, speaking to suspects and sifting through clues, but he didn't seem to care about Sarah or what she wanted. So, the question was, how could she make him care?

It took a while for her to think of it, but in the end the solution seemed obvious, though she knew it would still not necessarily guarantee success.

'How did you get my number?' demanded Crozier when she called him.

'You gave it to me,' she said.

'I did not.'

'When you phoned me back, remember? It was stored on my phone's call log.'

He grunted his understanding of that. 'I didn't say you could call me. I told you I wasn't interested.'

'And since I couldn't get you to help me, I thought you might prefer it if I helped you instead,' she suggested.

'What do you mean?'

'I am willing to pay for your time,' she told him bluntly,

'in the form of a further donation to your community centre.'

There was a pause while he seemed to consider this then he asked, 'How much?' It appeared he was interested now.

'A hundred pounds,' she said, 'in return for one hour.'

'Done,' he agreed. 'But don't expect miracles.'

Sarah took it easy on the way to Alnwick in the unfamiliar car. Edward Crozier lived in a bungalow on the edge of town within sight of the ancient castle. He must have seen her pull up and he came out to meet her. Crozier was in his early seventies, a tall, wiry man dressed in a cardigan and a check shirt with a collar. His shoes looked like they had been shined recently.

'My mystery benefactor,' he said dryly. 'You'd better come in. The meter is running.' Sarah had only been promised an hour of his time and it seemed he was going to hold her to that.

They sat at his kitchen table, sipping tea from plain white mugs while the former detective quizzed Sarah about her interest in Lucy Woodfell's disappearance. She explained her aunt's close friendship with the woman but did not mention her conditional inheritance, in case he assumed money was the sole reason for her being there. His questions continued until they took up enough time for her to enquire, 'When does the clock start ticking on my hour?'

'It started when you walked in here.'

'Then don't you think I should be the one asking the questions?'

He appeared to find that amusing and she wondered if he had been deliberately trying to hijack their meeting. 'Go on then,' he urged her.

'I've read a lot about the case but I wanted to speak to someone who actually worked on it. I know the official version but not the unofficial one.'

'How do you mean?'

'I would like to know what you thought happened to Lucy Woodfell back then,' she said, 'and what you think about the case now.'

'I don't know,' he said simply. 'If I knew that, we would have solved it.'

'Do you think she is dead?'

'It seems highly unlikely that she just walked away. There have been no credible sightings of her since. I would put my money on her being dead, yes.' He looked away from her then and stared out of the window, 'Except . . .'

'There was no body,' she said.

'We never found one or even a trace of one, and we searched everywhere with sniffer dogs. If a body had been dumped somewhere or buried locally, they'd have found it. We brought in extra officers to do fingertip searches on every inch of land around the house and all the way down to the beach. We examined the cars of every family member or anyone else at the house when Lucy Woodfell disappeared and never found so much as a hair from her head. In any case, no one left the estate that afternoon.'

'According to who?'

'Everyone. Three family members, a nanny, a cleaner and a gardener. They all said no cars had driven away.'

'And obviously you searched the house?'

'From top to bottom.'

'Including the priest holes?'

'Yes. They showed us the priest holes and there was nothing inside them.'

'Was there any resistance to that search? From family members, I mean.'

'It wasn't as if they were obstructing us exactly, but I don't think they liked a bunch of oiks traipsing over their carpets.'

'Even if that involved finding Lucy?' she probed.

'They weren't the easiest people to deal with,' Crozier admitted. 'I got the impression they thought we were amateurs who didn't know what we were doing.'

'But you weren't?'

'Twenty-six murders I've investigated. We cleared up all but two. If Lucy was murdered, that is.'

'But your feeling is, she was.'

'On the balance of probability, I'd say so.'

'Who do you think did it then? I'm not asking you to prove anything, just for your off-the-record opinion.'

'It wasn't that simple,' he said. 'Usually, even if you haven't got proof, you've got a good idea of the culprit, but not this time. The first thing you do on a murder case is ask yourself, who stood to gain? The answer here was no one. If Lucy Woodfell was murdered, we never worked out why.'

'What about her share of the trust fund. Who got that?'

'The amount wasn't that significant and she was never legally declared dead, so no one got it.'

'Even after all these years.'

'They didn't even bother to try and claim it.'

'So, if money wasn't the motive?' she asked. 'What could it have been?'

'If it was someone close to the victim, then you are usually looking at motives like love, lust, jealousy, revenge. Nobody in her family seemed to have a motive.'

'That you were aware of,' she countered.

'That we were aware of,' he conceded.

'What if the killer was not known to the victim?'

'You mean if it was Warren Evans or David Young?'

'Young was on the run already,' she reminded him, 'and desperate, presumably.'

'He was in the area and sleeping rough. We even got a description from an eyewitness in the village who spotted a big, scruffy young man with muddied clothes who was the same height as David and had the same hair colour. Some said he had nothing to lose, so why not kill more women if the result was going to be the same – a long prison sentence? Others pointed out that he freely admitted killing a woman who was close to him but always denied murdering Lucy Woodfell. They think he would have fessed up to both killings if he had committed them.'

There was something about the way he said *others* and *they* that made her sense he was not in agreement. 'But you don't?'

'No.' He didn't explain why. It was as if he was making her work hard for it, testing her even, to see what she could work out for herself.

'Neither do I.'

'Why not?'

It was clear she was going to have to earn this. 'Because

owning up to one murder gets you a life sentence but it doesn't actually mean life. With good behaviour, you could be out on parole in twelve years, and a confession that saves the cost of a trial will earn you remission. On the other hand, if you admitted killing two different women in separate incidents, they would lock you up and throw away the key.'

'My thoughts exactly.'

'Do you think he did it then?'

'He was an obvious suspect and we pressed him hard during questioning, but we never could prove that he was there that day or had interacted with Lucy before. It is so difficult when you have no testimony from the victim and no body to examine for physical evidence. Our DCI figured we would nail him for the murder he confessed to and he would get jail time for that, so it wasn't like he was going to walk free if we let this one drop due to lack of proof.'

'What was he like?'

'Barking, obviously. He killed that poor girl, so he obviously had ... what do they call it these days? Anger management issues. He snapped,' he explained, 'so maybe he snapped more than once. Who knows?' He shrugged as if that was the end of the matter.

'Did you press Warren Evans hard too?'

'We did. Warren was seen on the beach. He was there for most of the afternoon and confirmed that he was lying on the sand at the exact point where Lucy should have emerged from the path, if she was indeed heading towards the sea. If four people said she walked that way, while he was on the beach, then it surely follows that he must have seen her. If he had admitted that and said she had walked off to the south or the north we might have accepted it, but he denied seeing her at all, so he quickly became a person of interest. His girlfriend painted a picture of a jealous and really quite angry young man. My DI fancied him as the culprit. He reckoned Lucy was the first woman he saw after his girlfriend walked away from him, and he took it out on her.'

'His girlfriend walked out on him and he was upset,' she conceded, 'but instead of going after her, he sat down and waited until he saw a stranger walking towards him and he pounced on her instead? He would have had to have attacked Lucy on the beach, in full view of anyone who happened to be walking by, or perhaps intercept her on the path before she got there.'

'That is what my DI surmised.'

'But the path isn't one long straight road. I walked it and it arcs round.' She demonstrated this by curving her arm. 'You wouldn't actually see someone coming until they were fifteen yards away.'

'I walked it too and fifteen yards is long enough.'

'Is it? Only if he was waiting for a victim along a path not many people use. Think about it. He's sitting on the beach and all of a sudden a woman appears. How long does it take him to turn around, notice her then think, I want her? Then he has to get up and walk towards her, slowly, so as not to scare her, then grab her and do what? Drag her off into the dunes then rape her, kill her and dispose of the body somehow, all without a vehicle?'

'I know it's thin,' he admitted, 'but in the absence of any other plausible theory . . .'

He had a point. Warren's guilt or innocence in the matter would be hard to prove, either way. 'I wish I could talk to him,' she said, almost to herself, 'but I have no way of finding him.' He passed no comment on this, so she returned to the Woodfells and the period following the initial search for Lucy on the estate.

'What was it like dealing with the family in the aftermath of Lucy's disappearance?' she asked.

'Not easy. They had a certain amount of influence. We had to tread carefully.'

'Which you wouldn't have done under normal circumstances?'

'If someone disappears, your priority is to find them, not worry about upsetting other members of her family. The welfare of Lucy Woodfell was our biggest concern, of course, but we were told to be discreet and respectful at all times in our dealings with family members.'

'How did that work in practice?'

'We never went in hard when we interviewed them. There was a lot of *I think the first time you recalled this, sir, you said that it happened slightly differently, could you just take a moment to help us clarify the matter?*

'Whereas usually . . . ?'

'I'd accuse someone of being a lying little scrote. That kind of pressure used to get results, but it's hard to apply politely.'

'I can imagine. Did they lie to you, then?'

'Let's just say they were a bit muddled over the timeline of when Lucy disappeared and who saw her last. It didn't help that Oliver Woodfell was a drug addict and an alcoholic. They're not the most reliable of witnesses. Drug users are often more than a little paranoid. They think *everyone* is out to get them so you can imagine how they feel about police officers.'

'Did you believe his story?'

'What part of it?'

'Specifically, that he saw Lucy walking to the back of the house towards the coast road.'

'That he saw her, yes. We just weren't sure exactly when. It was plausible. She liked to go to the beach, she liked to swim in the sea when she could and it was a warm afternoon. His brother Freddie and sister Sephy saw her too, as well as the child's nanny, Margaret Malloy. That's four people with no obvious reason to lie, who saw Lucy walk down to the beach.'

'What did you make of Freddie and Sephy?'

'Freddie was quite arrogant and had that upper-class sense of entitlement. They all did. Born to rule and all that. I thought his sister was brighter and, although she was quite often sharp with us, she was more cooperative. I think she felt Lucy's disappearance more keenly than he did, but I would add that there were times when I saw both of them visibly distressed by it.'

'You ever get the feeling they might have been involved in it in any way?'

'We didn't like them much but that doesn't make them killers.'

'What was your impression of the nanny?'

'She was obviously loyal to the family but I don't reckon she was so loyal she'd lie to the police to protect them.

She lived quite a sheltered life and I think we frightened her, to be honest. She was like a little rabbit when we interviewed her.'

'Toby Ramsay was a bit old to have a nanny, wasn't he? I thought they only looked after younger children, but he must have been twelve around then?'

'Thirteen,' he corrected her, 'and yes, we wondered about that. It was something to do with him being home-educated at the time and she helped to keep him focused on his work or something.'

'Sounds a bit vague.'

'It was a bit vague,' he agreed. 'Anyway, it can't have done him any harm, judging by where he is now.'

'Clearly,' she said. 'Does the nanny still live locally?'

'I think she retired and went back to Scotland years ago. Died a while back, or so I heard.'

It was to be expected that not everyone would still be alive after all these years, but Sarah would have liked to have asked Margaret Malloy about the family, and specifically why they felt the need to employ her to look after a thirteen-year-old and why he was being home-schooled. That seemed strange even for an eccentric aristocratic family like the Woodfells.

'Did you interview Sephy's husband too?' she asked.

'Captain Ramsay? Yes, we did. He was buttoned down, hard to read, but he answered all of our questions. Where was he when she went missing? *At his home in London.* When had he last seen his sister-in-law? *Some weeks earlier.* Did they get on? *Well enough.* Did he know anyone who might want to harm her? *He did not.* It wasn't that he was evasive, just lacking in emotion. I put it down to his war years. I understand he saw a great deal of death back then, so the disappearance of a sister-in-law he got on passably well with might not have impacted on him as much.'

'Passably well? My aunt thought that he and Lucy Woodfell were close.'

'We were not given that impression,' he replied, but that did not necessarily mean it wasn't true, thought Sarah.

'When did you get to speak to him, if he was in London, I mean?'

'He came up as soon as he heard Lucy had gone missing.'

Sarah considered this for a moment. 'Must have arrived very late then, if he drove up from London. Lucy went missing in the afternoon and I imagine it was a few hours before anyone raised the alarm. Could he have been in the area already?'

'The timings seemed plausible,' Crozier said. 'He was there the following morning when we interviewed them all, once Lucy Woodfell had been missing overnight.'

'And a couple of years later, he was dead too,' she reminded him. 'What did you make of that?'

'Coroner said accident,' he shrugged, 'and he was well known for driving too fast on the roads near the manor house, but it could have been . . . something else.'

'Murder?'

'Murder?' He was surprised by that. 'I was going to say suicide, maybe. What made you think it might have been murder?'

'Village gossip,' she said. 'About his brakes being tampered with.'

'They do that in villages,' he said dryly. 'Gossip, I mean.'

'Why did you suggest suicide?'

'Don't read too much into that. It was just the speed he was travelling at.'

'How fast was he going?'

'I didn't investigate the crash myself, but it was estimated he was doing around sixty miles an hour when he hit that wall, which would have been reckless on a road like that one.'

'Would he have had a reason to kill himself?'

'He must have seen some pretty awful things during the war. That might have affected his mind.'

Patrick had said as much, but Sarah still wasn't convinced. 'The war had been over for more than forty years by then,' she reminded him.

'Accident then,' he said dismissively, 'or suicide for some other reason we are unlikely ever to learn.' He was clearly tired of discussing it now. 'Is there anything else?' he asked.

'If I pinned you down and you absolutely had to pick one of them to be the murderer, who do you think is the most likely?'

He pondered this for a while then asked, 'Off the record?'

'Off the record,' she agreed.

'I like a bet on the horses, been doing it for years. It's easy to look at the odds and find yourself attracted to an outsider. You start thinking, wouldn't it be great if that horse came in first because I'd make so much money, but you should never bet on an outsider. In reality, the favourite or second favourite horse wins more than fifty per cent of all races.'

He was trying to tell her something, but at this point she wasn't exactly sure what. 'Who is the clear favourite here then?'

'If I was a bookmaker writing down the odds for this one, I'd go with the guy who had already killed someone.'

'Despite the absence of evidence?'

'Despite the absence of proof,' he corrected her. 'The fact that he beat a woman to death is damning enough, surely.'

'Circumstantial evidence, perhaps,' she said. 'I understand David Young is back in the area?'

'He is,' said Crozier, 'but don't go and see him.'

'Why? Do you really think he's that dangerous?'

'Well, look at it this way, pet – he murdered one woman and may very well have killed another, so if you're not careful, you could be next.'

Chapter Twenty

Sarah had a lot to think about as she drove away from the detective's home. She wondered if the original investigation might have gone differently if the police had been allowed to go in harder on the family members and not treat them with such deference. Had her half-siblings been asked enough awkward questions about their relationships with the missing woman or probed sufficiently about her private life? It didn't sound like it.

Then there was the underwhelming response from Sephy's husband, Captain Ramsay, who had played down his friendship with Lucy, even though Evie had written in her memoir that they became close. Either she felt more for him than he did for her, or he was as buttoned down and unemotional as the detective had described him. There was a third possibility, of course. He was lying. But why do that unless you have something to hide? Like what? An affair with Lucy, or even the fact that he had killed her, perhaps? If he had murdered her, then guilt or remorse might explain his possible suicide two years later, if the crash that ended his life wasn't just an accident.

It was a shame that the nanny had passed away because Sarah would have loved to have talked with a woman who had lived and worked with the Woodfell family for so long. What an insight she could have given into their world.

Sarah really wanted to speak to Warren Evans too, to

challenge him about being on the beach that day but maintaining that he never saw Lucy. His story just didn't ring true. It struck Sarah that, if he really was the one who had attacked her, his claim to have never seen Lucy might have been a lie he had told from the beginning that he became trapped in, since he could hardly change his story, which left Sarah wondering if he might be the killer. Crozier's DI seemed to think so, but the retired Detective Sergeant had another suspect in mind. What were the odds of two murders being committed by two different men in the same region at around the same time? Crozier reckoned David Young would have been the bookie's favourite for this one, and when Sarah considered it like that, she had to concede he had a point.

So, if David Young was now her prime suspect, what could she do about it? Even if she could track him down, she couldn't just knock on his door and invite herself in for a cup of tea. Nor would she want to. Crozier had reminded her of just how dangerous he might be.

Sarah told herself she should not simply regard the testimony of the retired detective as if it was the truth. This would be a process of elimination, and before she could be sure that David Young was the culprit, she would have to discount everyone else. Until that point, everybody her aunt had mentioned was still a suspect.

The phone started ringing as she was opening the door to let herself in. Sarah went straight to the sitting room without taking off her raincoat. She heard Dickie's unmistakeable voice on the other end of the line. He already sounded apologetic even as he greeted her.

'Did you make any progress on the manuscript?' she asked him.

'I have some good news on that score . . .'

'Excellent.'

'. . . and some bad news too, I'm afraid.'

'Give me the good news first. It's in short supply at the moment.'

'We managed to track Sean down. Our former intern is in Vietnam but he responded to our entreaties and got in touch with us.' Dickie seemed quite proud of this. 'He explained he'd been typing up sections of your aunt's memoir and saving them in smaller files, with a view to putting them all together into one big one at the end, and this he duly did, or thought he had done.'

'You're not making a lot of sense, Dickie. Did he do it or not?'

'He swears he did, but I opened the file we had printed and bound for you and, as you said, it's not all there. He thinks it didn't save properly, so you received a copy of an earlier draft that doesn't have all the chapters in it.'

Sarah wasn't sure she was buying that. 'I actually got duplicated chapters.'

'Yes, something has obviously gone wrong there, but don't worry, in theory we should still be able to find the smaller files. I've got one of our people going through it all now, but it's an old laptop and there are a great many files on there – it's been used for a decade by a lot of interns. She needs to find them, place them in the right order and send the whole thing back to you.'

'And who have you given the job to?'

'Her name is Kirsten,' he said.

'I mean, is she another intern?'

'Er . . . yes . . . yes, she is.'

'Great.'

'She is young and keen, though, and understands technology, unlike me.'

'But are you paying her, Dickie? Because you know that does tend to motivate people and prevents them from messing up the job before heading off around the world without a care.'

'I will pay her a bonus once the work is complete.'

'Good, but tell her not to wait until she has stitched it all back together. Get her to send me what she finds when she finds it.'

'Will do. I really am very sorry about all this, Sarah, and I sincerely hope it doesn't hamper your investigation.'

She almost asked 'what investigation?' but didn't want to provide him with a disincentive to get the work completed. He was about to hang up when she asked, 'What about the original manuscript? Did you ask Sean about that?'

'I did and he swears he put it back in the desk drawer, like I asked him to.'

'But it's not there,' she said helplessly. 'Do you think he stole it?'

'I have to say I believe him.'

'Why?'

He sounded uncomfortable then. 'He strikes me as the honest sort and . . . er . . . I knew his father.'

And he probably went to the right school too, thought Sarah cynically. 'That doesn't rule him out, Dickie,' she said forcefully.

'I know, but it can be a bit chaotic here at times. Someone has probably just moved it somewhere.'

'Then where is it?'

'That is the question,' he admitted, but he didn't offer her an answer.

When she had finished speaking with Dickie, Sarah went to hang up her raincoat in the hallway. Before she managed that, the phone started ringing again. Dickie must have forgotten to tell her something.

'Hello?' She failed to hide her impatience.

The reply came from a deep, synthesized, male but robotic voice, which distorted the speaker's words till they were barely recognizable.

'Sarah Hollis?'

Was this a prank or was there something wrong with the line? 'Yes,' she managed.

She expected the voice to speak again but it did not. There was silence on the end of the line. 'Hello? ... Hello?' At first, she wondered if he had been cut off but something told her he was still on the line, listening.

'What are you doing at Cragsmoor?' the voice boomed at her. Whatever he was using to disguise his own voice was turning his words into a deep and threatening growl.

'Who is this?' Sarah was scared but also annoyed by the intrusion. 'Why is it any of your business?'

'What's your real agenda?'

'I don't have an agenda. What's yours?' Silence on the end of the line. 'Why do you care about any of this?'

'Why do you?' the robotic voice demanded.

Some of Sarah's fear turned to anger then. 'Because a

woman disappeared and she was probably murdered, and she was a great friend of my aunt, who recently died, but something tells me you know all of this already. I don't have an agenda. I'm just interested in the truth.'

'Truth is entirely subjective.'

'What are you talking about?' she demanded.

There was a long pause before he spoke again. 'Tread carefully.'

'Are you threatening me?' She was almost as outraged as she was frightened, but not quite. Sarah was not used to being threatened and there was something cold and sociopathic about the computerized voice. She could feel her heart pumping with adrenalin.

'Well, obviously,' he said, as if this was entirely reasonable behaviour. She was so shocked by this admission that she could not think of a response at first.

'I'm not frightened of you,' she said eventually, hoping that she sounded more convincing than she felt.

'You should be,' he said. 'Oh, and I wouldn't wear that blue coat again. It doesn't suit you.'

The line went dead then, leaving Sarah standing in the empty house holding the phone, her other hand instinctively moving to touch the collar of the dark blue coat she had been wearing. The one he had just described. Knowing he had seen her that same day, probably even moments earlier as she stepped from her car, made his anonymous threat far more chilling. Was he still watching the house, even now? In that moment, Sarah felt very alone.

Unsurprisingly, dialling 1471 did not give Sarah the number of the anonymous caller. He was not that stupid. The phone company weren't much help either, offering Sarah advice on how to block future calls, while pointing out the difficulty of tracking down the caller if they used a disposable burner phone, which seemed most likely as no one was going to be foolish enough to threaten someone on the phone from their own home. The number of a burner could still be traced, but that wouldn't give you the caller's identity if they purchased the phone anonymously. They recommended she contact the police, but when Sarah called them, they suggested contacting her phone company, so now she was going round in circles. The police did say they took her threatening phone call seriously but left Sarah under no illusions. They lacked the time and resources to investigate it further.

The anonymous call had two contrasting effects on Sarah, leaving her frightened and angry at the same time. Living in this creepy old manor house was bad enough without the additional worry of someone threatening to do her harm, when moving out wasn't an option. If she didn't see this through until the end she wouldn't even get to keep the twenty grand, leaving her in a dire financial state. That thought made her even more determined, and she told herself that they wouldn't be trying to scare her if they weren't worried about what she might find.

Sarah had always despised bullies. Her aunt was the same. Standing up to them was draining but necessary if you wanted to live a life free from other people's control. Of course, in the normal world, most bullies were cowards and less likely to resort to physical assault or even murder to get their way, but this time she could be dealing with an actual killer, or people who had a lot to lose if the future PM was damaged by some embarrassing revelations about his family. Even so, she didn't contemplate leaving. Where the hell would she go? She was in this till the end, like it or not, and she would not give in.

Chapter Twenty-One

July

The plot of Sarah's book had changed. The missing guy wasn't missing at all, just lying low. He had contacted his former lover and together they were now trying to prove his innocence, but could she really trust him, and how would she convince the detective that her man wasn't lying? Sarah had no idea, and if she didn't know then this new book of hers was going nowhere. She had spent days writing and rewriting then scrapping those rewrites and going down a different path altogether. This mystery, which had originated entirely in her own head, was as frustratingly elusive to resolve as the real-life one she was meant to be investigating. Sarah had reached the stage where she felt bad when she was writing instead of trying to solve the disappearance of Lucy Woodfell, and guilty when she was investigating that cold case and not focusing more fully on her book. They were both incredibly important to her future and each of them had a deadline that was fast approaching.

Somehow, a month had passed since her arrival at Cragsmoor and she was still far from used to the place. During the day, it felt too large to live in. At night, when Mrs Jenkins and Patrick had finished for the day and gone home, she was left there on her own, which meant hours to think about the warning she had received from her anonymous caller. Every sound outside the house made her go to the window and peer out nervously in case someone was prowling around. Once in bed, she slept fitfully, her rest filled with nightmares, as every creak and groan from the timbers of the ancient house and its decrepit plumbing system caused her to picture someone breaking in downstairs and coming up to silence her forever. Then there was that whispering sound. Some nights she would hear it and convince herself someone was in the house, while trying not to think about the possibility that it was the tormented spirit of Lady Alice, trying to communicate from beyond the grave with her lament. Some nights Sarah didn't hear it at all but still found herself lying awake, half expecting it to begin at any moment. Often, she woke feeling more tired than when she had gone to bed and this affected her ability to concentrate on her writing, which suffered as a result.

Though Sarah had expended considerable time and energy looking into Lucy Woodfell's disappearance, she had not made the progress she had hoped for, mainly because she couldn't get anyone to talk to her. None of her letters to the Woodfell siblings received a reply. Evelyn had been right about them and Sarah wrong not to listen to her. Now she had clumsily announced her presence at Cragsmoor Manor and been brutally ignored by them all. If she was going to speak to the Woodfell family at all, Sarah was going to have to be far more forceful.

As expected, Toby Ramsay was confirmed as the new leader of his party and prime minister of the country, and his face was all over the television. The coverage often focused on the tragedies he had experienced, including his aunt's disappearance, the loss of his father in a car crash and the accidental death of a university girlfriend, in a fall from a balcony that could have been an accident or suicide. Toby Ramsay's ability to bounce back from tragedies that would have felled lesser men was considered to be one of his strengths.

'He's a populist with no political principles or particular world view, so he is basically a blank canvas,' said one political reporter. 'His gift is to be all things to all men without being one particular thing to anyone. As a youth he was quite the scholar and is fluent in both Latin and Greek. The party faithful describe him as better looking than Boris and cleverer than Cameron, which makes him electoral gold, and he is tipped to win the next general election by a landslide as long as he can avoid any major controversy.'

So, the last thing Toby Ramsay would want to do now would be to speak to someone investigating the mysterious disappearance of his aunt. Even if she could get a message to him somehow, she knew his PR people would never allow it.

That afternoon, Sarah received an email from Kirsten, the new intern at Dickie's firm. The young woman had been working diligently through the many smaller files on the company laptop, opening them all, and was now starting to send the relevant ones on to Sarah. They didn't always reveal all that much and often didn't feel as if they had been worth the effort or the wait. Annoyingly, they weren't in chronological order either, so they tended to dart around between the sixties, seventies and eighties too. The handwritten manuscript had still not been found, which left

Sarah reliant on Kirsten's emails for new information, and her frustration increased along with her impatience.

Sarah read the latest extracts without much enthusiasm, until she eventually reached one that harked back to Evie's first visit to Cragsmoor, which had ended badly.

My stay at the Woodfell family home was not without its difficulties. I did not always feel comfortable there, especially when Lucy's father was in residence. There were enormous rows in his study whenever anyone questioned his judgement. 'You'll do as I say!' and 'That's the end of the matter!' were two of his favourite ways of signalling an argument was over, his voice carrying across the house.

Lucy was less often the victim of his tirades than her half-siblings, but one day I found her in tears in her bedroom. Her father had told her he wouldn't be paying for a university education, as this would be wasted on a woman. A husband was acceptable, or a job if she simply must have one, but not college. When I ventured the possibility of her defying her father, she told me that no one ever did, and I pursued it no further.

Near the end of my stay, everything went very wrong very quickly, and this time Lucy's father had nothing to do with it. It was all because of Oliver, Freddie and Sephy.

Taking advantage of her father's latest absence, Sephy had a boyfriend to stay. The pretence was that James was actually Freddie's friend. We were told they were all out on the lake, so Lucy and I headed down there, expecting to see them pottering about in a rowing boat or picnicking by the water. Lucy appeared as shocked as I was by the spectacle that greeted us. It had been a while since my first introduction to Freddie, when he had calmly towelled his naked body dry in front of me after a swim, and the memory had begun to fade. Now here he was again, lying on his back, stretched out on a towel, shamelessly letting the sun's rays touch every part of his body. Next to him lay Oliver who wasn't wearing a stitch either. If that were not shocking enough, Sephy was lying not far from them both, with her boyfriend James by her side, both as naked as her brothers.

'Sephy!' Lucy exclaimed in shock and, when her half-sister didn't respond, Lucy's embarrassment at their exhibitionism spilled over. 'I might have expected it from Olly and Freddie, but not you!'

'Don't be so bloody bourgeois, Lucy,' Sephy said. 'No one can see us from here.'

'What if one of the servants came down, or a villager?'

'Well then,' said Olly, 'they'd get an eyeful.' And he made no effort to cover himself.

'And you don't care?' Lucy was apoplectic, her face beetroot red.

'Thousands of people do it,' said Freddie. 'You can read all about it in *Health and Efficiency* magazine. It might even broaden your very narrow mind.'

'It's disgusting.'

'And yet, you're still here,' smirked James.

Sephy got to her feet then, the better to address Lucy. I tried not to look but couldn't help myself. She was so womanly and curvaceous, with the kind of body you might find on a classical sculpture. Her breasts were full but firm and she didn't even bother to hide her pubic hair. She just didn't care. I recalled the girls in the dormitory at St Hilda's, who would undress furtively, removing garments from beneath outer layers or disappearing off to bathrooms to get into nightgowns, so no one saw an inch of flesh. Here was Sephy not giving a damn and there was something shocking but a bit wonderful about it too.

'You used to come down here naked with us all the time,' Sephy retorted and I thought Lucy was going to explode with anger and embarrassment.

'I was five then and knew no better. It's not the same.'

'Why isn't it the same?' asked Sephy, placing her hands defiantly on her hips.

Lucy couldn't find the words. 'Because . . .' she began, '. . . it just isn't.'

Freddie stood up then and moved next to Sephy.

'Why isn't it?' he asked, as if genuinely curious. Then he glanced down at himself. 'It's just a bit of hair.' And with that he wiggled his hips and set his penis moving from side to side like the pendulum of a clock and I couldn't help myself.

I giggled.

Then I glanced at Lucy and saw how furious and embarrassed she was, but I still couldn't help myself.

I giggled again.

It was a nervous reaction and not meant in any way to undermine my friend, but Lucy didn't see it that way. Before she could react, Sephy told her, in a bored tone, 'Stop being a little bastard.'

'Don't call me that!' Lucy hissed.

'No one cares if you were born on the wrong side of the blanket,' said Oliver. 'You're hardly going to inherit.'

'Doesn't look a bit like any of us though, does she?' interjected Freddie, 'I wonder why?' It was clear what he meant. Lucy wasn't their mother's child but he was implying she wasn't even their father's.

Lucy turned and stormed off, and I was left standing there, mouth agape, not knowing what to do for the best. Freddie looked bored now that the object of his torments had run off. James walked up behind his girlfriend's brother and placed a hand on his bare shoulder and kneaded it. 'You're starting to burn there,' he said in a low voice.

'Better go after her,' Oliver told me. 'Now that you've had a good look.'

It was my turn to be embarrassed and I looked to Sephy, hoping for support, but she just laughed, as if Oliver had said the funniest thing. I turned and ran too.

I arrived in the hallway in time to hear Lucy's feet thumping up the staircase as she ran to the very top of the house. I knew where she was going and followed slowly, not wanting to get there too soon. She'd have time to calm down, before I offered her some solace.

The hatch was open and I bent low to peer in. I found Lucy crouching there with smudged panda eyes and fresh tears on her cheeks. Before I could think of anything consoling to say, she rounded on me.

'For God's sake, Evie!' she shouted. 'Do you have to follow me absolutely everywhere? Can't you go off on your own, just this once?'

Her words were as shocking and painful as a hard slap across the face. Devastated, I turned and ran down the stairs and out through the back door. I didn't stop running until

I was across the lawns and had reached a welcoming shield of trees. I didn't want anyone else to see how hurt I was.

I spent ages wandering glumly around the estate, wondering if I should return to the house, pack my bag and ask if one of the servants could drop me at the railway station so I could go home. Instead, I doubled back on to the path that led down to the empty beach and sat there for the rest of the day, feeling a wretched sense of injustice, because Lucy had turned her full ire on me and not other, more deserving parties, like her older sister and brothers.

Was I not a loyal friend? Why did I always experience this constant state of exclusion? By now, I almost wanted to feel hard done by, so I could renounce other people entirely and resign myself to a solitary life.

I returned to the house in the evening and went in through the kitchen, where I was informed by the cook that I had missed dinner. She must have sensed something was wrong, because she guided me towards some bread, fetched some butter and jam and left me to help myself. I ate it silently until I'd had my fill then went up to my room. It struck me as I climbed into my bed that no one had bothered to come and look for me and, for all the family knew, I could have been lying dead in a ditch somewhere.

At breakfast the next morning, I expected either an apology or an inquest. Where had I been? What on earth was I playing at, worrying everyone like that? A normal family's reaction, in other words, though my own family was far from normal.

Instead, not a word was said. I'm not sure whether I felt even more crushed by this or relieved by the lack of an interrogation. Both at once, I think.

When everyone was gone, Lucy did approach me but all she said was, 'Oliver's in hospital,' then she told me, 'and Father's back. He said you've to go.'

I hoped we would put the incident with Oliver, Freddie and Sephy behind us and be firm friends again once we were back at St Hilda's, but I never got to speak to Lucy on her own. I tried too hard, in fact, and that made her lash out.

'Still following me around like a lost puppy?' Lucy said it loudly enough for the other members of the set to hear and all eyes turned gleefully towards me, then she walked out of the room I had just entered. The rest followed her. I was heartbroken. Having been in the set for a while, I was out of it again. It was a cold, brutal exclusion and all the more upsetting because I had spent half the summer with Lucy at Cragsmoor. I judged myself more harshly for this than Lucy. I had ruined everything.

From then on, I kept almost entirely to myself, speaking only when spoken to. My unhappiness had reached its zenith. I wasn't content at home and never fit in at St Hilda's, except, it seemed, for a brief and glorious period, before and during the trip to Cragsmoor, when I actually began to think I might be normal.

This state of affairs continued right through term until there was a drama that had nothing to do with me. A new girl, from some grand old aristocratic family, had started at St Hilda's and was instantly elevated to the level of visiting princess, due to her beauty, family status and the fact that she didn't seem to give a damn what anyone thought of her. Lucy was assigned by the headmistress to be her guide and mentor and they soon became firm friends, at the expense of the rest of the set, breaking an unwritten rule.

When the new girl left abruptly just before the Christmas holidays, a jealous member of the set saw an opportunity to get even. You were allowed to have a 'pash' on another girl, especially if she was in a year above you, and almost everyone had a pash on this girl. It was accepted because it wasn't real, just a practice crush, until we were grown up enough to be allowed to enter the world of men, for which we were entirely unprepared. But a rumour was started that Lucy's 'pash' on the princess of St Hilda's had gone beyond the 'huggy' status and had led to 'unnatural acts' being committed. They had been caught together and the new girl asked to leave. The fact that none of this was remotely true didn't prevent those rumours from sweeping the school. Now Lucy found herself talked about, laughed at or shunned when she entered a room. I could sense the jubilation of the other girls, who had been slighted by their former leader's time spent away from them.

When they decided that even I should be informed of these scurrilous rumours, I decided enough was enough. 'Don't be bloody stupid,' I told the execrable Marjorie Gallagher, chief tormentor of her now fallen idol. 'If a word of that was true, why is Lucy still here? The girl most probably left because her father thought mouldy old St Hilda's was beneath her.' That rankled Marjorie enough to think she could say anything in reply.

'Oh, do bog off, Plebby,' she told me. 'You're just jealous because she never had a pash on you.'

Without thinking, I slapped her so hard across the face she actually fell to the floor. I knew from the shocked looks on the other girls' faces that I had gone way too far but I was so angry I didn't care. I leaned over Marjorie and called her every swear word I knew then told her if she ever spread another rumour about either Lucy or me, I would pull her hair out. I left her lying there sobbing.

I knew I was in big trouble and expected the worst, including an expulsion I would have welcomed, but nothing happened. I can only assume that if she had reported my assault on her, Marjorie would have had to explain what had provoked it. Either that or she was worried I would tell on her for making accusations of forbidden sapphic behaviour against a girl who was popular with the staff and another who was considered minor royalty.

I was sitting outside on my own as usual when Lucy came to see me.

'I heard what you did to Marjorie,' she told me, 'and why you did it.' I wasn't sure if I was supposed to express satisfaction or regret about the event until she said, 'She bloody deserved it, the bloody bitch.' And we both spontaneously laughed at the double bloody in Lucy's sentence because it had been said with such relish.

'You should have seen her face,' I said.

'I heard it was redder than a beetroot after you slapped it and that she cried all night. It'll teach her to stop spreading stupid rumours.' She looked away then, as if she half expected me to ask if they really were stupid.

'How dare she make stuff up like that,' I agreed.

'I'm through with her. Actually, I'm through with the lot of them. They're all completely vile.' She sat down next to me, both of us looking out over the playing fields. 'I was vile too,' she said solemnly without looking at me directly, 'to you.'

I was about to protest but she said, 'Oh, I really was, and I'm so sorry. I shouldn't have snapped at you then ignored you like that.'

'I'm sorry too,' I said, 'for crowding you.'

'I think that every time I saw you it reminded me of Sephy, Freddie and Oliver by the lake,' said Lucy. 'They were so horrible to me after you left. Seeing you here brought it all back, but it wasn't you, do you understand? You offered me friendship and I threw it back in your face,' she continued, determined to take all the blame. It was a trait I would see in her regularly over the years. Perhaps it was a Catholic thing. That need to confess out loud and seek absolution. 'I would like it if we could be friends again,' she said, 'like we were before I ruined everything.'

I sensed she didn't want me to deny she had ruined everything and I was only too happy to absolve her. 'I'd like that very much.'

For the remainder of our time at St Hilda's we were an unlikely double act, each of us helping the other to laugh off our previous humiliations, fortifying ourselves against the need to ever crawl back to other members of the set.

I woke every morning fully expecting Lucy to eventually tire of our splendid isolation and re-join the set, but she never did. I no longer cared what the rest of the school thought of us. We floated high above it all.

Chapter Twenty-Two

The siblings all ganging up on Lucy by the lake stayed with Sarah and she found herself thinking back on it over the next few days. Was this normal behaviour between brothers and sisters or something much darker? Did Sephy, Oliver and Freddie have it in for Lucy because she was the child of a second marriage, and did they really believe she wasn't their father's child or was that just a spiteful taunt to goad her?

Sarah still hadn't received a reply from any of them and doubted she ever would. She couldn't force them to see her, but perhaps she could simply turn up on their respective doorsteps and see how they reacted? Not well, she imagined, and perhaps that was best kept as a last resort. Instead, she decided to see if she could get hold of phone numbers for them. She rang Dickie to see if he had them on file somewhere.

'We do,' he told her. 'I'm sure of it. Just wait a moment.' He left her hanging on the line until he eventually dug them out for her and she duly noted them down.

'Think you can persuade them to talk to you?' He sounded sceptical.

'Don't know,' she admitted. 'Worth a try.'

Sarah decided to waste no further time. Given the suspicious demise of Captain Alex Ramsay, first on her list was Persephone Woodfell. It wasn't Sephy herself who answered the phone at her cottage but someone who described herself as 'Mrs Ramsay's carer'.

'I'd like to speak to Mrs Ramsay if I may?' she said. 'I'm Sarah Hollis, my aunt Evie owned Cragsmoor Manor. She passed away recently.'

'And you want to speak to Mrs Ramsay about Cragsmoor Manor?' There was a definite tone of disbelief and Sarah decided it might be wise not to risk lying about her true intentions.

'Actually, it's about her half-sister, Lucy Woodfell. She was a great friend of my aunt's and . . .'

'I know who she was,' the woman cut her off in mid-sentence but did not add anything further.

'So, may I speak to Mrs Ramsay, please?'

There was a pause then before the other woman said, 'I'll pass on your request.'

Silence followed but Sarah had not been cut off. She strained her ears in the hope of overhearing some background dialogue between Sephy Woodfell and her carer, but if there was any, it did not reach her. Presently, the woman returned to the line.

'I'm afraid Mrs Ramsay cannot speak to you.'

'Could I call back another time?'

'Mrs Ramsay has no wish to speak to you on the matter at all,' and before Sarah could protest, she said, 'goodbye.' And the line went dead.

Sarah was left helplessly holding the phone and wondering why Sephy would not speak to her. A charitable conclusion might be that her sister's disappearance had been devastating for her and that any mention of Lucy would dredge up terrible memories from long ago, which she was keen to avoid. Sarah wasn't feeling very charitable, however, not to a woman who was suspected of affairs that may have driven her husband to suicide, if she herself hadn't been the one to actually kill him by tampering with his brakes. The fact that her husband and her sister had become close may have at least hinted at a possible motive, involving jealousy or revenge. Within two years, both the captain and Lucy were dead and, if that was not suspicious enough, Sephy refused to talk about her missing sister, which made Sarah wonder what she might have to hide.

Getting through to Oliver Woodfell took longer. His phone rang and rang and Sarah almost gave up, but she reminded herself that the oldest Woodfell sibling was in his late seventies, so perhaps he needed time to get to his phone. He did eventually answer but his voice sounded thick, as if he had a cold or had been woken from an afternoon nap.

'Yes?'

'Oliver Woodfell?'

'Yes.' The S at the end of the word became elongated till it sounded like a hiss.

'My name is Sarah and I am the current . . .' what was the right word? '. . . resident of Cragsmoor Manor. It used to belong to my aunt Evelyn and . . .'

'Fuck's sake.' She wasn't sure if this was directed at her or uttered to himself in exasperation. She pressed on regardless.

'I sent you a letter and I was hoping I might be able to come and see you to, er . . .' She had hoped for a more normal reaction from him, before deciding whether to mention Lucy or just lie. '. . . talk about . . .' She stopped then because he was mumbling something unintelligible down the phone at her. At first, she worried he might be having a stroke, but then she realized Oliver was drunk. He was very drunk, in fact. He was trying to berate her but the only words she could actually make out were '. . . bloody dare you . . .' and a repetition of '. . . for fuck's sake . . .' Before she could even think of a way to communicate with a man this inebriated, he put down the phone.

Aunt Evelyn had been right. Members of the Woodfell family, drunk or sober, didn't want to speak to anyone about Lucy if they didn't have to. She fully expected the same reaction from Freddie, who picked up on the third ring and was thankfully a lot sharper and more coherent than his older brother.

'Bloody Evie,' he said, as if he hadn't heard the name in years. 'I read that she'd carked it.' He obviously wasn't too concerned about Sarah's grief. He surprised her even more when he said, 'I was hoping someone would ring me.'

'Were you?'

'Well, I figured somebody would inherit and there's much to discuss.'

'What is there to discuss?'

'The manor house,' he said. 'I want to buy it back.'

Chapter Twenty-Three

Freddie lived in a small but pretty cottage not five miles from the estate. He opened the door, dressed smartly in jacket and tie, and could have passed for a man a decade younger. He still had a boyish look about him, even with silver hair.

He welcomed Sarah in and offered her some Earl Grey. When she declined, he wandered off, poured himself a cup and brought one back for her anyway then commented that she had taken her time to get in touch, since her aunt had died a while back. When Sarah mentioned that she had written a letter to him he simply said, 'I don't like to open the mail. It rarely brings good news.' As if this was an entirely normal way to live your life.

'So,' he said. 'How do you feel about it?'

'About what?' she was confused.

'Selling the house to me.' He must have assumed that was why she had arranged to come round.

'You're serious about that?'

'Of course.' He seemed put out that she had doubted him.

Why on earth would Freddie want to buy back the house that had been the cause of so many of his family's troubles, particularly the financial ones? Was it because he still had such belief in himself that he truly thought he could turn it into a profitable venture, even now? Was he really that deluded? Sarah would have challenged him on this but she had more important things to ask him about. She didn't want to run the risk of Freddie becoming defensive then clamming up and telling her nothing. Instead, she enquired, 'You have the finances?' She was trying to put it delicately, having assumed he was almost broke, apart from his trust fund and the cottage.

'I'm going to put a consortium together,' he assured her. 'A bit of Middle East money and some chaps from the US.' This sounded incredibly vague to Sarah but she decided to play along with it. 'We are thinking conversion into a boutique hotel, high-end spa and golf course.'

'That will take some funding,' she said but he didn't seem deterred. 'I haven't decided what to do with the house yet but I would be willing to listen to offers.'

'I hope you won't listen to offers,' he snapped. 'Got to give me a chance to buy back the family home first.' And she felt like telling him she was under no obligation to do anything of the kind. 'I'll get the money, you'll see.'

'There's no hurry.' She was keen to end the discussion about the house and move on to her real purpose, but Freddie still wanted to talk about Cragsmoor.

'Your aunt stitched me up,' he said. 'She got her solicitor to keep the buyer's name confidential until after the sale. I had no idea she was behind it until the deal went through. I would never have sold to her.'

'Why not?'

'Because she bought it for the wrong reason,' he said, 'her obsession with Lucy.'

'I'm not going to stitch you up, Freddie,' she assured

him, 'and my aunt has been an excellent custodian of the estate, keeping the house from falling apart, for one thing.'

He ignored this. 'It's too big for one person.' She wasn't sure if he was referring to Evie or herself. He spent five more minutes telling her of his plans before she interrupted to explain that the real reason for contacting him was Lucy's disappearance. Freddie was far less enthused. 'Why do you want to discuss that?'

'Unfinished business,' she said. 'I promised my aunt I would carry on where she left off. She never stopped trying to discover the truth about Lucy.'

'I know,' he said, 'and fair play to her, though I did think it was morbid of Evie to put so much of her book money into buying our family home. She insisted on paying over the odds for the place, but only if she got it lock, stock and barrel. She should have let it go. Personally, I find talking about Lucy painful,' he said.

'But you kept the investigation going,' she reminded him, 'for years after the police had given up on it.'

'I paid private investigators to follow up on sightings of Lucy, yes. I suppose I hoped someone would find something, but they never did. It was a waste of time, I'm afraid.'

'How did the others feel about that?'

'They supported my efforts in trying to find Lucy. I don't think I can adequately describe the distress her disappearance caused everyone in our family. I can still picture her now, heading off down to the beach. We assumed she'd probably gone for a swim and she'd be home in time for tea but we never saw her again.'

When she pressed Freddie about his half-sister and

whether they'd got on, he admitted there had been arguments between them but explained that the whole family was often at each other's throats. 'Because of the estate. It was an absolute bastard to run and almost impossible to turn a profit from it. This caused us all a great deal of worry and I suppose I was the focal point, because Father left me in charge instead of Oliver.' Then he sighed. 'I didn't want it, you know. I pretended I did. I was going to be the family saviour but really it was all a massive headache and I didn't know what to do for the best. Nor did anyone else, by the way, despite what they might tell you. They didn't always like my ideas but no one ever came up with better ones.'

'Did Lucy not like your ideas?' she probed.

'No,' he admitted. 'She wanted to open up the place to the public and stick in a gift shop and tea room, but there wasn't much future in that. Cragsmoor is hardly Blenheim Palace and I told her we wouldn't get the footfall.'

'Was the zoo your idea, then?'

He seemed to physically sag at the mention of the failed zoo. 'Not one of my best plans, that.' But then he pressed on, 'The golf course, though,' he smiled at the notion, 'that could have been a goer, still might be, but back then we ran out of capital, almost at the planning stage.'

'There was a book too, wasn't there?'

'A coffee-table book, I called it.' And he smiled at the memory. 'I had ten thousand copies printed and it looked gorgeous.'

'What went wrong?'

'Couldn't persuade the retailers to take it. They had no imagination.'

Sarah noticed that it was all the fault of the retailers and not Freddie.

'And the gold mine?'

'It was always a risk.' And she could tell by his tone it was one that had not paid off.

'All of these . . .' she was going to say failures but changed that to '. . . projects must have been costly.'

'We were throwing good money after bad and could barely keep up the maintenance of the house towards the end.'

'Was Lucy angry at you for losing all that money?'

'I suppose she was, but then so were Oliver and Sephy. Like I said, they thought they could do better.' A thought must have struck him then. 'Lucy and I may have argued about the estate but that doesn't mean I did anything stupid. Why would I? She couldn't do anything to stop me in any case.'

'Did she try?'

He looked furtive then. 'I don't know what you've heard,' he began and Sarah sat there poker faced, because she'd heard nothing about it but had guessed Lucy might have tried something to stop Freddie from blowing all the family's money. 'But that injunction thing was never going to work.'

'She took out an injunction on you?'

'Tried to but didn't get very far. She claimed I was mismanaging the estate.'

'You mean she tried to get you thrown out?' He gave a slight shrug at this, as if it was just a small family matter. 'Did she act alone or were your brother and sister involved?'

'I never did find out. I strongly suspect Oliver would have been in cahoots with her. I don't know about Sephy.'

'You never asked her?'

'That's not how we do things in our family. We're more subtle than that.'

Machiavellian would probably be a more accurate word, thought Sarah. 'You continued to see Lucy,' she observed, 'she continued to stay at Cragsmoor even after she tried to oust you?'

'It was her home too,' he said. 'We just put it behind us and moved on.'

'You didn't resent her at all?' She was finding this hard to believe. 'Even though she could have ruined you if her court case had come off?'

'Like I said, it didn't get very far. I don't think she was all that serious about it. It was just a shot across the bows.'

'A warning to get your act together?'

'If you like.'

'I must say, you took it very well.'

'It was all a long time ago now. I can barely remember it.'

'Some people would have found it hard to forgive,' she told him, 'and some might have worried that she could try again. I'd imagine you would have been very keen to prevent that from happening.'

'I know what you're implying,' his voice turned icy now, 'but you're barking up the wrong tree. I didn't kill Lucy. I never even considered her to be a threat. It might have been different if I had, but I didn't.'

'All right,' she said, 'was there a big family falling-out at the end, when you were forced to sell up?'

Freddie considered this for a moment. 'Our family came apart over a long period of time. Lucy was already gone and Sephy's husband killed by the time we finally sold up. What did Oliver, Sephy and I have in common any more, except a lot of unpleasant memories and a fair amount of bitterness at how everything turned out?'

'Do you still see them?'

'Oliver and Sephy? No.'

'I imagine it would be hard to look your older brother in the eye when he was ousted by your father and you lost the estate anyway?'

'Do you really think Oliver would have done a better job than me? He has been stoned or drunk virtually every day of his life.'

'What about Sephy?' she asked. 'Were you close?'

'We were,' he admitted, 'but that was a long time ago. Sephy is quite an angry person. She never forgave Father for his rather outmoded views on women and thinks her life would have been very different if he'd been more enlightened. She might be right about that. He was a hard man to please.'

'Did Lucy please him?' she asked. 'She had a career in publishing and no husband.'

'She never married,' he said, as if he was quoting some-one. 'That's what all the newspapers said back then, and everyone knew what they were implying.'

'Do you think that Lucy was . . .'

'On the other bus? I never asked and she never told.'

'And your father?'

'I don't think he gave it much thought. Sephy gave him a grandson in the end,' he laughed, 'and now he's the bloody prime minister. Even the old man might have been pleased about that.'

'Do you ever see Toby?'

'From time to time.' He didn't seem to want to elaborate on that, so she pressed on.

'You never married yourself or had a family. Weren't you under pressure to, from your father?'

'I was too busy trying to prevent everything from falling apart and it was quite hard to start a serious relationship with our family plastered all over the newspapers like that.'

'Because of Lucy? What do you think happened to her?'

'I used to hope she had run away for some reason. I clung to that theory for years. She'd show up or we'd find her in the end. Eventually, I had to accept it wasn't true. Lucy is dead. It's the only explanation that makes any sense.'

'Then who killed her?'

'I would have thought it was obvious, wouldn't you?' And when she didn't reply, he said, 'David Young.'

'You think he did it?'

'The man murdered a girl a week or two before Lucy went missing,' he scoffed. 'He was on the run and seen in the area not long before she vanished, so yes, I would say he was the likeliest candidate. Whenever someone goes missing or is found dead, it's usually the most obvious person who did it, and David Young was clearly the prime suspect.'

'Actually,' she corrected him, 'it's usually the person closest to the victim that did it; their partner or a family member.'

'Well, Lucy didn't have a partner,' he said, ignoring the reference to family. 'I don't think we will ever discover what happened, but obviously I wish you *bonne chance* and do please keep me informed. If you find anything, I'd like to be the first to know.' After their interview had concluded, he walked her to the door. 'You should be careful, you know.'

'What do you mean by that?' she asked.

'It's cursed,' he said. 'The house, I mean. I had a spiritualist look at the place years ago and she confirmed it. She told me it's because of Lady Alice who died a prisoner there but not before cursing her entire family. Everyone who has inherited Cragsmoor has experienced misfortune. Even Evelyn died before her time. Now the house is yours,' he concluded, 'and so is the curse.'

Did he genuinely believe this or was he trying to scare Sarah into selling up? 'If it carries such bad luck, Freddie, then why ever would you want it back?'

He let out a little embarrassed laugh when he couldn't contradict her logic. 'I don't know,' he said. 'Perhaps I'm a glutton for punishment.'

Chapter Twenty-Four

Freddie Woodfell wasn't the most likeable man but, as Crozier had pointed out, just because you don't like someone, it doesn't make them a murderer. He'd obviously had a complicated relationship with Lucy, but the same could be said about the other members of his family, though only Lucy had openly tried to have him removed from control of the estate. When Sarah considered this, she couldn't help but feel that Freddie was trying to make light of that whole situation, but in reality it would have surely caused him some considerable distress. If Lucy's case had gone against him and he was ousted, then what would he have left? Not much, in reality, and she couldn't imagine him in a conventional job. He may have claimed to have moved on but must have known that Lucy was hardly going to forget her concerns and let him lose even more money with one high-risk scheme after another. What had he said to Sarah about that? 'I didn't kill Lucy. I never even considered her to be a threat. It might have been different if I had, but I didn't.'

It might have been different if I had.

What if she really was a threat to him? Was that an admission of sorts?

Whether Freddie was a guilty man or not, he had blamed David Young for Lucy's fate. Sarah had given the convicted murderer a lot of thought but hadn't yet tried to contact him. She knew she couldn't delay it much longer, but what normal person would actually want to sit down and calmly discuss a case with a convicted killer, a man who had beaten another woman to death in a jealous rage? Even if it turned out he had nothing to do with Lucy's disappearance and was able to prove that somehow, Sarah would still have to come face to face with a murderer, but ultimately she couldn't think of a way to dodge this. David Young was right at the top of a pile of suspects and was the only one who had definitely killed someone before. She needed to look him in the eye to see for herself whether guilt or innocence was written on his face.

Sarah spent some time trying to work out how to get in contact with Young, who was out on licence and back in the community but at an unknown address. The press coverage of his release included condemnation from appalled journalists and alarmed locals, but it contained one detail that was of specific use to her. He was under the care of a Doctor Phillips, who was in charge of a revolutionary new outreach programme for serious criminals. Crucially, offenders were expected never to avoid responsibility for their actions but to embrace it, via interaction with their victim's family members. Sarah could hardly claim to be one of those but she implied she was to the receptionist at Doctor Phillips' clinic, convincingly enough for her to be put through.

'I'd like to speak to David Young,' she told him.

'What about?'

She told him the real reason and reminded him of the promise made in his programme's policy statement. He heard her out then said, 'The Lucy Woodfell case? I am of course aware of it and we do encourage interaction with the outside world in the outreach programme. We also urge offenders to admit what they have done and take ownership for their actions. That way they become stakeholders in their crimes and the consequences.' Sarah despised the management-speak he was coming out with, but this sounded hopeful. 'However, in all the time that I have been dealing with David, he has never admitted to any involvement in that woman's disappearance.'

'Why would he?' she asked.

'To experience closure.'

'But he was never convicted of that crime, so he could still be arrested and charged with a second murder, which would probably get him a whole life sentence without the prospect of parole.'

'Then what makes you think he would admit anything to you now?'

'I don't think he would, necessarily, but I'd still like to ask him a few questions.' Then she added, 'With your permission, of course.'

'I will speak to David and put your proposal to him. If he agrees, we can arrange an appointment for you to speak to him.'

'Where would that take place?'

'At his home.'

She wasn't sure she liked the sound of this. 'Would I be on my own?'

'He doesn't have prison warders outside his front door, if that's what you mean, but I could be present?' he offered.

'That would make me feel safer.'

'You've really got nothing to worry about on that score, but I should come along anyway, to ensure fair play.'

'Fair play?'

'David has had bad experiences in the past,' he explained, 'with journalists trying to trap him.'

Poor, innocent little flower, thought Sarah. Listening to the doctor, one could almost have forgotten that David was a murderer. On the one hand, she was pleasantly surprised that she'd been able to get this far and might actually be able to put her questions to the murderer, but on the other, it appeared that Doctor Phillips would be policing the interview and it sounded as if he was most definitely on David Young's side.

'I have no traps,' she assured him, 'only questions.'

Cragsmoor Manor was cursed, according to both Freddie Woodfell and Mrs Jenkins. That would make sense. The place appeared to have a will of its own, and the way it seemed to creak, groan and whisper to Sarah made it feel like a living entity. It wasn't so bad during the day, with Patrick in the house or garden and Mrs Jenkins busying herself going from room to room, cleaning, dusting and hoovering. But when they had finished for the day and gone home, the entire atmosphere of the house changed.

Sarah couldn't decide if it was the occasional sound coming from outside or sometimes within the house, or if it was the absolute silence that was more disturbing. She would break it by playing music on the radio or her laptop or by streaming a film, but she would always keep the volume low, in case she missed the sound of someone prowling around outside, trying to break in. At night she would leave lights on randomly in downstairs rooms, in an attempt to confuse anyone who might be watching the house, and before climbing the stairs to bed she would obsessively check every door and window to ensure they were all secure, though that hadn't stopped someone from getting inside before.

She hadn't forgotten the way Lucy's portrait had been turned around while she slept, nor the threatening phone call. She was sure that wouldn't be the end of it and there would be further threats or warnings, but what form would they take? And how long would it be before the person making them lost patience with her continued presence at Cragsmoor and decided to silence her for good? That thought preoccupied her as she climbed into bed and lay there trying to sleep, while night creatures shrieked or hooted outside and the house seemed to moan in reply as its timbers contracted. Occasionally, she would hear a scuttling sound that she hoped was birds on the roof and not rats running around in the attic or worse, along the unused third floor directly above her. Sarah realized that she was in an almost constant state of fear.

It had been weeks since Sarah had had the bright idea of contacting the TV historian, Marcus Fernsby. When an unknown number came up on her phone, he was the last person she was expecting to hear from, but she recognized that mellow, upper-class voice immediately.

'Sarah Hollis?'

'Yes.'

'It's Marcus Fernsby. You sent me a message.'

'A while ago now, er, yes, I did.'

'I was away filming,' he said by way of explanation, 'in Budapest and Vienna. I'm very familiar with Cragsmoor, obviously, but I'd welcome the chance to take a look at the property, privately, as you suggested.'

The conversation that followed was short and pleasant. Marcus was quite charming, in fact, and even claimed to be as enthused by the prospect of meeting her as of seeing the manor.

'Priest holes?' he said then, as if only just remembering this. 'You mentioned there's more than one.'

'Yes. We have one at the top of the stairs and I know there are a couple of others, but I've read that there may be another one tucked away somewhere.'

'Oh goody.' He didn't bother to contain his excitement and said he would 'swing by soon', if that was all right with her?

It was.

Having arranged for Marcus to explore the house, Sarah walked into the kitchen in a cheerful mood. There she found both Mrs Jenkins and Patrick. He was on his haunches peering into a toolbox, while the housekeeper busied herself by the draining board.

'Would you like some tea?' Sarah asked them both. 'I'm making some.'

'No, thank you.'

'I'll have one,' said Patrick cheerfully.

She made the tea and gestured for him to sit with her at the kitchen table while Mrs Jenkins carried on clearing up around them, dropping cutlery into a drawer instead of placing it there, stacking plates and putting them back into cupboards then moving pans from the draining board to corners of the kitchen where they normally resided.

Sarah didn't think this was a deliberate intrusion, but it was irritating, nonetheless. Having a conversation was impossible while it was going on. After the umpteenth bang of pot against countertop, Sarah looked over at Patrick and they exchanged one of those sheepish smiles you share when someone is getting on your nerves and probably doesn't even realize it.

When she had finally put everything away, the housekeeper walked out of the room and Sarah seized the opportunity to ask a question she'd felt too foolish to raise before.

'Patrick? Are you very busy today?'

'Why?' he asked lightly. 'What do you need?'

'I know it's going to sound silly, but I'd like a lock on my bedroom door.'

'Not silly at all,' he replied. 'You're up there on your own at night. I'd say that was a sensible precaution.' And she was pleased he hadn't mocked her for being overly cautious. 'Leave it with me. It'll be done by bedtime.' He made that sound like a promise and she could have kicked herself for not asking him sooner.

Mrs Jenkins walked back in then and asked, 'Are you tending to the garden today, Patrick?'

'I am.'

'Very well then,' she said, as if it was her job to grant him permission to do this, 'but if you tread mud on to my clean floor, even your combat training won't save you.'

He laughed but she wasn't smiling when she left the room.

'Combat training?' asked Sarah.

He was immediately dismissive. 'I was in the army.'

'When was that?' She tried to make her tone conversational and not interrogatory because she sensed Patrick didn't really want to talk about himself.

'A while back.'

'What regiment?' she persisted.

'Er . . .' Then he suddenly dropped an 'oh' into the conversation and immediately frowned at his watch, as if they had been carelessly sitting in a pub for hours, not sipping tea for a few minutes. 'I'd better crack on or I won't get finished,' he smiled at her. 'Evelyn didn't pay overtime.' And before she could say anything, he rose from the table, picked up the mug, drained the last of its contents and said, 'Thanks for the tea.' He took the mug to the sink, washed it and left it on the draining board, then he was gone.

'That went well,' she said aloud, even though there was no one else left in the room.

Sarah took a fresh cup of tea to the library. She planned to spend some time reading the latest extracts from the memoir but first she had a closer look at the library's contents. As well as a lot of books, it contained boxes of paper and three large chests that appeared to be almost as old as the house. She opened one and started to look through the documents inside. They appeared to be very old and when she tried to read one of them she couldn't decipher the text. More bloody Latin, she realized, and when she scanned the other papers she could see they were the same. She put the papers back in the box and closed the lid.

There was a glass case that contained a stuffed bird of some kind, possibly a kestrel or a kite, and another beautiful writing desk with intricate marquetry and a series of little drawers. She had noticed it before but now Sarah took the time to open them. She found some blank sheets of headed notepaper in one that looked quite old. Each sheet had a drawing of the manor house on it, along with the Woodfell family name and a Latin inscription she had not come across before: *Sit Dormiens Canibus et Mentiuntur.* It meant nothing to her, but Sarah carefully folded one of the sheets and placed it in her pocket so she could check it later. Whatever it meant, it had enough significance to be placed on the family letterhead, and Sarah wanted to know why.

Chapter Twenty-Five

Some people look better on television than they do in real life. Sarah fully expected to be underwhelmed when she finally met the academic-turned TV presenter in the flesh, but Marcus Fernsby was actually more handsome in person than on screen. It was quite distracting at first.

'I like this,' he said as he surveyed the entranceway and staircase then the Latin motto above the fireplace. 'I've been doing my research on Cragsmoor.' He immediately took control, moving from room to room and touching things that interested him most. 'Nicholas Owen stayed here,' he told her.

'Who?'

'The Jesuit. This house has three priest holes, all built by Nicholas Owen or possibly an apprentice of his. Shall we have a look at them?'

'I'd love to,' Sarah said. 'I mentioned I'd found the one at the top of the stairs, but I need your help to locate the others.'

'This should be fun,' he said. 'The location of each priest hole here was marked by a clue.'

'What kind of clue?'

'I'll give you the example of the one you know about,' and he took her to the bottom of the staircase and showed her a wooden carving that was off to one side, on the wall near the bannisters. He read the Latin inscription to Sarah:

'*Ad caelum ire primum necesse est cadere*,' which he explained broadly translated as 'To ascend to heaven a man must first fall.'

'Now, if you were to come across those words, you might mistake them for a biblical verse or religious saying, meaning that the path to everlasting life comes to the humble or penitent, but that's not what it means at all. The clue to the location of the priest hole is in the words *ascend* and *fall*.'

'Ascend the stairs and fall into the hole?' she offered.

'Exactly! Climb down, more accurately, but that would have been a bit of a giveaway. He wanted to be more subtle than that.'

'But how could he be sure the priests would be able to work out the clues and not the Queen's men, who were presumably every bit as clever?'

'I don't think the messages were for the priests. The Woodfell family knew the locations of the priest holes already. As soon as word reached them that the Queen's men were on their way, they would have directed the priest to his hiding place.'

'Then why carve messages at all?'

'My opinion? It was a game. He was trying to show the Protestants that he was cleverer than they were.'

'Sounds risky.'

'It was, but remember, only the creator of those messages knew they were clues to anything, let alone the location of a priest hole. They would be viewed as simple religious homilies adorning the walls of the house.'

'They were almost a private joke,' she mused.

'I think you are right, Sarah. They were. He was sticking

two fingers up at the Queen's men and thoroughly enjoying himself in the process.'

He turned back to the panel. 'Now, let's have a look at the next Latin motto, which is not far from the first one.' He pointed at the wall again and recited. '*Vitam regit fortuna, non sapientia.* That's Cicero.' Then he translated: 'Fortune, not wisdom, rules lives.'

'Okay, and how is that a clue?' she asked, because it didn't sound like one.

'It's a commentary on the specifics of our next hidey-hole.' He smiled. 'You still can't see it, can you, the hole, I mean?' He indicated the ancient brickwork next to the staircase with its wide vertical supporting beams.

'If I could, it wouldn't be a very effective priest hole, would it?' she told him.

'No,' he admitted. 'Right, I hope I'm correct, or at least that the book I read about this is.' And he counted the beams from left to right. 'One, two and three.' Marcus placed his hand on the top of the third beam and gave it a gentle but firm push. To Sarah's delight, the beam swung out and upwards, leaving a space wide enough for a person to pass through the wall. 'Take a look.'

Sarah peered into a small, dusty room that opened out from behind its false beam door, but there was still only enough space to allow someone to shelter there for a while in some discomfort. 'That's amazing,' she said, 'but quite tiny. Much smaller than the one at the top of the stairs.'

'I think this one was reserved for those desperate moments when the Queen's men were breaking your door in and there was less time to hide. If anyone did discover this, they would not necessarily find the priest hiding in it anyway. There was a false screen that stretched over here, like so,' he waved a hand at the front section, 'which made it look like a small hidden cupboard for storing valuables. When the Queen's men approached, the priest would go in through here, then the false screen would be placed back over the gap to cover him. The lady of the manor could put some of her jewels in the front section. If it was discovered, well, no matter, it was only a kind of Elizabethan safe. That's what was meant by *Fortune, not wisdom, rules lives*. It's another joke, you see. Fortune as in *money* but also as in *luck*. If the priest was lucky, the Queen's men would assume it was just a strongbox for hiding valuables, while the true treasure – God's emissary – hid behind it.'

'Was it ever discovered?'

'Not back then, nor for fifty years or more after that.'

'I'm impressed.'

'You should be,' he told her. 'Now, do you want to see one that wasn't discovered for almost two hundred years?'

He took her up the stairs, to the top floor of the building and into a room that was quite bare apart from a couple of old wardrobes, a bed with no sheets and a fireplace with a chimney that had another Latin motto. '*Ignis non exstinguetur*,' he recited. 'The fire will not be put out.'

He reflected on this. 'Quite deep, that one. The fire being the old faith, of course. What do you notice about this fireplace?'

She stood and stared at the grate for some time. 'It's not real,' she said eventually.

'What makes you think that? Other than the obvious fact that I'm showing you where the priest hole is?'

'The dark marks at the back of the hearth look like stains from soot and smoke but they appear to have been painted on.'

'Very good,' he said approvingly. 'Anything else?'

'The chimney,' she answered.

He gave her a questioning look.

'There isn't one. On the outside, I mean.' And she placed a hand on the part of the chimney that was visible from inside the house, which went up the wall and appeared to carry on through the ceiling. 'This doesn't go anywhere,' she told him. 'There are no chimneys on this side of the house.'

'My turn to be impressed, Sarah.' He beamed at her and she had to admit she enjoyed being well thought of by him. 'You'd make a damned good research assistant, you know. The ones I get lumbered with are hopeless, always too young and never know how to think for themselves. You should join me for a weekend's filming.' He said this brightly, as if it had just occurred to him and was an entirely reasonable suggestion. 'I've got Prague coming up next, then Milan. Think about it.' Then he carried on as if he hadn't just invited her for a weekend in Europe with him.

Marcus patted the false chimney. 'The priest would climb up into a gap here that is even smaller than the one downstairs. Nobody ever found this priest hole during the time it was needed. It was another two centuries before someone finally wondered why there was a fireplace here that appeared to go nowhere.'

When they went back downstairs, she commented, 'Your Nicholas Owen was a clever man.'

'Not clever enough, sadly. He was caught in the end

and died under torture but revealed nothing to his inquisitors. They aimed to break his body and did so. They hoped to break his will but could not. He was canonized by the Pope in 1970.'

'Poor Saint Nic,' she said. 'What do you think of the rumour about a fourth priest hole?'

'I'd heard about it,' he said, 'but in generations no one has ever found it.'

'You don't think it's a possibility, then?'

'Harvington Hall in Worcestershire has seven priest holes and some of them weren't found for many years. The possibility of a fourth one here remains,' he said, looking around for effect. 'But where the bloody hell is it? That's the question. It's amazing what you can find in these old manor houses – hidden doors, false walls, secret passageways. If it is here, I can promise you one thing.'

'What?'

'I shall be the one to find it.' Sarah wished she had an ounce of Marcus's self-confidence. 'Leave it to me!'

'All right,' she agreed.

They walked back downstairs and Sarah took him towards the carving which hung above the fireplace. 'I wondered if this might be a clue to the location of the fourth priest hole?'

'Afraid not,' he said. 'That is mounted on an actual fire. Stick a priest behind that wall and he would roast.'

'Why put it there, then?' and she recited the Latin motto. '*Respice ut ante videas*. I did a check on the internet and it roughly translates as "look behind in order to see before". Which confused me.'

'Indeed it does, though *respicere* also means to look back, not just look behind something, and *ante* can also mean "in front of" or what is ahead of you.'

'But what did he mean by that?'

'I believe he was paying homage to a great family, withstanding the turbulence of being Catholic in a Protestant age. He was telling them to look to their glorious past for inspiration in order to see the way forward.'

'He was kissing their arses, in other words?'

'You had to do that back then,' he told her. 'A patron would expect it.'

'It's a clumsy phrase, though. It doesn't exactly mean what it says.'

'Why doesn't he just say what he means, eh? You make an interesting point,' and he smiled at her as if she was a bright student again. 'Your priest hole man was a genius, no doubt about it, but there wasn't a lot of book-learning in his world. He was apprenticed to a joiner as a young man of thirteen or fourteen and would have focused almost entirely on his trade for the next seven years. He did know enough Latin to have carved these mottos and some of it translates exactly as it is meant to, but here it's a bit ambiguous and easy to mistranslate, so you came up with *look behind* instead of *look back*.'

'Thank you, Marcus. This has been really interesting.'

'My pleasure, Sarah. Now, before I go, would you mind if I had a peep in the library?'

Sarah took him there and as soon as he saw its contents he clapped his hands together in glee. 'I've been longing for this.' He went to the shelves that contained the old bound papers then he approached the ancient chests, pulled them open and peered inside. 'The Woodfell family archive – much of it is five hundred years old. Most of it is in Latin, of course, but it's absolute treasure,' he told her. 'Please tell me you'll allow me to come back and examine it all, and in return, I'll see if I can find anything that might shed more light on your fourth priest hole, if it exists.'

'Yes, I'm happy with that,' she said. 'As long as you let me know if you find some plans for the house.'

'There may be something in amongst this lot,' he said, 'though it might take some finding. What do you want it for?'

'I thought it might be useful if we're looking for the priest hole. A plan would . . .'

He smirked and interrupted her, 'I don't wish to sound condescending, Sarah, but they are hardly likely to mark secret priest holes on a plan of the building or they wouldn't stay secret.'

'I know that,' she told him sharply, 'but if you'd let me finish, I was about to say that we could take a look at the plan of the house and see if anything on it differed from the building we are standing in. A priest hole wouldn't be marked on a plan, but if it was added later, as I understand they all were, we could search in parts of the house that look different from the plan. The priest hole in the fake chimney is a case in point, because the chimney wouldn't show up on the original plans.'

He seemed to contemplate this for a moment. 'Actually, that's not a bad idea, Sarah. Not a bad idea at all.'

'It isn't,' she agreed, 'and you were.'

'I was what?'

'Condescending.'

'Was I? Sorry.' He laughed. 'I'll go and sit on the naughty step, shall I?' Then he smiled. 'I'll keep my eyes peeled for a plan of the house and let you know when I find one.'

'Please do,' she said and resisted the temptation to add, *I look forward to you mansplaining it all to me when you find it.*

She took the headed notepaper from her pocket. 'Before you go, do you think you could help me with this one? I found it in a drawer. Might be some sort of family motto, perhaps?'

He read the Latin words aloud. '*Sit Dormiens Canibus et Mentiuntur.*' Then he smiled. 'Interesting.'

'Do you know what it means?'

'It's not a proper Latin phrase,' he said, 'more of a botched modern-day translation, I'd say. *Canibus* means "from dogs",' he told her, 'and *Dormiens* means "sleeping". *Et Mentiuntur* translates as "they lie", but that's "tell a lie" rather than lie down. *Sit* means "Let it be". So, to summarize, *Let it be sleeping dogs they lie.*' And he smiled.

'Let sleeping dogs lie?' she asked.

'Pretty much.'

'It's a little family joke, isn't it?'

'I imagine so,' he agreed, 'or possibly a warning.'

They left the library and walked back to the main door just as Patrick appeared, wearing work clothes that were grubby from whatever task he had been in the process of completing. Marcus greeted his arrival with 'The Lord of the Manor, I presume?' and Patrick gave him a look that showed he wasn't impressed.

'This is Patrick,' Sarah began, genuinely wanting to talk

him up but suddenly realizing she didn't know how to describe him, since he did a bit of everything. 'He's brilliant,' she settled on, 'and such a great help with the house.'

'Not your significant other then.' Marcus sounded happy about that.

'Patrick, this is Marcus Fernsby. You might recognize him.'

'From the telly-box,' said Marcus, flashing his smile at Patrick.

'No,' said Patrick quietly, 'I don't.'

The two men shook hands then Marcus made a point of rubbing his palm with his other hand to remove the dust he had picked up from Patrick, who surveyed him coldly.

'Better be off,' said Marcus, 'but I'll see you again soon, Sarah,' and he went past Patrick without another word.

Chapter Twenty-Six

Patrick walked briskly on into the kitchen and Sarah would have gone after him to explain Marcus's presence in the house but she was distracted by the phone ringing. It was Doctor Phillips coming back with a response from David Young. The killer had agreed to speak to her because he wanted to assure Sarah that he'd had nothing to do with Lucy Woodfell's disappearance. Apparently, she could come that very day, if she wished? She told herself that this was a good thing while still not being entirely convinced that it was.

She met Doctor Phillips outside David's apartment and David Young opened the door. He waited to take his cue from the doctor, who indicated that Sarah should enter the flat. David was a very big man in late middle age. He looked powerful and she tried not to think of how he had once used that strength. Sarah could read nothing in his blank expression.

The flat was starkly furnished and the living room doubled as the kitchen. Sarah chose the only armchair. The doctor sat down easily on the sofa next to his charge, making them look like co-conspirators, ready to answer her questions together.

'I don't want to go into the details of what happened between you and Megan,' she began. 'I am sure you've been over it many times.' David gave her a half-smile to acknowledge this. 'I want to ask you about what happened afterwards, when you went on the run. You managed to elude the police for two weeks?' He nodded to acknowledge the truth of this. 'During that time, where did you sleep?'

'I slept rough. The weather was warm and I tried sleeping in the woods, but I kept getting bitten by insects so I moved to the beach.'

'The beach near Cragsmoor Manor?'

'No,' he said quickly, 'further up.'

'Whereabouts?'

She could tell he didn't like that question.

'I didn't sleep near the towns or villages, so I never knew exactly where I was.'

'But you never slept near Cragsmoor? Not once? It's right near the beach.'

'No.' He said it too quickly and looked down, avoiding her gaze. He definitely looked nervous.

'You grew up ten miles from there. There are woods nearby to hide in. It was an ideal spot.'

'No,' he repeated firmly.

'Okay,' she said. The doctor gave her a slight smile then. She got the impression it was born of pride in David.

'You kept that up for two weeks,' she said, 'sleeping rough. Then you handed yourself in. Why did you do that?'

'Living like that is hard.'

'You were still on the run when Lucy Woodfell disappeared.'

'I never saw her.' He said this quickly and it seemed like a well-rehearsed answer to a question he must have known was coming, but had the doctor rehearsed David or did he do it himself?

'There were witnesses who saw you near the village close to the manor?'

'That wasn't me.'

'A big, scruffy young man with muddied clothes who was the same height as you and had the same hair colour.'

'Not me. I was far away then.'

'And yet you handed yourself in to a police station not that far away from Cragsmoor.'

'It was,' he argued.

'If you walked the coastal path you could have made it there in a day.'

'But I didn't.' He looked scared, worried and angry all at once. He also looked as if he was trying to hide all of that from her. 'And I don't want to answer any more stupid questions. You're trying to trap me because you think I did it.'

'Did what?'

'Killed Lucy.'

'She might still be alive,' said Sarah and he snorted at that. 'How do you know she is dead?'

He turned to the doctor then and said, 'You see. Trying to trap me. I know what she's doing.' And he turned to Sarah as if she hadn't just heard him and said, 'I know what you are doing!'

'David . . .' she began but he got up out of his seat.

'No!' he said firmly. 'Stop the questions. I don't have to answer them.'

'I would be far less suspicious of you if you did.'

He spun round then and roared at the doctor. 'You see! Get her out of my head!'

Then he marched off through the bedroom door and slammed it behind him.

There was silence for a moment while Sarah and the doctor looked at each other. 'Let's not pretend that went well,' he said. 'I think you should leave.'

The image of David Young storming off to his bedroom, leaving Sarah with a disapproving Doctor Phillips, stayed with her. She had rattled him and didn't find his answers at all convincing. If he had admitted to her that he was in the area but hadn't killed Lucy, it might have been more convincing. He showed nervousness and flashes of anger whenever she challenged him.

It seemed that no one she spoke to about Lucy Woodfell sounded entirely convincing, but unlike the others, David had beaten a woman to death. Was he a psychopath or just a man with anger issues, particularly when he was under pressure? Was he lying about being near Cragsmoor because he had something to hide or simply because he worried that Sarah might be more suspicious of him if he admitted he was close to Lucy's last known whereabouts?

Someone's lying, she told herself on the drive back. Or maybe they all are, but does anyone actually know the truth about Lucy? Somebody must, she reasoned: the person who killed her.

Chapter Twenty-Seven

August

Having questioned Freddie, Sarah was even more determined to speak to his sister and try again with Oliver. As far as she could tell, Sephy might have had even more reason to, at the very least, dislike her half-sister for being close to her husband, but Sarah's letter remained unanswered and her phone call had not even reached Sephy.

For some time, Sarah had been at a loss as to how to contact the woman. She supposed she could show up at Sephy's house and knock on her door, but would she even answer? And if she did, she would surely decline an interview. Perhaps there was a way to entice Sephy to come to Sarah instead, though, and the more she thought about it, the more convinced Sarah became that it might just work.

She drove down to the old woman's house in the Triumph Sunbeam, pulled up close to it by the side of the road, and switched off the engine. She didn't go up to the house or even leave the car. Instead, she waited there for Sephy to glance out of a window. Meanwhile, she read news items on her phone and even found some different articles about Lucy Woodfell to scour. An hour passed before a curtain in the cottage finally twitched and, moments later, just as she'd hoped, the front door opened.

A frail but distinguished-looking woman in her mid-seventies stepped out of the house and walked slowly down the path, her eyes fixed on the car she had once owned. When she reached it, Sarah wound down the window. Sunlight illuminated the old woman's features. Her face was pale and the skin dry. It reminded Sarah of parchment paper, but she could still tell that Sephy had been striking once. Age could not disguise that kind of beauty.

'I haven't seen *this* in a very long time,' Sephy announced as she placed a bony hand almost reverentially on its bonnet. 'The times we had.'

'It still handles well,' Sarah told her, 'once you get used to the steering.'

'Yes, it was a bit hairy on corners,' the old woman agreed. Then she took her eyes from the car and focused on Sarah. 'So you're . . . what? A relative of Evelyn's?'

'Her niece.'

'The one who wrote to me,' she said, 'then you called.' She announced this flatly to show she was unimpressed. 'You want to speak to me about Lucy?'

'That's right.'

'I thought when your aunt passed that it might be the end of this. You were told I had nothing to say to you,' she observed, 'but you came here anyway. Must be a family trait.'

This was not the first time Sarah had been compared to her aunt Evie though it did not sound like a compliment. She got out of the car then and followed the old lady back to her home. Sephy seemed to accept that the tenacious younger woman would persist until she had been granted an audience.

The cottage Sephy lived in was small but tastefully

furnished. There was no sign of Sephy's carer so the two women were alone. Sarah began by offering Sephy her congratulations.

'On what?' She seemed genuinely unsure.

'Your son has just become prime minister,' Sarah reminded her.

'Oh that. Yes, it is rather jolly.' She said this as if he had just been promoted in a normal job.

'Have you spoken to him?'

'Not yet. He is busy.'

'Still, I would have thought he'd phone his mother after such a big moment.'

'I haven't seen him in a little while. Like I said, he's very busy.' Sarah got the impression it might actually have been quite a long while. From the way Sephy spoke of her son, it appeared they might even be leading quite separate lives, and Sarah wondered if there might be a reason for this.

Sephy changed the subject, by offering Sarah her condolences about Evelyn, without saying anything positive about the woman she had first known as a callow young girl and later as the successful woman who had taken her ancestral home. Sephy claimed not to have placed the blame for that necessary purchase on Evelyn but squarely upon the shoulders of her brother.

'Never moved with the times,' she observed. 'Freddie kept thinking he was going to keep the house no matter what, but the figures didn't add up. Not to me, anyway, but Father didn't believe in sending girls to university and that's probably why none of them ever listened to me.'

'What would you have done differently?'

'Let's see,' she pretended to think for a while. 'Would

I have wasted hundreds of thousands of pounds on absurd ideas and vanity projects like a book, gold mines or a zoo? The answer to that is no, but my brother wanted to do something big, to make a statement.'

'Did you fall out with him over it?'

'We all did. Constantly. When it was finally sold I was informed never to tell him *I told you so* and that was that. My brothers both still think they were victims of circumstance. I don't see either of them any more. Haven't for years.'

'Because they lost the estate?'

'I'm a forgiving soul, but when a man messes up everything in his life and fails to even acknowledge his share of the blame, let alone apologize for it, that does rather make him somewhat irredeemable, don't you think?'

'I suppose so.'

'Have you spoken to my brothers?'

'I couldn't get hold of Oliver.' That was a partial truth at least.

'Try him in the mornings, dear. Don't bother in the afternoons.'

'I spoke to Freddie, though.'

'About Lucy?' Was that a trace of alarm in the older woman's voice?

'About the house, initially. He wants to buy it back.'

The old woman stared at Sarah for a moment, her face frozen, then suddenly she burst out laughing. 'Buy it back? With what? Oh, what a fool he is.'

There seemed little point in discussing Freddie's foolishness further or explaining his theory that David Young was the killer. Sarah wanted to hear what Sephy had to say on the matter. She also wanted to confront her about the rumours surrounding her husband's death and Lucy's closeness to him, but knew she would have to tread carefully with her questions or the other woman would ask her to leave.

For now, she settled on, 'Did you ever think either of your brothers might have had anything to do with Lucy's disappearance?'

'God, no!' It was a snort of derision.

'Because they were family?'

'Because they had no reason to,' she countered. 'Wouldn't you agree?'

'I don't suppose Freddie had a very high opinion of Lucy. Not after she took out an injunction on him.'

'Oh that,' she was as dismissive as her brother had been, 'it was just Lucy making a point.'

'The point being that she considered her brother to be incompetent and she wanted him gone.'

'Well, he was incompetent. As for wanting him gone, what she actually wanted was for him to grow up and start being more practical in his running of the estate. The way she went about this wasn't subtle, I'll grant you. Good for her, I say.

'Look, I don't know what you were expecting to achieve by coming here today, but if you were after some astonishing insight, I'm afraid you will leave disappointed. I haven't the faintest idea what happened to Lucy.'

'What do you remember about that day?'

'Nothing out of the ordinary, until she went missing.'

'You saw her walk away from the house?'

'I was in the kitchen with Freddie, Toby and his nanny. Oliver was upstairs. We all saw her walk off in the direction of the beach.'

'Wasn't Toby a bit old for a nanny by then?' Sarah wondered if Sephy would provide her with the same answer she had given to the detective.

'Margaret had been with us for years,' she said. 'She was my nanny, Lucy's too, and the boys'. We brought her back to look after Toby and when we started educating him at home, I asked her to stay on to keep him focused on his work.'

'Why did you home-school him?'

'It was only for a year or so,' she said dismissively, 'he was having a tough time at school. It happens, and one does one's best for one's children.'

'That was good of you,' said Sarah. 'Why was Oliver there if he had been passed over?'

'He was attempting a rapprochement of sorts with Freddie. Father and Lucy's mother died within a year of each other,' then she added archly, 'natural causes, before you get the wrong idea. Anyway, Oliver contested the will at that point and things dragged on for an age but he didn't get anywhere. The legal fees were draining away what was left of his money and I think he realized he was never going to win.'

'When he saw Lucy, was that before or after you spotted her from the kitchen?'

'Before, presumably, though with Oliver you could never tell for sure. He had an addictive personality. To start with it was gambling, then drugs and finally drink. If you expect him to remember things, he won't. There will be large gaps.'

'How did you feel about Lucy? Did you ever resent her?'

'Why would I resent her?'

'She was the baby of the family, born to the second wife. You might have been jealous if your father paid her more attention.'

'Lucy was family,' she said, as if this was explanation enough. *'Familia ante omnia,'* she quoted before translating the Latin, 'family is everything. We may have fought each other but we stuck together against the world. That's how it works. Do you have siblings?'

'No.'

'Then you will never understand.'

'Did you all fight with Lucy or was there someone in particular she fought with?'

'I've already explained she argued with Freddie about the running of the estate, just as I did. She even argued with me because I wasn't forceful enough with him, not that he would have listened. She fought with Oliver because he almost destroyed himself and us.'

'She must have been relieved when he was passed over, at least initially.'

'She was, as we all were.'

'Was that your father's decision or did you all have a hand in it?'

'Father's decisions were always Father's. You couldn't sway him even when the right course of action was patently obvious; you had to wait for him to make up his own mind. Lucy did try to speak to him about Oliver once. I think she thought she might get away with it, being the youngest, but all she got for her pains was a slap across the face.'

'Her father struck her?'

'He could be a bit of a monster,' Sephy explained. 'In

the end he worked it out for himself when Oliver almost died of an overdose.'

'Did Oliver know Lucy had spoken to her father about him?'

'Probably, yes – what does it matter?'

'He may have harboured a grudge.'

'He didn't kill her,' said Sephy firmly. 'Freddie didn't kill her and nor did I.'

'Who else was around that day?'

'No one.' She seemed to think for a moment and Sarah wondered if she had forgotten about the staff or was deliberately keeping that information from her for some reason. 'Except the cleaner, perhaps, and I think the gardener was still around outside.'

'What about your husband?'

'Oh yes, Alex, of course. He came up from London as soon as he heard.'

'I understand your husband and Lucy were close.'

She blinked then, her response a little slower than usual. 'They got on. He liked to go for walks and I didn't. Lucy would take him off my hands and they'd leave me in peace for a while.'

'Was there ever more to it than them just getting on?'

Sephy shook her head and grimaced as if this was an absurd suggestion. 'She was my sister. Do you really think she would sleep with my husband?'

'I don't know.'

'Well, she wouldn't, and as for Alex . . .' she seemed to struggle to find the words, 'he wasn't the sort to . . .'

'Have affairs?'

'He was entirely devoted to me,' she said emphatically.

'And were you entirely devoted to him?'

She bridled at this. 'Who have you been talking to?' And when Sarah did not answer she drew her own conclusion. 'Malicious gossip.'

'What is?'

'The idea that I did not love Alex, that I somehow needed . . .' again she struggled to find the words.

'Someone else?'

'You wouldn't understand.'

'I might. He was older than you, by quite a lot, and I understand he struggled after the war. I could see how, under certain circumstances, it might be tempting to embark on an affair.'

'You really have been listening to gossip, haven't you?'

'I'm not judging you,' said Sarah. 'Having an affair is not a criminal offence.'

'No, it isn't,' said Sephy dryly, 'or they'd be locking up half of England.'

'You are right,' conceded Sarah. 'I have been listening to gossip and I probably shouldn't, but we all do, don't we? We can't help ourselves. Some of that gossip suggested you might have had a lover, or more than one.' Sephy snorted at this suggestion but it was hard to tell if she was rebuffing this idea or indicating it was nobody else's business. Sarah noted that she hadn't actually denied she was seeing someone else back then. 'Then there was the other gossip,' she said.

'You mean about Alex,' said Sephy, 'and the crash? Nonsense, all of it. I didn't kill Alex,' she said, aghast, as if those village gossips had invented something really quite incredible.

'There was talk about his brakes,' said Sarah.

'Let's see, shall we,' and she started counting the different pieces of gossip on her fingers. 'There was talk about Alex and talk about me, there was more talk about Alex and Lucy too, presumably, and talk about me and a mystery lover. Only where is he, this mystery man of mine, and why didn't we run off together? They tend to forget that bit, don't they, the gossips?'

'I didn't say I believed it all,' said Sarah, 'but I did wonder what you made of it?'

'I think it showed me just how vile some people can be.'

'Alex did struggle, though, because of what happened to him during the war. Did he ever display any violent tendencies?'

'Alex struggled, yes, but so did many thousands of other men after that and all subsequent wars. It doesn't make them killers in civilian life.' Then she said, 'Now if you don't mind, I don't like to talk about my husband. It upsets me.'

Sarah decided not to pursue it further. 'Who *do* you think might have been responsible for Lucy's disappearance, then?'

'I don't know,' Sephy admitted. 'Don't you think I might have said something if I did?'

'The police thought she could have been meeting someone that afternoon. Did she have a boyfriend, a lover?'

'If she did, she never mentioned him to me, but if you're looking for someone to question, I would start with that boy on the beach.'

'Warren Evans?'

'Ask him how he could have been sitting there all afternoon and not seen my sister walk by. Impossible, right?'

'You think he killed her?'

'It is certainly possible,' said Sephy. 'The police thought so.'

'They did for a while but never charged him. No body and no evidence.'

'A body could easily disappear in that sea,' Sephy insisted. 'Have you seen how wild it can get?'

'Perhaps if it was thrown from a boat or even off a cliff, but I doubt a body would disappear completely if someone just pushed it into the sea from the shallows.'

Sephy had no answer to this, so she ignored it. 'I always suspected him. Do you know he hit that girlfriend of his?'

'I did not know that.'

'Slapped her outside the pub in the village, apparently, during a jealous row before this business happened with Lucy. That's what people said. A boy like that can't control himself. A man who hits a woman is no longer a man,' she concluded.

'I'll bear that in mind,' said Sarah, though Sephy seemed to have forgotten how her own father had also slapped a woman, his own daughter, Lucy. It also hadn't escaped Sarah's attention that Sephy had only offered her theory about Warren Evans being responsible for Lucy's disappearance in response to Sarah's own suggestion that her sister might have been secretly meeting someone that day. A deflection? Possibly. The first unanswered question was why, and the second, who. If Captain Ramsay had been less than honest about when he'd set out from London, could Lucy have been planning to meet him that day?

Chapter Twenty-Eight

As Sarah drove back to Cragsmoor Manor, she went over the conversation with Sephy in her head and recalled the bits that jarred with her. It wasn't the flat denials that anyone in the family could have been responsible for Lucy's disappearance that troubled her, or the way Sephy was so dismissive of the gossip surrounding her. Not denying that she might have succumbed to an affair was interesting, though, because it showed a certain selfishness – but did not of course make her a killer.

She had also been dismissive of her half-sister's personal life and quickly moved on from that topic, while refusing to talk any further about her late husband. Instead, she steered Sarah towards Warren Evans as a suspect. That did not make him an innocent man, necessarily, but it did leave Sarah feeling even more determined to speak to Warren to see what he could tell her about that day. She could then make up her own mind about him and not simply rely on Sephy's opinion, but how could she find the man? He had no social media presence and there wasn't any information about his current whereabouts online. As far as the internet was concerned, he was a ghost, his only presence there being in archived articles about Lucy's disappearance.

Perhaps Dickie would sign off some expenses to hire a

private detective who might be able to locate him. That might be a conversation worth having.

That evening, Sarah opened three new emails from Kirsten. The extracts revealed that Evie and Lucy's friendship deepened when they both managed to get jobs in publishing. Evie became a regular guest at Cragswood Manor during holidays, occasional long weekends and even a Christmas or two. Evie visited her friend throughout the sixties and on into the seventies.

Some of the latest extracts from her aunt's memoir told Sarah little that she had not already worked out for herself since her time at Cragsmoor, but there was one section that was both timely and interesting. It concerned Evelyn's thoughts on Sephy and her marriage to Captain Ramsay.

There was excitement when it was announced that the captain was arriving to spend the weekend with the family. This was generally understood, by even the lowliest member of the household, to mean that he was coming to spend the weekend with Sephy. She had broken up with James months ago and Lucy said it was 'more of an audition than an engagement', but she did not make clear who was auditioning.

Sephy had an aristocratic background, a little money from her family and would surely be a suitable match for any man, with her beauty and 'breeding', which everyone in their world seemed to care about. Captain Ramsay, meanwhile, may have been more than twenty years her senior but he was a war hero, with medals to show for it, and was described, in a society magazine, as 'handsome, dashing' and 'a man on the rise'. There were rumours he was heading for parliament.

I read up on the captain before his arrival. He had been featured in a book on his regiment that was in the family library. Apparently, he was a paratrooper who led his men into missions behind enemy lines before D-Day. There was a high casualty rate and he was wounded twice, but they achieved their objectives and he was always in the thick of the action, having 'personally despatched a good number' of enemy soldiers. I was intrigued. What was a good number of killings? Two? A dozen? More? I wondered if all that brutal killing, even in war, would not have a detrimental effect on a man.

'Never expect your men to do anything you might baulk at doing yourself' was his motto, and they apparently loved him for it. He did admit to a terrible fear of heights, however, which must have made life difficult when he joined the parachute regiment. 'I was always worried I was going to chicken out when we had to jump out of an aircraft, so I gave my sergeant strict instructions to stand right behind me and, if I hesitated even for a second, he was to shove me through the door.'

After the war the captain left the army to work in the City, but his thirst for action could not be sated in banking. Instead, it was quenched by mountain-climbing expeditions and treks across deserts. I wondered then if marriage to Sephy, who was something of a home bird, and a career in parliament might not make him restless.

When the captain finally arrived, Sephy met him from his car and took his arm to lead him into the house. The servants seemed to appear all at once to take a look at the war hero, the men almost standing to attention.

Captain Ramsay was a tall, distinguished-looking man, who gave me the impression he noticed everything, even me, as I lurked on a first-floor landing. I looked down as he glanced upwards and would have instinctively stepped back had he not possessed what I can only describe as a kind face, for someone so used to killing people.

'Does Sephy love the captain?' I asked Lucy later. We always called him the captain, as if he was a pirate, and never used his actual name. It locked him into his earlier life, which we still thought of as having honour or glamour.

Lucy gave a half-shrug. 'Sephy wants an easy life. What else is she going to do?'

Sephy was never encouraged to have a job, so marriage and a family seemed to be the logical next step for her. 'Still, she doesn't have to marry the captain. There are lots of other men around.'

'Younger men, do you mean?' She pounced on that as if I was saying something distasteful, but there was a twenty-year age gap between them, which surely every-one had noticed. I sometimes wondered if Sephy had worked out that she might be free of him by the time she was in her forties. I immediately felt guilty for hav-ing that thought, but I never once saw Sephy show any sign of affection towards the captain. He, on the other hand, would gaze at Sephy as if she had just emerged, naked and beautiful, from a shell, like Venus in that painting by Botticelli. I think she realized that, with Alex Ramsay as her husband, she would always be able to do whatever she wanted. In any case, they were married within the year.

I was pleasantly surprised to be invited to Sephy's wedding, though I was only there to keep Lucy company. It was a grand affair and the weather held for her. I had a little too much champagne, which I was not used to, but managed to stay sober enough to keep a writer's eye on proceedings. One day you'll all end up in my novel, I told myself, and, for once, I was right about that as they and Cragsmoor became my subconscious inspiration for *The Gallows Tree*.

My overriding memory of that day was of Sephy. She seemed to be thoroughly enjoying herself but didn't spend very much time with her new husband. Instead, she flitted from group to group, accepting congratulations and compliments about her hair, her dress, her radiant beauty. I specifically recall her being at the centre of attention from a group of quite young men, one of whom was her old boyfriend, James. She was clearly flirting with him and the rest of the group, and I recall thinking 'You are going to miss this.'

That gathering only broke up when the captain, presumably tiring of his wife giving her attention to numerous other men, made his presence felt. I saw his face and one look from him was all it took for the younger males to be reminded of their place and they melted away. I also recall that Sephy's smile went with them.

Chapter Twenty-Nine

Sarah had not expected Sephy's marriage to Captain Ramsay to have been a love affair exactly, but she was surprised that Sephy hadn't made more of an effort with him on their wedding day, at least for the sake of appearances.

It took her ten minutes to find the book Evie had mentioned in the library, but it was still there. She wanted to see how the captain was portrayed in the history of his regiment and what this might reveal about his character. There was a portrait photograph of a handsome young man, captioned: *Captain Alex Ramsay, shortly before D-Day. He distinguished himself behind enemy lines. Ramsay survived the war only to be killed in a road accident in 1988.* Sarah realized that this could not possibly be the book her aunt had mentioned, as that had been published long before Captain Ramsay's death, before he had even married Sephy, in fact. This was a far more recent history, written by a man called Julian Hastings, a former officer in the same battalion as the captain but from a later era. Had the two men perhaps known each other personally? She decided to write to Julian to find out.

Sarah remembered Patrick telling her that the men who took the wreck of Captain Ramsay's car afterwards claimed it had been tampered with, an act of sabotage that would surely indicate murder not suicide, but if you wanted to kill someone this wasn't necessarily the right way to go about it. If someone did tamper with his car, how could they know he would lose control of it on such a long, fast stretch of the road?

Perhaps the mechanic who had checked the vehicle was simply wrong. Did his claim start out as a rumour which was repeated until it became accepted as fact? There was only one way to find out.

The business was part garage, part scrapyard. Out front, there was a sizeable workshop with two large, open doors and Sarah walked through them, hoping to find the owner working on one of the four cars awaiting his attention, but there was no sign of him.

'Hello?' she called, wary of stepping further inside without invitation. She called twice more before deciding she didn't look like someone who had come to steal spare parts, so she ventured further in. He couldn't be far away, judging by the unlocked front doors, so she walked through the workshop and emerged at the back in a large open site with a wire perimeter fence. It was filled with scrapped cars that had been broken down and cannibalized for parts. Some of them were stacked on top of one another to save space. As soon as Sarah turned a corner, she was spotted by a very large and vicious-looking German Shepherd and the dog immediately went for her.

She had a split second to digest the fact that an aggressive dog with bared teeth was bearing down on her at speed. It was too close and there was no time to run. Sarah was a trespasser and it was going to savage her. Instinctively she turned away to protect her face from a mauling, which was why she didn't see what happened next.

There was a harsh sound of metal grating against metal and when the dog did not land on her after all, Sarah felt able to risk a glance in its direction. It was barking furiously and desperate to reach her but had been prevented from doing so by a very long chain, which was secured around its neck and connected to something at the other end of the scrapyard. Sarah prayed it would hold because the dog was still absolutely determined to get to her.

'Down!' A man had appeared suddenly because of the din. 'Tyson! Get down!' and mercifully, Tyson complied, calmed by its owner's presence and his commands. Sarah was glad to see him, until he demanded of her, 'What were you doing?'

'Looking for you,' she told him. 'If you're the owner?'

'I'm Colin,' he told her by way of confirmation. 'You're lucky I didn't let the dog off the leash,' and she realized he was holding a newspaper and had just emerged from a Portakabin, presumably having been to the toilet.

'I'm sorry. There was no one in the workshop.'

'What are you after?' he asked.

As Sarah began to explain, she wondered if he would tell her not to waste his time. Patrick had given her the details of the scrapyard business Colin had inherited from his father, so she had taken a chance and driven over to speak with him. He seemed like a no-nonsense kind of guy who might just think his father was wrong about the captain's car being sabotaged, or that it was all far too long ago for anyone to remember anything about it now. Instead, he heard her out silently.

'My dad used to go on about it. I was only a bairn when the crash happened but it was a big deal at the time.'

'What do you think happened that day?'

'Oh, he was murdered,' he said, in the calm tone you might use to offer someone a cup of tea. 'The brake line was cut. That's what my old man said.'

'If it was that obvious, how come the police didn't spot it?'

'Don't know. You'd have to ask them.' Then he added, 'Maybe they weren't looking for anything suspicious because it looked like an accident.'

'How did your father spot it?'

'Someone bought the exhaust so he had to get under the car for it. That's when he noticed.'

'Did he go to the police?'

'He said they weren't interested. He'd had the car for months by then and they thought he was making it up to get attention or a reward or something.'

'There's no way a brake cable could be cut by accident or during the crash?'

'He thought it looked deliberate. He reckoned it was probably that wife of his. It's usually the wife, isn't it? If the husband turns up dead, I mean. More often than not it's the husband who kills the wife but it works just the same the other way around. She was younger, wasn't she? He thought she might have wanted to be free of him.'

It didn't seem to Sarah that Colin's father would have had much to gain by going to the police with this story if it wasn't true, and why would he wait months to make something like that up? He must have genuinely believed that the cable had been cut and that Captain Ramsay had been murdered. The scrapyard owner's casual assumption that the captain was murdered by his wife in order to free herself from him became the root of the gossip that had targeted Sephy for years, though it did fail to recognize an obvious fact. She could have just divorced him instead. They might have been Catholic and divorce was frowned upon, but not as much as murder. Perhaps wanting to be free of her husband was not a good enough reason to kill him, but what if he had been having an affair with her half-sister, or Sephy suspected he might have actually killed Lucy? Revenge was a much better motive.

But if it wasn't Sephy who was responsible for her husband's death, then who else could it have been and why would they have done it? Sarah was far from understanding the truth behind all this yet, but with every passing day she was becoming more convinced that whoever was responsible for it, the death of Captain Ramsay and the disappearance of Lucy Woodfell were inextricably linked.

Chapter Thirty

Sarah's book finally seemed to have a life of its own, judging by the direction it had now gone in after a few days of intensive writing then rewriting in order to make up some lost time. This had been needed following a period dominated by investigating the Lucy Woodfell case. The protagonist of Sarah's work-in-progress was possibly in league with her missing partner now and trying to outrun the police as they attempted to close in. For the most part she was able to stay just ahead of events and the police. In short, her character was far more in control of events than Sarah was in real life.

Her anxiety was building with every passing day, knowing that each one brought her closer to the deadlines for the closure of her investigation and the delivery of the first draft of her novel. Progress in both directions seemed excruciatingly slow. Her book as yet had no ending and her investigation lacked a crucial ingredient that had also eluded the police: proof that any of the suspects had killed Lucy.

When Sarah did finally get a break, it came from an unlikely source. Out of the blue, former Detective Sergeant Crozier phoned her to pass on an address. 'You didn't get this from me, you understand? I've been thinking about it for a while. I've still got friends.' She took this to mean he had them on the force. 'You said you wanted to speak to Warren Evans but you didn't have an address for him. Well, I've just given it to you. Or rather I haven't, if you catch my drift?'

'I do,' she said. His reticence meant that he could only have received the information from a serving member of the police and, though it was clearly an abuse of power, she had to admit she was glad of it, having no other means of tracking down Warren Evans. 'Thank you.'

'That's all right, pet. He still has questions to answer, I reckon,' he said. 'And why should he escape being pestered by you when I didn't?'

The first thing Sarah had noted from the online newspaper archives she'd trawled through was that Warren Evans was rarely referred to by his actual name. Immediately after Lucy's disappearance, the man-on-the-beach was urged to come forward in newspaper reports and televised appeals. That label stayed with him for years afterwards.

He was interviewed and reinterviewed by detectives and hounded by the tabloids. 'Police name the man on the beach' ran one headline, as if they were also naming the actual killer of the missing woman.

'Do you deny you were the man on the beach?' questioned one reporter, even though Warren had never denied it.

It took him a suspicious amount of time to come forward, claiming he never watched the news and had no idea the police were searching for him, which must have endeared him to under-pressure detectives.

'The man on the beach was jealous and controlling.'

That was the headline from a piece involving his former girlfriend, who accepted money for a tell-all interview. She said that he was an angry man who could snap at any time. The newspapers hinted that, at the very least, he must have seen Lucy, therefore he had to know something and if he continued to claim that he did not know anything, then he had to have a sinister reason; ergo he was her killer. It didn't help that he himself would not speak to those same tabloids who were now implicating him, so they damned him with insinuation. He was 'a loner with few friends', he had 'only ever had one girlfriend', he was jealous of his 'free-spirited former belle', who had 'fled to London to pursue a modelling career'.

Sarah thought of trying to call Warren but in the end she decided to turn up on his doorstep instead, having first checked that he lived in a quiet suburb in a house overlooked by others, so she would feel comparatively safe there. The memory of David Young's outburst when she had questioned him was still comparatively fresh in her memory and she'd had the protection of his doctor with her in the same room at the time. There would be no professional person with her when she spoke to Warren and he was an unknown quantity at this point. Her strategy where he was concerned was to hear him out, to judge for herself whether he had never seen Lucy that day and if he had a plausible explanation.

The man who answered the door to her was in late middle age and scruffily dressed but he still looked a lot like the young man whose face she had seen on the internet. Warren Evans regarded her warily and when Sarah told him why she was there, he flared up. 'I don't speak to journalists,' he hissed. 'How many times do I have to say it?'

'I'm not a journalist,' she told him, 'or a police officer or a private detective.'

'What are you then?'

She almost said 'I'm family' but instead launched into a long-winded explanation about her aunt's wish to discover the truth about Lucy.

'I don't know how long I have to keep on saying it. I did not kill that girl!'

'I don't think you did. You had no reason to.'

He seemed taken aback by that, as if having no reason to do something wasn't mitigation enough for most people. She hoped that doubting he was the murderer might win him over. In truth, she had lied about that part. Sarah did not necessarily believe that he *was* the murderer but had certainly not ruled him out either.

'Then why are you here?'

'I just want five minutes of your time, please, for you to tell me about that day from your perspective, so I can understand it?'

He seemed to be deciding whether to trust her or not.

Warren glanced over her shoulder then and she turned to see a couple walking down the road close to his house. They looked over towards him and though they seemed innocuous, with no particular interest in him, this was enough to rattle Warren.

'Christ,' he hissed, 'will you get in?' and he gestured for her to come inside. As she walked through his door, she did consider the wisdom of entering a potential killer's house, but it was broad daylight and two people had just seen her standing on his doorstep. Would that be enough to protect her? She pulled out her phone and fake-dialled it then held it up to her ear.

'Hi Patrick,' she told the dead line. 'Yes, I'm with him now. At his home, that's right, so I'll meet you where we said later. Thanks.'

'Who was that?' he asked.

'My lift home.' She had parked the Sunbeam around the corner because it was so conspicuous. She now had the additional security of knowing that Warren thought she had just given her location to a male friend.

He sat down in a chair and she took that as an invitation to take a corner of the sofa.

'The anniversaries are the worst,' he told her. 'You get a new set of reporters but they're exactly the same as the last ones. You can't trust them. If I talk to them, they twist my words, so I don't speak to them and they stitch me up anyway. They write things down that I never said and they make . . .' He was searching for the right word.

'Insinuations?'

'Yes.' He seemed surprised that she actually understood.

'I've read their reports. They do make things sound bad,' she told him, 'and that interview with your ex-girlfriend was . . .'

'Disgusting.' He was still angry about it, even now. 'She wrote to me, you know?' Then he clarified, 'Jane. She wrote to me to apologize. Hah!' It was clear the apology had not been well received. 'She was sorry for all the things she'd said about me – she was just a silly little girl back then and dazzled by that reporter, who'd made up half of what she said.' Sarah could tell Warren didn't believe Jane's account, even though he'd had similar experiences himself with the press.

'That girl ruined my life. Her and the bloody Woodfell family. This has stayed with me. There isn't a day when I don't think about it. I haven't been able to move on.' He shook his head as if reliving the trauma of that time. 'The police wanted to lock me up and throw away the key. They kept on and on at me, telling me to confess. "Get it off your chest, son, you'll feel better." Maybe I should have done.' He added hastily, 'Even though it would have been a lie. I didn't do it. I didn't do anything. I was just there, that's all. But maybe if I had copped for it, I wouldn't be living like this.'

It was a strange thing to say when the alternative would have been life in prison, but she could see Warren was clearly not at peace.

'I'm sorry to go over it all again, but I want to find out what really happened to Lucy,' she explained. 'If I can learn something from you that helps me work it out, then maybe you will get some peace of mind.' He seemed to accept this. 'Did you know Lucy Woodfell before she disappeared?'

He shook his head. 'Not at all. That was another thing the police didn't believe. They kept saying the village was a small place, but she didn't live in the village, did she? She lived at the big house and didn't hang out with the rest of us. I'd never even seen her around.'

'You can see why the police wanted to talk to you?' she said. 'A number of people saw you sitting there on your own, you'd had an argument with your girlfriend and must have been angry, you were close to the path and Lucy would have walked right past you. She was never seen again.'

'And I never saw her either,' he assured her.

'That's the bit of your story that no one believes,' she told him. 'Four witnesses saw Lucy leave the house to walk to the beach that day: her oldest brother, her sister, the other brother and the nanny. They all saw her heading that way.'

'Right,' he said. 'I never disputed that but I didn't see her.'

'I've walked that path. It's not so very long and only a small number of people used it to get from the house to the beach. I'd say it's unlikely that someone hid to one side of it on the off-chance that one of the Woodfell girls would come by so they could grab them.'

'I don't think anyone would try and grab someone there,' he agreed. 'It's too close to the beach and people walk by with their dogs.'

'So we think she left the house and we reckon she safely navigated the path to the beach, which means she had to have come out right by you. Yet you still say, after all these years, that you never saw her. How can you account for that, Warren?'

'I can't. Don't you think I want to?'

'Did you give the police any explanation?' she asked, her frustration building now. 'Did you say you fell asleep?'

'No,' he said, 'because I never fell asleep.'

'Were you facing the sea?'

'Yes.'

'And you saw other people go by?'

'Yeah, and they saw me. They told the police I was

there but no one ever said I was talking to Lucy or that I was even with a woman, apart from Jane – but she wasn't there long.'

'What was your argument about?'

He looked frustrated then too. 'I was jealous,' he admitted, 'because Jane kept flirting with other guys. I got angry and we had a row, and yes, I do know how that makes me look.'

'Like someone who might take out his anger on another woman, do you mean?'

'That's pretty much what the police reckoned, yes.'

'How long did you stay on the beach after Jane left?'

'Hours,' he said. 'I was pissed off and upset and I just wanted to be on my own.'

'But didn't you get bored? What did you do, read a book or something?'

He shook his head. 'I listened to music.'

'You had a radio.'

'No. A Walkman, it had those headphones, you know.'

'Were you sitting up or lying down?'

'Both. I mean, I sat for a while and lay down for a while.'

'Did you close your eyes?'

'I didn't go to sleep but I may have done, for a few minutes.'

'So if you were lying there with your eyes shut and your music coming out of your headphones, could Lucy have slipped past you?'

'That's what I said.'

'No, you didn't.'

He corrected himself then. 'Not to you. It's what I said to the police when they interviewed me.'

'What did they say?'

'They didn't believe me.'

'Why not?'

'I think they'd made their minds up about me by then and that was that.'

'But they let you go in the end.'

'Only because they had nothing on me. There was no evidence, I didn't know the woman and they never found her. Oh, and that other guy showed up and turned himself in.'

'David Young.'

'Yes, and that guy was an actual killer so, you know, he got their attention for a while.' He shook his head in annoyance. 'I still get mentioned in the same breath as him and he killed a lass with his bare hands. How is that right? He did life, you know.'

'I do know,' she said, 'and now he is out.'

'So for him it's over, but for me it never ends. I just want to forget about it. All I want is for everyone to leave me alone so I can move on. Then this nightmare might finally be over.'

Chapter Thirty-One

September

Later that morning Sarah received the latest extract from Kirsten. In it, Evie gave Sarah a glimpse of the world inhabited by another Woodfell: the oldest sibling, Oliver.

If you absolutely must burn through a sizeable family fortune then you would be advised to take up the two most expensive hobbies known to man: gambling and drugs.

Oliver gambled with the urgent rashness of a man who had already lost a shameful amount of money and had to win it back quickly, before anyone noticed it was gone. His sense of wretchedness at his own weakness led him to seek oblivion in more drugs and his habit was not just costly but life-threatening. Twice he overdosed and had to be rushed to hospital. It was clear that something had to be done and he was eventually persuaded to check into a rehab clinic in Switzerland. Somewhat surprisingly, he pursued a course of treatment for some months. Even Lucy was guardedly optimistic and she drove out to the airport to pick him up and bring him straight home before he could come into contact with anyone who might lead him astray again, then she stayed at the manor house with him.

After all the therapy and rehab, it was entirely typical of Olly to ruin everything with one rash act. He had only been back at Cragsmoor for a couple of days before he took a massive overdose of heroin and died.

Oliver was dead for four and a half minutes. That's how long it took to bring him back. Later, Freddie said it was like watching someone trying to start a clapped-out car with jump leads.

When Oliver came round, he denied that the drugs he had taken in his room were his, claiming they had been deliberately left there by someone else to tempt him. By then we were all used to Oliver's lies and this one was the final straw for his father, who started legal proceedings that eventually led to Oliver being disinherited in favour of his younger brother. Freddie told members of the family that he would take on the responsibility of the estate, to secure it for future generations. It had something of a hollow ring to it even then.

Once in charge, the first thing Freddie did was to buy himself an old Jaguar car, in racing green. He used to tell everyone that Jag could go from nought to sixty in nine seconds and it once belonged to a racing driver; Stirling Moss, I think. He liked to roar up and down the roads around the estate in it, terrifying the locals. His sister tried to get him to slow down. She was worried he might run over a child. Freddie used to laugh at the notion that he might not be fully in control, but he was about to embark on a series of disastrous projects that brought the family to its lowest point in five hundred years.

A photographer took photos of every corner of the house for his glossy 'coffee-table' book. They littered the library because it took him ages to choose the right ones for the book. When it was finally published, no one bought it. Lucy and I were both working in publishing by then and had warned him against it but, characteristically, he refused to listen to us.

His next idea was to open part of the house as an upmarket hotel, complete with golf course. It never got off the ground but it was a better idea than his zoo. We will never know how much he spent on the tigers, lions, zebras and giraffes he housed there, but it didn't last long.

The depleted finances and insurmountable problems with the estate would have severely taxed a brilliant man, and Freddie was far from brilliant. Sephy offered to help him out and she came back to Cragsmoor almost every weekend for months, to provide support then solace, as one scheme after another failed and more money was lost. If her husband objected to this, he did not let on in public. She may have been able to restrain Freddie from his wildest excesses but she couldn't save the estate. By now everyone could see how this was going to end. It was just a matter of time.

After reading that extract, Sarah decided that Oliver Woodfell should be next on her list for a surprise visit. She was keen to discover just how he had dealt with being disinherited by his father, only to see his younger brother make an even bigger mess of managing the family estate than he had. Oliver must have harboured resentment towards his siblings, none of whom seemed to have supported the idea of keeping him in charge. His greatest rancour would surely have been directed towards Freddie, however, and not Lucy, unless there was something about his relationship with his half-sister that Sarah had not yet discovered.

As she drove out to see the eldest of the Woodfell siblings, she made sure to follow Sephy's advice by arriving at his home in the morning, before Oliver was too far into his drinking. When she rang his doorbell she found Oliver up, dressed and coherent, and he peered at her suspiciously. Oliver was a cadaverous figure. Years of drug and alcohol abuse had turned him into an emaciated, undernourished soul.

Sarah explained who she was and why she was there. To talk about Lucy. Unsurprisingly, he did not appear to have any recollection of her earlier phone call.

'And why would I talk to you about Lucy? Why wouldn't I just tell you to fuck off?' he asked her.

'Because I might be the only person who believes your story.'

'What story?'

'The one about the drugs you overdosed on,' she said. 'You claimed they weren't yours and that someone had left them there. I believe you.'

He narrowed his eyes suspiciously. 'Why? No one else did.'

'I understand you were in that Swiss clinic for months. Even if you knew how to score in Geneva, I don't think you would have risked bringing heroin home on the plane and Lucy met you off it, so you couldn't go and meet any of your druggie mates.'

'That's right, she did.'

'Something also tells me that you wouldn't have hidden

heroin in your bedroom when your family and the servants would have been looking out for you to relapse and you had managed months in that expensive clinic without any. I don't think you would have taken an overdose unless someone put it there on a plate for you.'

Oliver regarded her closely. 'It almost sounds as if you were there,' he said, meaning she had hit the nail on the head. 'Are you some sort of private investigator?'

'No.'

'And you're obviously not a police officer?'

'I'm not a police officer. I told you, I'm here because of my aunt, Evelyn.'

'Which magazine or newspaper is paying you to dredge this all up again?'

'No one. Like I said, I'm just Evelyn's niece and I have a couple of questions about the day Lucy disappeared, then I promise I'll leave you alone.'

'People are always promising to leave me alone,' he told her, 'but they never do.' Then he leaned into a space behind the door and pulled out a coat which he struggled into. 'I'm off to the pub,' he announced. 'If you want to ask your questions there, you can, on the strict understanding that you're paying for everything.'

'All right.'

'Good, but be warned, I have quite a thirst.'

Chapter Thirty-Two

The pub was no more than two hundred yards from Oliver's home, and when they reached it he sat down heavily on a bench seat outside at one of the quieter tables, which was set slightly apart from the others. No one else sat outside. The weather wasn't warm and it was threatening to rain, but perhaps he didn't want to answer her questions in public.

'You're going to the bar,' he ordered. 'I'm having a pint of bitter and a large Bushmills. You're having whatever you're having,' and he waved a hand imperiously. 'Now run along, my girl, and don't dawdle.' Sarah supposed he thought he was being amusing, but she considered his rudeness a small price to pay for his cooperation.

The landlord eyed her suspiciously because he must have looked out and seen who she'd arrived with. 'Tell him from me, if he gets loud or nasty he is barred, and this time it will be for good.'

She came back with Oliver's beer and Irish whiskey, as well as a Coke for herself, because she was driving, though she would have preferred something stronger to tolerate Oliver's company. She didn't tell him what the landlord had said, in case he marched inside and started an argument, then they would both be thrown out.

He took a very large gulp of his beer. 'It was an absolute stitch-up,' he recalled. 'I'd been clean in that clinic, went through the whole godawful process, with all the withdrawal symptoms. I stayed clean for another few days in the UK and tried desperately not to think about drugs. I had put myself in a position where I couldn't score even if I wanted to, because I was miles from the nearest dealer, then I went up to bed one night and it was there, waiting for me.'

'Are you saying that someone put heroin on your pillow?'

'In my bathroom, actually, but yes, someone had placed it there, along with all the paraphernalia I needed: a baggy, a needle and syringe, a lighter, even a bloody silver spoon. That's a laugh, isn't it? Born with a silver spoon in his mouth – they say that, don't they?'

'They do,' she agreed.

'Seeing it there made it far harder to resist, though I did try. It's one thing to get in your car, drive to the city and cruise round taking a massive risk until you find that one dealer you might actually know well enough to score from. You can tell yourself it isn't worth it, but when it's on a plate for you like that, it feels like a banquet for a starving man. I couldn't help myself.' He took another gulp of his beer. 'If the maid hadn't found me, I'd have been a goner.'

'Who do you think gave you the drugs?'

'Who do you think?'

'It's obvious who stood to gain the most from your dis-inheritance,' she remarked. 'And that was Freddie.'

'He was most probably behind the idea,' Oliver agreed.

This did not seem like the same thing to Sarah. 'But you don't think he planted the drugs in your bathroom personally?'

'He made sure he was well away from Cragsmoor that day, so it was all very deniable.'

'Did you accuse him anyway?'

'I did, but funnily enough he denied it, and strangely no one sided with the man who had just overdosed on heroin. They all thought I had made it up. They said I must have had the H on me.'

'So, if Freddie was behind the idea to plant drugs in your bathroom, who actually placed them there?'

'No idea,' he said quickly. 'Could have been anyone.'

'Hardly. I think you could have narrowed it down to only a few people with access to your room.'

'People used to come and go a lot more back then,' he said evasively.

'But surely it was only a few servants or family members that could have done it?' she suggested. 'A servant would have been risking a lot, for what? A few pounds from Freddie, perhaps?' He didn't argue that point. 'But a family member could have gained a lot from the removal of a man whose judgement had been weakened by drugs, especially as no one knew at that point what a disaster Freddie was going to be as the heir to the estate.'

'Yes, he did rather fuck everything up, didn't he?' He seemed quietly amused by that.

'Was Sephy there when you overdosed?'

'No.'

'Which leaves Lucy.'

'I can't remember if Lucy was around.'

'But we've already established that Lucy picked you up from the airport and my aunt said she stayed with you when you first came out of rehab.'

'Maybe,' he said, as if he really couldn't recall.

'An overdose when you were already in the last chance saloon would have been just what was needed to push your father over the edge and get you disinherited, but it almost went very wrong, didn't it? You nearly died.'

'Technically, I was dead,' he said, 'for a while.'

'Then you must have been incredibly angry afterwards,' she probed, 'towards the person who gave you the drugs. So, who was it, do you reckon? A servant or Lucy?'

'No bloody idea.'

'Oh, come on, Oliver, you must have.'

'Even if I had my suspicions, I didn't have any proof.'

'You don't need proof to harbour a grudge, and that overdose put you in the wilderness for years. When your father died, Freddie inherited everything instead of you. When your legal bid to overturn the will dragged on, you started to run out of money, which is why you were at the house that day when Lucy disappeared. You were trying to come to some sort of compromise with Freddie and your other siblings. Am I right?'

'I was trying to be reasonable.'

'And you were waiting in your old room, having a drink on your own, when you looked down and saw Lucy? The woman you must have suspected of being Freddie's accomplice. The one who might very well have planted the drugs that almost killed you.'

'I never said that.'

'You had to have considered it, though. It would have been quite the betrayal. She had the opportunity and the motive to get you disinherited. Maybe Freddie put her up to it then made himself scarce.'

'You think that's what happened?' he asked her.

'No,' she admitted, 'but it doesn't really matter what I think, only what you thought at the time. You were at a very low ebb then, Oliver, weren't you? You were back in your family home at Cragsmoor, a place that should have been yours by rights, you must have been feeling very resentful and then you spotted Lucy looking like she hadn't got a care in the world. Is that what happened?'

'That doesn't mean I did anything about it, except pour myself another drink. Sometimes shit just happens and you have to deal with it.'

'Did you deal with it by killing Lucy?'

He shook his head. 'No. Lucy and I didn't get along, that's no secret, but I didn't kill her. I wouldn't kill my father's daughter over a scrap of land and some money. In any case, by that stage, I wasn't in the best shape physically. Climbing the bloody stairs was tricky. Do you think I could have run after a young woman and overpowered her? No chance.'

'Who did it, then?'

'I don't know. No one does. Nobody even knows if she was killed.'

'The direction she was heading in when you saw her would have taken her towards the path to the beach.'

'That's right. She went there often. She liked to swim.'

'Was she swimming that day?'

'I seem to recall she mentioned earlier that she planned to go for a swim that afternoon, yes.'

'You gave the police a description of what she was wearing – blue denim jeans, white top, green jacket?'

'That's right.'

'And she didn't have anything with her? No bag or anything?'

'No bag or anything,' he repeated facetiously.

'And her costume?'

'What?' He had almost finished the beer by now and was holding the nearly empty glass in his hand and frowning at it in a not-too-subtle way.

'I'll get you another pint in a minute,' she told him, 'but I was wondering about her costume.' When he looked confused, she said, 'You said she definitely didn't have a bag with her.'

'Oh,' was all he said in response.

'I suppose she could have worn it under her clothes,' offered Sarah. 'That's probably what I would have done. She probably wouldn't have wanted to get changed on the beach.'

'Yes, yes, I'm pretty sure that's what she would have done. More modest.' She could tell he was grateful for the answer she had provided. There was definitely something off about this.

'But still, no towel.'

'Huh?'

'Surely, if she was going off for a swim, regardless of whether she was wearing her costume or not, she would have taken a towel.'

'Maybe she did?' he offered weakly.

'Well no, because you already said she wasn't carrying one. *No bag or anything*, remember?'

He stared at her as if he had belatedly realized she was capable of trapping him. 'I *did* say that, didn't I?' he said with an exaggerated tone of incredulity. 'Perhaps I didn't see a towel and she had one all along? Who can say? I mean, I noticed Lucy walking away but I didn't give it much thought because it didn't seem all that important at the time. How was I to know I would never see her again?'

'You were the only witness who was on their own, weren't you?' she asked him, while wondering to herself if he could be lying about seeing Lucy heading towards the path at the rear of the house or even seeing her at all. His story about the sighting would have corroborated the other witnesses' accounts if he had not been so vague on timing, but was this because he had been drinking or was it deliberate on his part? If he had really seen Lucy from an upstairs window, then he was less likely to have been the killer, but what if he wasn't really sitting alone in his room for all that time? Could Oliver have slipped out and followed her somehow or intercepted her before she took the path to the beach? 'Sephy and Freddie were in the kitchen with Toby and his nanny, right?'

'Apparently so, but of course I wasn't there. You'll have to ask them about that.'

'I have,' she explained, 'though not Toby, obviously. He's too high profile these days and your former nanny is dead, of course.'

'Dead!' He reacted sharply to that. 'When did that happen?'

'I'm sorry,' she said, confused now, 'I was told she died years ago.'

'What? No! She sent me a birthday card two months ago. She never forgets. Margaret's not dead, unless it happened recently.'

'Then I apologize. I was misinformed about that.' It had been the retired detective who had told her he thought Margaret had been dead for a while, but it seemed this information was false. 'She must be very old.'

'In her eighties,' Oliver said. 'She's not that much older

than me. I think Father went for her because she was young and pretty back then. Wouldn't surprise me.'

'Does she live nearby?'

'No,' he said firmly, 'and I want you to leave her alone.'

Sarah smiled. 'Of course. Same again?'

He seemed to hesitate for a moment. Perhaps he was weighing up whether it was safe to drink more in her presence, but his greed for beer and whiskey outweighed his caution. 'Why the fuck not?' he announced jovially, as if this was a rare day off.

When Sarah returned with more drinks, he immediately reached for his new pint and took an enormous gulp as if it was much needed. The whiskey that accompanied it went down quickly too.

'You dropped your legal case against the will just weeks after Lucy disappeared?'

'I was left with no choice,' he argued.

'What happened?'

'My lawyer informed me that mounting a very public legal case involving money was not a good look for a heroin user whose sister had just vanished. He suspected no one would be particularly sympathetic towards an addict whose family had kicked him out then experienced a very public tragedy. He urged me to drop the case and make a statement in support of my brother as the de facto head of the family. He also said he could not continue to represent me.'

'No wonder you gave in.'

'I was also being blackmailed by the family.'

'What could they blackmail you with, Oliver? You were

232

already disgraced and very publicly disinherited. What's worse than that? Except perhaps murder?'

'Murder?' He sounded outraged. 'I told you I didn't kill Lucy. It wasn't anything that I had done. It was about the money.'

'What money?'

'When I was kicked out of the family home I had nowhere to go, so Father arranged for me to live in the cottage. At least I had a roof over my head and some income from the trust fund, which continued to pay out, but when the lawsuit dragged on, Freddie threatened to kick me out of the cottage and stop the trust fund. He said my drug addiction could be cited to stop all funds from any source linked to the family, on the grounds that I would spend it on something that could kill me. Ironically, I had been clean for over a year by then and he knew it. I came to the house that day for a meeting with Freddie to see if we could work out some sort of compromise, but the bastard knew he had a winning hand. That's why he kept me waiting, so I stayed upstairs in my old room and had a few drinks. Freddie saw me eventually but he didn't budge. In the end, I had to back down or I would have been penniless as well as homeless. It was game, set and match. I almost admired his ruthlessness. The little bastard.'

Sarah left the eldest Woodfell sibling sitting outside the pub with a fresh pint. It had turned cold by now and was threatening rain, but Oliver would have probably continued to sit there in all weathers, as long as he still had a beer. Sarah didn't know what to make of him. Parts of his story sounded convincing and she believed his explanation about the overdose and the blackmail, but if he did suspect Lucy of leaving drugs in his room for him then surely that would be a motive to kill her. He'd been at rock bottom when he'd gone to Cragsmoor to plead with his brother and Freddie had left him waiting in his old room, where he'd done what he usually did these days – he drank – and then he'd seen Lucy. If he considered her to be the cause of all his problems, then maybe he did kill her. He told Sarah he was too unfit to attack a young woman, but how could she know if that was the truth back then?

It seemed to Sarah that almost every time she tried to rule out a suspect, they ruled themselves back in again by being evasive or through outright lying. Eliminating them from her enquiries wasn't working. The trouble with the Woodfell siblings and everyone else linked to Lucy's death was that they all seemed to have something to hide.

Oliver couldn't necessarily be trusted to tell her the full truth about anything. How could he even remember what he had seen if, on his own admission, he'd had a few drinks? Had he really not noticed Lucy wasn't carrying a bag or towel or find it strange at the time? To be fair, he wasn't alone in that. The police never seemed to question it either. If Lucy had walked down to the beach without a towel or a swimming costume, it would give more credence to the theory that she might have been meeting someone instead. Sarah recalled the other path that led away from the beach and carried on all the way to the village. Lucy could have gone that way to avoid suspicion and met somebody there, but who? The captain, perhaps, if he had left London earlier than he claimed, or someone else entirely – and why would she need to keep it a secret from the rest of the family?

Chapter Thirty-Three

That same day Sarah got another call from her aunt's solicitor. Dickie seemed a little uneasy but he went on to tell her about two enquiries he'd received regarding buying Cragsmoor, which he was legally required to inform her about, even though she was unlikely to ever be in a position to sell the place herself. There was also a request from Literary Heritage, a charity that wanted Evelyn's personal papers for an exhibition they hoped to open, to showcase notable British authors.

'There's something else, isn't there?' she asked when he didn't conclude their call. 'And you've saved the worst till last?'

'I'm afraid so,' and he suggested that she go online to read a news item that had been posted on a tabloid web page that morning, then ring him back if she felt the need. It sounded ominous.

MURDER THEY WROTE!

Author's 'Mad Aunty' leaves entire estate to her but only if she can solve a murder.

Sarah felt sick. Now everyone would know what she was really doing here, including Mrs Jenkins and Patrick, and that she had lied about that to them both.

The article went on to explain the terms of the famous but eccentric Evelyn Moore's will. It also claimed that Lucy Woodfell, a woman who had disappeared but was believed to have been murdered, was probably Evelyn's lesbian lover, during an age when coming out was not an option. Grief and torment over her missing soulmate had led Evelyn to write her monster-hit novel *The Gallows Tree*, which had sold millions of copies in thirty countries.

Her obsession with Lucy had led to her ploughing some of her fortune into buying the ancestral home from the victim's bankrupt family. Here she had 'created a shrine' to her lover and spent decades pining for her, changing nothing. The reporter went on to describe Sarah's aunt as fearsome and reclusive, with a fortune she was now prepared to leave to her niece, as long as Sarah delivered justice to her auntie from beyond the grave.

The newspaper claimed that Sarah thought her aunt was crazy but was willing to comply with the terms of her will in order to receive her fortune. He then described Sarah as 'a failed novelist'.

'Tell me you didn't leak this, Dickie?' she asked, as soon as the solicitor answered her irate phone call.

'Of course not.'

'Then who did?'

'I don't know. You didn't tell anyone that your inheritance was conditional on solving a murder?'

'Of course not.'

'Then, regrettably, I have to entertain the notion that it could have been someone from our firm,' he said with resignation, and she had to admit it was the most likely option, given the detail in the article about her aunt's legacy and its terms.

'Can nothing be done about it?' she asked. It hadn't quite sunk in yet: she had been named in a derogatory newspaper article that would likely be read by thousands of people online. I'm all-in on this investigation, she thought, and can't just abandon it, otherwise I would very happily walk away from it right now.

'I already put a call in to their editor,' Dickie explained. 'He was neither helpful nor sympathetic and in no way keen to alter a word. The article has been viewed thousands of times already, so the cat is well and truly out of the bag, I'm afraid.'

'Is there a case for libel?'

'A libel action is ruinously expensive and you haven't inherited that kind of money, yet. You can't libel the dead, by the way. It's open season on them once they're gone, so I assume you mean that they have libelled you in some way.'

'They said I described my aunt as crazy. I would never do that.'

'Yes, I suggested as much, but he pointed me in the direction of a YouTube clip where you were doing a talk at a murder mystery event.'

'But that wasn't filmed,' she retorted.

'Someone did film it,' he clarified, 'on their phone, clearly without your knowledge. I'm afraid you described Evelyn as "my lovely, mad aunt".'

'But I meant that affectionately. I didn't mean she was crazy.'

'I'm sure you didn't, but in a court of law that would be a risky one to challenge.'

'What about describing me as a failed novelist? I'm not a failure.'

'I suppose they could argue you could be viewed as one, in comparison to your very successful aunt, sales-wise, I mean. I'm sorry, but that's what they would say.'

'What should I do, then?'

'Let it go,' he told her. 'This nonsense will be forgotten very quickly.'

'No,' she told him sadly, 'it won't. Every time someone puts my name into an internet search, that article will be right at the top, forever.'

After her call with Dickie, Sarah went straight out and got into the car. She took the Triumph for a long drive to clear her head, with no destination in mind, and occasionally crossed the boundary of speed she would normally have been comfortable with.

She couldn't help herself. She was angry. In fact, she was boiling mad. Failed novelist? Mad aunty? I'll show them who is really mad.

There was no one else at home when she returned to Cragsmoor, and later Sarah was assured that neither Pat-rick nor Mrs Jenkins was responsible for leaving an old, quite faded newspaper article lying face up on the kitchen table waiting for her there when she walked in to make a cup of tea. Marcus had been in and out of the house a few times by now, wading through the family papers in the library, but he would also deny all responsibility for it, causing her to lash out, not necessarily at him but the world in general.

'Then who *is* responsible for it?' It was a cry of

frustration, caused by the knowledge that, aside from herself, only Patrick and Mrs Jenkins were supposed to have keys for the house and Marcus was always let in by one of them when he showed up to pore over the archive.

The article from the local paper seemed innocuous enough at first. It dated from the early eighties, a little under two years before Lucy Woodfell had disappeared. She was in the centre of the photograph that accompanied the piece. It was a report from the annual summer fete and Lucy, being a local dignitary by birth, had been invited to declare it open. She was in the process of doing this by cutting a ribbon across the entrance to the field, while several onlookers waited to be admitted to the stalls behind her. Lucy was smiling, happy, her hair flowing in a breeze. The onlookers all appeared to be watching the tape she was about to cut or peering beyond her to see what treats awaited them. Several of them were children, but there were two middle-aged women in the picture and one man who had handed her the scissors, probably a local politician, judging by the way he was already applauding and looking straight at the camera, to make sure his face would be in the local paper. But it was the final figure who caught Sarah's eye. A young man of perhaps sixteen with a face that was nevertheless unmistakeable. It was Warren Evans, the man who had claimed not to have known Lucy Woodfell at all or even to have seen her around the village. Yet here he was now, gazing at Lucy, with a look of absolute longing.

Whoever had left this article wanted to put Warren Evans at the centre of Sarah's thoughts. But were they doing this for noble reasons, or hoping to deflect her from looking more closely at someone else? The fact that they had got into her house somehow to leave it face up on the kitchen table made her thoughts lean towards the latter theory.

Either way, though, the photo implicated Warren, so she decided to go straight round to his house and ask how he could reconcile this picture with his earlier account. She wouldn't go inside this time, in case he turned nasty when caught in a lie. For her own safety, she would stay on his doorstep in full view of the street.

There was no answer when she rang the doorbell. Sarah glanced over at the window and realized the curtains had been removed. She moved closer and peered in. The living room was empty, all its furniture gone, and so too, presumably, was Warren Evans. He had talked about wanting to be left alone so he could move on. Guilty or not, it looked as if that was exactly what he had done, or perhaps he was worried she was closing in on him somehow and he had done a runner before she found any more damning evidence about him, like the photo in the newspaper. Sarah was left doubly frustrated. She had lost the opportunity to confront him with it and now she had no idea where he was.

This is my fault, she told herself. I warned him I was looking into the case and now he has disappeared. If he really is the killer, I just let him slip right through my fingers.

Chapter Thirty-Four

She was trying to write in one of the reception rooms, because this was one of Marcus's days at the manor. He had been coming and going infrequently, between lectures and filming dates, but when he was at Cragsmoor, he spent hours busying himself in the library and it was hard to concentrate if he was moving around in there, rustling papers and occasionally muttering to himself while he tried to focus on something, shattering her own concentration in the process. She had barely written anything of worth that day when there was a fake cough from the door, which was designed to get her attention. Marcus was standing in the doorway. 'I think you should come and look at this,' he told her. 'I finally found those plans you were looking for.'

She followed him into the library. Marcus had taken over one end of it and had been removing papers and placing them on a table where there was good light from a nearby window.

Sarah examined the ancient document he had uncovered. It had yellowed with age, was crisp to the touch and there were wrinkles in the paper, but you could still make out the plan of the house. She studied it for a while then felt the familiar tinge of disappointment.

'The plans mirror the house exactly,' she said. 'No hidden nooks or built-over add-ons, apart from the chimney that we already know about.'

'It was always a long shot,' he told her.

Then something else on the plans attracted Sarah's attention. 'What's this line that goes right through the building?' It was actually two very faint dotted lines, and she would have missed them altogether had she not been peering at the plan so intently. Sarah traced them with her finger to the end of the building and on across the now blank part of the plan, right to the edge of the page. 'Is this a tunnel?'

'Let me see.' He leaned forward, put his reading glasses back on and looked more closely. 'It could be.' Then he looked at Sarah approvingly. 'I think so, yes. I found a document that said the family was named in a court case over a smuggling operation back in the eighteenth century, which caused a bit of a scandal. This could be how they were doing it.'

'What were they smuggling?'

'Wine, spirits, even tea. Anything with a prohibitive import duty could be lucratively smuggled into the country then. The manor house backs right on to the coastline, so if a ship could get near enough, a cargo could be offloaded in rowing boats, almost to the back door. If there was a tunnel connecting the manor house to the coast,' he followed the line with his finger, 'it would have been a lucrative sideline for a family already down on its luck.'

'Then how do we find this tunnel?' she asked.

'All we have is two faint lines, with no precise location of an entrance or exit,' Marcus said thoughtfully.

'But the entrance to the tunnel must still be here in the house somewhere? It will be just like looking for a priest hole,' she observed. 'Which is your speciality.' Then she smiled encouragingly at him. Judging by the look on his face, Marcus liked that idea.

'I'll give it my best shot,' he assured her.

Sarah couldn't help wondering if he really would be the first person to find the tunnel in over two hundred years, or if someone else might have already beaten him to it back in the 1980s. If they used the tunnel, someone could have left the house without being seen. It would have been the ideal way to remove a body. Even Lucy, if she had known about its existence, could have used it to disappear.

'We have to find it,' she told Marcus.

Chapter Thirty-Five

Sarah tried to do some writing, but for the rest of the day her phone rang steadily with enquiries from the press, which she greeted with a firm, 'no comment'.

Dickie called again to check she was all right. She had been hoping to speak to him. 'Has your new intern resigned or gone on a go-slow, Dickie? Perhaps in protest at not getting a living wage? I haven't received a file from her in a while.'

'Oh, yes, that . . .' he began, and as usual he seemed reluctant to get to the point when there was bad news coming. 'There's been a bit of a hitch, actually.'

'What kind of hitch?'

'It seems that some of the files on the laptop have been corrupted. So she can't open them.'

Sarah was immediately suspicious. 'How did that happen?'

'Well, I'm no *techie*,' he admitted unnecessarily, 'but our IT man thinks that it might be because our previous intern may have used the laptop at home to view things he shouldn't have.'

'You mean porn? Christ,' she said.

'We've sent the laptop off to an expert to get it debugged and whatnot.'

'I hope your expert knows what he's doing,' said Sarah. 'Those files could contain vital information.'

'Indeed they could, and since that laptop also contains

a decade's worth of other information that we desperately want to retrieve, we are treating this issue with the utmost seriousness, I can assure you of that.'

She sighed. 'Keep me informed, will you?'

'Of course.'

'And Dickie, next time you hire an intern, try paying them.'

'That would be a radical departure from the norm, especially for a firm the size of ours.'

'Perhaps, but in this, as in everything, you get what you pay for, and you didn't pay anything. Now you have a laptop with a sexually transmitted disease and your precious client files have probably all been hacked.'

Seemingly chastened, he said, 'I do take your point.'

When Patrick walked into the room later, his face showed his concern. 'Are you okay?'

Sarah had just loudly told a journalist, who had called her back for the third time, to 'fuck the fuck off!' and he must have heard her from the corridor.

When she did not immediately reply, he asked, 'Anything I can do?'

'You can pour me a glass of wine?' She gave him a weary look. Though this was probably not what he'd had in mind, he headed for the kitchen. 'Pour yourself one too.' Sarah didn't want to drink alone and needed company.

Almost as soon as they sat down with the wine, Patrick said, 'I read the article.'

'Oh.'

'People were talking about it in the village. I told them it was probably a made-up story.'

She could have opted to say nothing but thought it might be better to reveal the truth. He deserved that. 'It isn't a made-up story.'

By the time she had finished telling him about it, their glasses were empty, so he refilled her glass then his. 'I won't be here forever,' she admitted, 'just a few more months, unless I get a very lucky break – with the case, I mean.' Patrick made no comment. 'You're going to say that I should have told you from the beginning?'

He looked confused. 'Why would you tell me?'

'I don't know,' she admitted, 'but doesn't everyone want openness about everything these days?'

He thought for a second. 'I don't.'

'You prefer secrets?' she asked. 'You've hardly told me anything about yourself, Patrick.'

His tone suggested this was not a deliberate tactic. 'What do you want to know?'

'I don't know,' she shrugged. 'Why did you leave the army?' It seemed a good place to start.

He took a long time to answer her. 'I was . . . invalided out,' he said quietly. 'A mental health thing.'

'That's nothing to be ashamed of,' she said gently.

He nodded. 'I lost . . . people that I knew . . . friends . . . in Afghanistan.' The pauses between his words were quite long and this was clearly a struggle for him.

'I'm sorry,' she managed.

'We were blown up . . .' and then he laughed, even though it was far from funny, '. . . twice.' He mock frowned at her, 'I was lucky, I suppose. My injuries were quite minor, whereas the others . . .'

'I really am sorry for asking. I shouldn't have.'

'It's fine to ask,' he waved away her concerns. 'I just struggle to give answers.'

'I'm not sure there is an easy way to describe the trauma of losing friends in a war.'

'Anyway, I had a bit of a . . . I don't know if breakdown is the right word, but I felt that I couldn't carry on after that. I mean, if I'd been blown up three times it would have been some sort of record. I was sent back to the UK for a bit and then they let me leave.'

'Is that when you came here?'

'No, I wandered around for a year or two.' Sarah started to understand how Patrick might have ended up here. He had clearly struggled to find a home and a sense of purpose on leaving the military. 'I travelled a little, worked a bit, just bars and other places. I came back when my mother died, fully intending to be on the move again, but Evelyn popped by one day,' he smiled.

'Did you know her?'

'I knew *of* her but I didn't know her. She'd known my mam for years, though. "Your mother said you're handy," she said. "Are you? Can you fix things?"' He had done a first-rate impression of the way Evelyn spoke to people, interrogating and a little imperious, as well as challenging. 'And I said that yes, I could fix most things. She then asked if I would like to fix some things for her and I asked, "Are you offering me a job?" and she said, "Possibly."'

They both smiled at Evelyn's bluntness.

'That was eight years ago.'

'You must like it here.'

'I like that I can live here and work just down the road. I enjoy being able to fix old things. Working outdoors in the garden seems to suit me. I don't think I'd do well in an office. There's always plenty to do here. I was supposed to paint the inside of the house months ago but only started this week, which reminds me, do you want to see what distracted me today?'

'Okay.'

They left their wine and she followed Patrick up the stairs. He took her to her own bedroom, which felt a little strange. When they got there, she realized he had painted the windowsill there and it looked much brighter. The window was open for the paint to dry and her bed was still set back from it.

'You were on the phone when I found this, so I didn't want to interrupt you.' Then he said, 'Those sounds you were hearing, the whispering, the lady's lament.' He indicated for her to look behind the headboard of her bed where there was now a gap between it and the wall, because he had pulled it out to gain full access to the window frame.

Almost at the foot of the wall, there was a small vent made of metal. It looked old but certainly not from Elizabethan times when the house was first built. 'These were put in to deal with the damp, I think,' he informed her. 'They let air in from the outside but magnify other sounds throughout the house. It could explain the whispering you heard.'

'So that's my ghost?'

'I think so.'

It seemed like an unglamorous explanation for what Sarah had been hearing but she was happy to finally have one. Of course, even though this explained why noises in the house, like voices or footsteps on creaking floorboards, were magnified, those sounds were still very real.

They went back downstairs and finished the bottle of wine, while they talked about the other, as yet unsolved mysteries concerning the house and family.

Because Patrick hadn't overreacted about the newspaper article, she felt easier trusting him with more of the story, so she told him about the anonymous call she had taken and how she had been threatened.

'Would you recognize the voice again?' he asked.

'It was heavily distorted.'

'What did it sound like?'

'Like a terrifying robot man.' Sarah shrugged helplessly because that was the best she could do and she felt sure he would be unimpressed. 'I'm living in a horror film, aren't I? I'm staying in a creepy old house, taking calls from a maniac.'

'Then you'll be fine,' he was playing along with the joke. 'Just don't go down to the cellar on your own.'

'Are you kidding? That's where the wine is.'

'Good point. Maybe I should bring a few bottles up to the kitchen.' He turned serious again. 'I don't suppose you had any luck tracing the number?'

'I spoke to the phone company but the best they could do was offer to block the number in future.'

'If he went to the trouble of using a voice synthesizer, I'd be astonished if he didn't use a burner. They'd be able to trace where that phone was purchased from but not who bought it.'

'The phone company said that, too.' She tried to make light of it. 'It was just a phone call.'

'Warning you off,' he reminded her.

'The man who threatened me has a touching faith in my ability to get to the bottom of this,' she told him. 'One that I don't currently share.'

'What will you do?'

'Carry on,' she said. 'I don't really have a choice.'

She decided to fully confide in Patrick then. She wasn't sure why, but she felt the need to unburden herself to someone and there was something about Patrick's easy demeanour that made him seem like the least judgemental person she could tell it all to. She explained the difficulty she was having with her latest book, how her new editor wanted her to simply cash in on her aunt's legacy and why she was so viscerally opposed to this idea. She even told him about the failed relationships, money worries and her general disappointment with herself, while he quietly listened. 'For some time now, I've had the feeling that my life has been slowly unravelling. Does that make sense?'

'I felt like that when I came home, after my mother died.' She wondered if he would unburden himself further but all he added was, 'That's why I was glad of the job from Evelyn. It gave me some certainty.'

'That's it,' she said, 'that's exactly what I need. Some certainty in my life. I feel like I'm being buffeted from all sides and I'm completely overwhelmed by it all. I thought I would be more anchored to something by now. Do you know what I mean?'

'I think so,' he said. 'So what would make you feel more anchored?'

'Where to start?' she asked rhetorically. 'I need to finish the worst book ever written then solve an unsolvable mystery that has baffled everyone for three decades before deciding what I'm going to do next.'

'Write more books, surely?'

'I don't know. I've not admitted this to anyone before, even to myself, but lately I've started to question whether I have much of a future as an author. Perhaps I should just go and do something else.'

'Like what?'

'I have absolutely no idea. The trouble with having that one thing that you've always wanted to do is that when it doesn't work out you're not left with any other options. It's like putting all your money on a really long shot, against all logic and reason.'

He was silent for so long then, she wondered if he was simply not going to offer an opinion on that, but in the end, he said, 'I think that you're probably a writer first, last and everything. I don't see how you can stop being one and I don't believe you should give up now.' Then he shrugged. 'For what it's worth.'

Even in that moment, Sarah had to admit it did mean something for someone to have faith in her. 'Thanks, Patrick.'

When the wine was gone, Patrick announced that he should be going. Sarah was tempted to offer to open another bottle but she didn't want to make him uncomfortable. Technically, she was his employer, even if that wouldn't be for long, and she didn't want him to feel obligated to stay and drink with her out of duty.

Sarah felt a little better for having had some company and time away from her constantly ringing phone. She tried not to think about how this was all going to end. The truth was that she was scared, but she didn't know how to simply walk away from it all – and where would she go if she did? She had no home now and little money, so leaving would be as frightening as staying and trying to ride this out, while hoping the people who wanted to stop her wouldn't go too far.

Chapter Thirty-Six

October

There was one witness Sarah still had not spoken to because, until Oliver had confirmed otherwise, she had assumed the nanny was dead. She had expected the woman to be quite a lot older than her charges, but when Margaret Malloy had looked after the first generation of Woodfell siblings – Oliver, Freddie and Sephy – she had not been all that much older than they were, thanks to their father's lecherous gaze falling on a young and pretty face. Now that young woman was in her eighties, but Sarah had no way to track her down and if Oliver knew where she was, he was not letting on.

Judging by her lack of presence on the web, she had probably not talked to anyone about Lucy since the police had interviewed her the day after Lucy had disappeared, even though the nanny had been one of the last people to see the young woman alive. An internet search simply yielded articles about other people all over the world with the same name as the seemingly anonymous old lady. It was only when Sarah tried again, by adding the words 'Toby Ramsay', 'prime minister' and 'nanny', that she came up with a single article from a local paper in Berwick.

The newspaper marked the retirement of a woman who had looked after three sets of children for the Woodfell family, including well-known politician, Toby Ramsay, who was 'tipped to be prime minister one day', and this from an article written years earlier.

Helpfully, the newspaper listed the street Margaret had retired to, and keying that information along with her full name into an online search got Sarah the number of her bungalow. Surely a local paper that had run a story on Margaret would have done so again if she had passed away in the interim, but there was no other piece on her and she had sent Oliver a birthday card within the past two months. Margaret was more than likely still alive and, Sarah reasoned, unlikely to have moved from her retirement cottage at her age. If she was well enough to remember birthdays, perhaps she could recall the events of the day when Lucy disappeared.

Before Sarah could do anything about this new information, she heard Marcus calling from the hallway. 'I've been looking for it all day,' he said, putting his head around the door frame. 'I was hoping the tunnel might be behind a fake wall or a bit of plaster, but, well, come and see for yourself.'

He led her out across the hall and towards the cellar door. 'I was thinking that if you needed to smuggle something, wouldn't you want your tunnel to lead straight into the cellar? That would make sense, no?' He opened the door and ushered her down the stairs. Marcus had left the lights on and they walked past the rows of wine bottles until they reached the far wall.

'I think *this* is your tunnel,' he said, and he knocked against the stone wall to emphasize its solidity. 'If you examine the stone, it's different from the other walls down here and I strongly suspect it was put in much later, possibly as recently as a couple of hundred years ago. I think they did this, once people began to suspect the smuggling operation. Your missing person could never have used the tunnel if its entrance was here, and I'm pretty sure that it was.' Clearly Marcus had seen the online article about her investigation into Lucy's disappearance.

'If this really was the entrance to the tunnel,' said Sarah, her hopes dashed again, 'can we at least try and find its exit?'

It didn't take a lot to persuade Marcus to join her on a hunt for the end of the tunnel. He was at least as keen as she was to find it.

'You said a big ship would have anchored offshore and the cargo would have been smuggled in small rowing boats?'

'That's the way they did it.'

'Then a tunnel would have to have been very close to the shore.'

'It was probably blocked up years ago,' warned Marcus.

But they went down to the beach anyway then slowly walked from one side of it to the other, moving northwards. As they travelled along it, they scrutinized the area immediately beyond the sand for any sign of a tunnel's entrance and explored the dunes and the land behind them.

When they reached the end of the beach, the cliff jutted out to sea, cutting them off. There were piles of rocks here and Sarah started to walk on them. Marcus followed and they found something, almost immediately. A cave.

'Looks like it was made by nature,' he pointed at its roof 'but widened by man.' It appeared that tools had been used to make the cave larger. They clambered into the mouth of the cave and Sarah shone the torch from her phone to illuminate a sandy-floored passageway. They managed ten more paces before the path abruptly ended with a large rockfall. 'I think it was blasted,' said Marcus. If this was the tunnel they were looking for, it had been deliberately blocked.

'There's a small gap at the top.' Sarah pointed.

'I would strongly advise against climbing into it,' he said. 'We don't know how safe it is.'

'I'll just take a look.' And before he could protest further, she started to clamber up the pile of loose rocks in front of them. They shifted beneath her feet and Sarah wobbled alarmingly at one point but she managed to keep going until she finally reached the top. This time her torch wasn't much use. All it showed her through the gap between the rocks was an inky blackness that seemed to go on forever. This had to be the tunnel, but there was no way Sarah could risk climbing through that tiny gap, even if she wanted to. It would have been far too dangerous to continue along the passageway in case the whole thing caved in on top of her, but she couldn't help wondering how long it had been since anyone had tried.

'Do you think we are idiots?' Edward Crozier asked her coldly. She had made the mistake of calling the former detective to enquire if he knew about the cave and whether anyone had thought to search it for Lucy's body.

'Of course we knew about the cave. We found it when

we searched the beach. We had to send an expert in through that gap you're on about, because it wasn't safe. He could only go so far, though, until it was completely blocked again.'

'How far?'

'He squeezed through the first rockfall then went another twenty yards or so, but there were more rocks and it was impassable.'

'Oh well,' she said, 'I thought it was worth a try.'

'Yeah, well, next time you have a bright idea that you think we haven't already thought of, feel free to waste my time by sharing it with me.'

Chapter Thirty-Seven

Sarah was on her second cup of tea when the phone rang. It was Dickie and he sounded sheepish.

'I found out what happened to your aunt's manuscript,' he said. 'It was our intern, Sean. He stole it.'

'What?' Wasn't this the young man he had vouched for when Sarah had suggested he might be the culprit?

'He thought he could waltz off with it then wait a while before sending an electronic copy of the manuscript to a publisher from a far-flung corner of the world. He tried to get them to pay him thousands for it. Of course, the first thing they did was send it back to me, to ask if it was legit and really for sale. I assured them it was not.'

'Well, at least you've got it back. Is that why he gave you the supposedly corrupted version, so that he was the only one with the complete manuscript?'

'I think so, yes. I would have said he had been quite clever if he hadn't also been so incredibly stupid.'

'What are you going to do?'

'I have already involved the police.' He paused moment- arily and she could hear his fingers tapping the keyboard in front of him, 'And I am forwarding the manuscript to you . . . now.'

Sarah spent the rest of the afternoon poring over every remaining word of her aunt's memoir. She wasn't expecting a great reveal or huge clue but was still left feeling frustrated when nothing immediately jumped out at her. There was one extract towards the end of the book that she read and re-read, however, because it shed a less than flattering light on both Freddie and Sephy, following their elder brother's exile. By now the story had reached the eighties.

The pressures of taking over from his brother saw Freddie also resort to drugs. Thankfully he avoided heroin. His drug of choice was cocaine, which was not quite as deadly but did help to fuel his growing paranoia, and he would often overreact leading to arguments over trivial things.

He got really mad at Lucy once, because she brought an old box of family photos to show the rest of the family before dinner. 'Not now, Lucy!' Freddie snapped. He accused her of hijacking the evening and said she knew he hated every photograph of himself as a boy, which was odd because the one positive thing you could say about Freddie was that he was a handsome chap. He snatched the box from her and left the room, leaving her in shock. Long-term drug abuse rewires the brain. That was the only explanation for such irrational behaviour.

Bankruptcy hung over the estate for years and, no matter what Freddie did to try and avoid this, it became inevitable. At least the trust funds gave the surviving siblings a modest income and a cottage. The only other thing Freddie saved was that old Jag he was obsessed with. It should have been sold off to pay debts when he was declared bankrupt, but he was crafty. An old school chum was the trustee of a car museum and Freddie donated the

Jag to it. Technically, it belongs to the museum, but he can take it out for a spin whenever he wants. Sometimes that spin can last for days and there's nothing the administrators can do about this. It was quite possibly the only really clever thing Freddie ever did.

Sephy's presence seemed to calm him at times, though they also fought like cat and dog.

'You would think she might do it the other way around,' I said when Lucy explained to me that Sephy stayed in London during the week then came up to Cragsmoor every weekend, arriving on a Friday afternoon train and leaving on Monday morning. 'She'd see more of her husband that way.' The captain must have been busy with his job during the week but free at the weekend, while Sephy was staying in Northumbria.

'It's one of those marriages,' said Lucy obliquely, leaving me to draw my own conclusions. By now, Sephy had at least belatedly provided the captain with an heir, but as yet there was no spare.

'It wouldn't surprise me if she had taken a lover,' said Lucy.

I recalled Sephy flirting with the younger men at her wedding. 'Who do you think it might be?'

She gave this question some serious thought. 'They've just hired James Lawless.'

'James? Her ex?'

'He's something of a celebrity these days.' Lucy explained that James was a landscape gardener and that Freddie was spending thousands to transform the gardens at Cragsmoor. This should have rung alarm bells with Sephy's husband, but he might not know about it or even that James was her former boyfriend. 'The magazines love him,' she told me before quoting one of them. '"He is as handsome as he is expensive."' Then she laughed, 'They call him James Pond, for God's sake. It wouldn't surprise me if Sephy isn't entirely enamoured of him again by now. I should go up there and catch them at it.'

So, even Lucy thought that Sephy did not love her husband and had more than likely taken a lover. That would tally with the scrapyard owner's theory about the severed brake cable. Sarah reminded herself not to bend the facts to fit the theory that Sephy may have murdered her husband. She still had no proof that linked his car crash to Lucy's disappearance, though they were two suspicious incidents in a relatively short space of time.

It seemed that Freddie was almost as much of a loose cannon as his elder brother. Small wonder that the estate fell into a bankrupt condition before Evie bailed them out, which was the point at which her memoir concluded.

Sarah thought she'd reached the end but realized there were still some pages left. Extracts from several letters from Lucy Woodfell to Evelyn had been transcribed and added to the manuscript. Her aunt must have included them here for a reason.

Dear Evelyn

The captain has hidden depths! It turns out he is a reader and an avid one at that. I think he may have even read more books than us. Once he realized I had been through much of the family

library, he saw me as a kindred spirit and lent me his copy of
The Traveller's Tree *by Patrick Leigh Fermor. I gave him my
copy of Daphne du Maurier's* The King's General, *because he
was a soldier. At breakfast, he told me he read a hundred pages
last night before turning in.*

Dear Evelyn

*The captain is actually quite misunderstood. Everyone thinks of
him as a man of war but he is a pussycat really. He likes to go
for walks in the woods but Sephy hasn't the slightest interest,
preferring to stay indoors with her magazines and records, so I
have been joining him. He knows every tree and can name any
breed of bird. Quite often, we end up at the pub in the village and
he orders beer — a pint for him, but I'm only allowed a half
because I'm a lady. Strange that a man who has seen war should
be bothered about the size of the glass a woman drinks from. On
the way back, we take the coastal path and walk along the sand
for a while. He always stops there to gaze out at the sea. I like to
think he is having deep thoughts.*

*I enjoy his company and provide him with moments of light
relief from my sister's constant disapproval. She isn't remotely
jealous when I offer to join him, even though she used to get the
green eye all the time with her old boyfriends. There's nothing going
on between us, obviously. He only has eyes for Sephy and only
needs me to share long walks, warm beer and to talk about lovely
books. I think he'd be quite lonely without me, poor thing.*

Dear Evelyn

*I'm worried about poor Alex. The other day he told me that he
had lost so many good men and had no idea why he was spared.*

He said war isn't about heroes or cowards, just luck. If a bullet or a bomb hits you, that's it. You could be the best, the bravest and the fittest soldier that ever lived but there is nothing you can do about it if you happen to be standing in the wrong place at the wrong time. He told me he feels guilty for making it through.

I told him he shouldn't feel guilty about surviving the war and he said, 'Perhaps I shouldn't, Lucy, but I do. I don't feel especially blessed or that God has any particular plan for me. Most of the time I don't feel anything at all.' I was quite disturbed to hear this, but he said that of course he still loved Sephy and Toby. He also said he felt a great sense of kinship with me and that our friendship meant a lot to him. I said it meant a lot to me too and I admit I was quite tearful. We had to sit in silence for a time until the feelings passed.

Lucy's letters started to take a darker turn in the year she disappeared and her concern for the wellbeing of the captain also increased.

Alex seems so sad for much of the time. I think he fears he will lose Sephy or has already lost her somehow.

He confides in me and says we are two halves of the same coin, though I don't see how that can be. Last night we stayed up long after Sephy had gone to bed and he told me a little about his war years; not the gory stuff but stories about people he met during the liberation of France and then Holland. He is quite the raconteur. I told him I think he is one of those few people who really does have a book in him and that writing it might help to banish the demons.

'I do have demons,' he confessed, 'but I don't think I would be awfully comfortable writing about them.'

Hours later, I was woken in the middle of the night by a pitiful sound. I'm not sure if I could more accurately describe it as a scream or a wail. I instinctively knew it had to be Alex.

I left my own bed, put on my dressing gown and went out on to the landing. I could hear sobbing below and Sephy's voice. I could not make out many words and I am a little ashamed to admit that I did not go back into my own room. Instead, I walked down the stairs and stood outside their door. I did this primarily out of concern for Alex but also for my sister.

I could hear my sister's consoling words. 'It's all right,' she was telling him, 'you're not there. You're here, darling. You're here with me and the war has been over for a very long time.'

'You don't understand,' he told her sharply. 'They are in here. They are inside my head.'

'It was just a dream,' she explained, 'just a very bad dream. Now lie down and try and get some sleep. We are all very tired.'

'It wasn't a dream,' he answered, 'it happened. They were on fire!' he shouted. 'My men were in the truck and they were burning and I couldn't do anything about it.' Then his tone became harsh. 'Do you even know?' he demanded.

'Know what?' She sounded stung by his tone.

'Anything. Anything at all of any use. Do you know what a phosphorus shell can do to a man? It sticks to his clothes then his skin and burns right through to the bone. They all died screaming!'

It was as if he was a different man and he was berating someone other than Sephy. He had woken from a nightmare that had trapped him in a memory and now, in his anger and frustration, he was lashing out at her.

Sephy shouted then. 'Alex, stop! I can't . . .' She never completed the sentence. They both fell silent for a time and I waited to see if he would snap out of it and realize he had been berating *my sister, when none of this was her fault. It wasn't his fault either, of course.*

'I'm sorry,' he said in a clearer but much softer voice, then the door abruptly opened and my sister emerged in her dressing gown. The first thing she saw was me and it was obvious I had been listening. She was furious.

'Oh, for God's sake, Lucy,' she hissed, 'go back to bed.'

She marched off to spend the rest of the night in another room and I sloped off back to mine, feeling I had betrayed her.

There was one more letter from Lucy and it was dated just a few days before she disappeared.

Dear Evelyn

Sometimes I think my brain will finally explode. I don't know how much more I can take. The stress never ends and the pressure is unrelenting. Everything is falling apart. There is no hope that it will ever get any better.

I trust too easily. I realize that now, and it makes the reality of life all the harder to bear.

I know things, I've heard things I wish I hadn't, but I cannot unknow them. Soon everything will come out in the open because we cannot go on like this. If we do, everything will be destroyed. Five hundred years, Evie! All of it ruined in a generation, and for what?

I'm sorry. I know I'm not making any sense but I promise to write again soon. By then I'll know what to do. You'll see.

What had caused Lucy to descend into this dreadful state and who had she trusted too easily? The captain? One of her siblings? If only she had named them or explained herself more fully, instead of writing to Evie in apparent despair before she had managed to organize her thoughts and decide on a plan of action. *By then I'll know what to do.* Presumably that plan had led to her death, but there wasn't enough information here to link directly to her disappearance. It was all still too much of a puzzle and it explained why Evelyn never managed to get to the truth.

Chapter Thirty-Eight

It had almost become a habit to end the day with a glass of wine together. Sarah always offered it lightly and made a point of saying he was under no obligation to drink with her. Patrick would nearly always say he had no particular plans or reason to dash off, before joining her, and there would be one less bottle to bequeath to the Conservative Party.

While they drank, she would tell him about her day and whether she had uncovered any new information about Lucy Woodfell. As she described the letters Lucy had written to her aunt she told him, 'I keep thinking Captain Ramsay's death and Lucy's disappearance were linked in some way.'

'Why do you think that?' he asked.

'Lucy and Captain Ramsay were close, odd as that may sound,' and she told him about their shared love of books, the walks they had taken together and the fact that they confided in one another.

'Do you think they were more than just friends?'

'I don't know,' she admitted. 'It's possible something happened between them, but in Lucy's letters to my aunt she categorically denied that her sister had anything to be jealous about. She seemed to think Sephy was happy for someone else to spend time with him so she didn't have to.'

'He'd have been distraught when Lucy went missing, then?'

'Presumably.'

'Unless he killed her,' he said starkly, and Sarah could not deny the idea had entered her head. It was almost a relief for someone else to have voiced it out loud.

'He was a troubled man who'd done some brutal things during the war,' she said. 'He killed a lot of enemy soldiers.'

'Killing can scar a man.' He didn't say whether he knew this from personal experience. 'He could perhaps have lost control, or maybe he thought of her as a better bet than his wife but Lucy wasn't having that? Maybe he forced himself on her and had to kill her or she'd tell?'

'Or perhaps they did have an affair and he was terrified she would tell her sister? I've thought of those possibilities.'

'It might explain things,' he agreed.

'If he did kill Lucy and got away with it, being a very troubled man anyway, it could have pushed him over the edge,' she suggested.

'Remorse driving him to suicide?'

'He was moving pretty quickly that day,' she recalled, 'but then he had a reputation for driving recklessly.'

'Which would explain why the police were quick to dismiss it as an accident.'

'He crashed down by the Dule tree, right?' she asked.

'That's right.'

'That bend where he hit the wall is pretty tight?'

'It is,' he confirmed.

'The crash scene investigators estimated he must have been doing about sixty miles an hour, but was that suicidal or just reckless?'

'Hard to tell.' He thought for a moment. 'Why don't we go down there and take a look?'

Sarah asked Patrick to drive because she wanted his opinion on the tightness of the corner where the captain had come off the road. There was no way she would have tried to take that bend at sixty, but she reasoned it was possible that the captain, a reckless man known for driving too fast, might have viewed it differently before losing control and killing himself there accidentally. Patrick could back this idea up or instead he might consider it a suicidal act.

They drove down to the corner where the accident had occurred and pulled over. There was no wall there any more but the Dule tree still overlooked the spot from its position in the field beyond. Patrick seemed to be surveying the bend.

'What do you think?' she asked him.

'Let's see, shall we?' and he turned the car around then started to drive back up the road again.

'What are you doing?'

'Just conducting a little experiment.'

'What kind of experiment?'

'I'm going to go back down the road until we're just beyond the last bend before the one by the Dule tree,' he explained, 'then I'll drive towards it, so we can see how fast the captain could have reasonably gone before a reckless act becomes a deliberate one.'

This did not sound good. 'How are you going to do that without killing us?'

'Don't worry, I'll be careful.'

'That doesn't sound careful.'

'Trust me, I know what I'm doing.'

'I get a very bad feeling when men say *I know what I'm doing.*'

He laughed at that. 'I promise I won't go too fast.'

They set off down the road until they reached the bend, and Patrick turned the car around and drove back towards the crash site, accelerating steadily. Sarah was torn between implicitly believing in him and feeling nervous, as he started to reach a speed she would not have risked herself. She could only hope he did actually know what he was doing.

She instinctively gripped the door and the side of her seat to steady herself. Patrick was still not slowing down. In fact, he was making the car go faster.

'Hadn't you better . . . ?' she began, but then she winced as she realized the crash site was hurtling towards them at speed and, wall or no wall, they were running out of road '. . . shit!' she managed just as he hit the brakes and turned the steering wheel hard.

Instead of ending upside down in a ditch, which she fully expected, Sarah experienced what appeared to be a hair-raisingly fast but controlled manoeuvre, as the front end of the car turned smoothly to the right and its back end seemed to slide towards the crash site but, before they could career off the road, Patrick expertly powered it forward again. He drove for another few yards then brought it steadily to a halt.

'Christ,' she said, 'you could have warned me.'

'I thought I did warn you?' He regarded Sarah in her shaken state and admitted, 'Perhaps I didn't warn you sufficiently.'

'You took that corner like a racing driver.'

'Thank you.'

'It wasn't a compliment.' Then she laughed. 'Is there anything you aren't bloody good at, Patrick?'

He took that question seriously enough to give it some thought, 'I'm a terrible singer.'

He turned the car round then drove it slowly back to the corner and they climbed out. 'Captain Ramsay was doing sixty when he went off the road? You thought we were moving pretty quickly but I couldn't have navigated the bend at that speed. He could have reached that speed but only if he had no intention of stopping.'

'So, you're thinking suicide?' she asked. 'Not accident or murder? But that doesn't explain the cut brake cable.'

'No, it doesn't,' he admitted.

Sarah thought about this contradiction for a moment. 'Oh my God,' she blurted suddenly.

'What?'

'I just remembered something I read about the captain. On D-Day, he parachuted behind enemy lines. He had to jump with all his men behind him but was worried he wouldn't be able to go through with it, so he told his sergeant to give him a shove if he hesitated even for a moment. His biggest fear wasn't dying but losing his nerve.'

'Maybe that's your explanation,' he said.

'Captain Ramsay severed his own brakes in case he tried to pull out before he hit the wall,' she concluded. 'That way the choice was no longer his. As soon as he pointed his car in the right direction and floored it, he knew that, no matter what, he was a dead man.'

Chapter Thirty-Nine

Sarah rose early the next morning, refreshed from a night's sleep that had been better than usual. The lock Patrick had put on her door had helped, and now that he'd shown her the cause of some of the sounds she was hearing in the house, most notably the whispering, she managed to sleep through it because she could dismiss it as a harmless hiss from the vents in her bedroom wall.

Having made such an early start, she decided to write a letter to Margaret Malloy, with a request to visit the Woodfells' former nanny in Berwick. Sarah did not wish to alarm an old lady by turning up on her doorstep unannounced, and she reasoned that Margaret might refuse to see her if she did. She decided on a partial explanation of her presence at Cragsmoor Manor, coupled with a request to hear about life there from someone who had worked for the family for so long. She was halfway through her letter when there was a loud banging on the front door. Sarah started. Who could be knocking at this hour, and why so urgently? She went quickly to the door and opened it. She was shocked to see who was standing there.

David Young's face was staring back at her and he appeared agitated. She would have slammed the door in his face immediately, if she had not been so stunned by the presence of the convicted murderer on her doorstep.

'I brought you something,' he said, sounding breathless, as if he had walked all this way at some pace, 'it's important.'

Competing thoughts raced through Sarah's mind all at once.

What is he doing here?

Is he crazy?

Does he want to kill me?

He reached inside a carrier bag and pulled out a bulging file and thrust it towards her. 'Read it,' he urged her.

'What is it?' She was stalling until she could work out how to get rid of him.

'Reports,' he said. 'From newspapers, magazines and the internet.' Then he clarified, 'About Lucy Woodfell,' and if this wasn't alarming enough, he added, 'I've been collecting them for years.'

'Why have you got articles about Lucy?' she asked him. Was he obsessed with his victim?

The look on his face betrayed his anger and Sarah grew more alarmed. 'You see, this is why I didn't mention it when you came to see me. I knew you'd think the worst! It's so I know everything there is to know about her. So that I can clear my name.'

'But you were never charged with anything involving Lucy.' She tried to say this gently, in order to calm him. 'So you don't have to clear your name.'

'Didn't stop you coming to my door, did it?' his voice grew louder as his frustration increased. 'You, the police, the psychiatrists and all the reporters. Do you know how many times I've been asked about her? I never met her! I don't go after women. I don't!' he said firmly. 'With

Megan, it was different. I lost my temper because I couldn't handle rejection.' Then he quickly added, 'Back then.' If he thought Sarah would be calmed by that, he was mistaken. He was clearly trying to contain himself and looked like he might be about to burst. It was time to take back control of the situation.

'I have to go now,' she told him firmly.

He moved forward to hand Sarah the folder, bringing him even closer to her door, which made her automatically step backwards to keep the same distance between them. He shook his head in frustration. 'I make you feel uncomfortable, don't I?'

How the hell could she answer that without making the situation worse? By being honest and admitting he freaked her out, or by lying and inviting him in for a cup of tea, which was an incredibly dangerous idea.

'All uninvited guests make me feel uncomfortable.'

'I see,' he said in a tone that made it clear he did not. 'I have changed. I'm just sorry you can't see that.'

'I'm sure you have, but . . .'

'Then take it,' he pleaded and he thrust the file full of newspaper cuttings towards her. Reluctantly, she took them, hoping to pacify him, quickly tucking the file under one arm so she could place her free hand back on the door.

'Now can I come in?'

'No.' Her voice sounded weaker than she wanted it to.

'I just want to talk about her,' he said, but Sarah was far from sure that was all he wanted to do.

'I can't,' she told him, seizing the initiative and moving

to close the door. Just as she had feared, he put a firm hand out to prevent this.

'Please!' he begged. 'They'll lock me up again. Please!'

Sarah's alarm was rising as David became more agitated. She was trapped with the door open and no way to close it, now that he had moved to prevent her. She didn't know what to do.

Then she heard Mrs Jenkins' voice behind him. It was calm but very firm and she was addressing the man blocking the doorway.

'I've seen you on the telly,' she told him. 'You're that murderer.' He turned to stare at her and when she reached him, he was still holding on to the door and barring her way. Mrs Jenkins used the same unperturbed tone as if he was the local weatherman or some other minor celebrity she'd seen on the TV. 'Are you going to kill us both, dear?' she asked him brightly then her voice hardened. 'If not, then buzz off. I've got chores to do.'

To Sarah's astonishment, he let go of the door and stepped to one side to let Mrs Jenkins in. She walked past David without another word and calmly closed the door on him. Sarah quickly bolted it.

'Thank you,' said Sarah when they were both inside. She experienced a huge wave of relief now that they had put a solid door between themselves and the murderer. 'You recognized him but you weren't even scared?'

'Oh, I was,' said Mrs Jenkins. 'Very.'

'You didn't look it.'

'I thought that was probably for the best,' she explained. 'That was amazing, Mrs J.' Sarah was aware that Mrs

Jenkins could have turned around and walked away as soon as she saw David Young standing by the door, but instead she had chosen to walk up and challenge him, saving Sarah in the process.

As usual, the woman showed no emotion. 'Cup of tea?' she offered. 'I think we've earned one.' Then she added, 'Oh, and we'd better check the back door, hadn't we? In case he still hasn't got the message.'

Sarah ran to the back door, half expecting to find David standing in the kitchen. She checked that it was definitely locked and bolted then came back to the front of the house and peered through the window, but he was gone.

Sarah realized she had triggered David in some way. The stress on his face when he pleaded with her not to implicate him in Lucy's disappearance was obvious, as well as his anger, which seemed like a sign that he was about to lose control. Did that mean he was responsible for Lucy's fate or merely panicked at the thought of spending the rest of his life in prison for a crime he did not commit, believing that Sarah could cause that to happen? Either way, he must have been thinking about Sarah ever since she had questioned him about Lucy. He was sufficiently motivated to come here and present his case to her in person, or perhaps that had been a ruse to gain entry to the house and silence Sarah for good.

Chapter Forty

'I can only apologize,' said Doctor Phillips, once a very irate Sarah had explained how David Young had arrived without warning. 'I thought we had made a lot of progress with David, on boundaries and not exceeding them.'

'I would say that turning up on my doorstep uninvited and scaring the hell out of me was crossing a boundary, wouldn't you? I don't know what's going on inside David's head but I want to make sure this never happens again.'

'I will ensure that it does not. I'll leave David in no doubt that what he did today was entirely unacceptable.'

'So you are going to speak to him about this, personally?'

'Absolutely,' he said as if that would be the end of the matter.

'Is that all?'

'I'm sorry?'

'Is that all you're going to do? What if he gets annoyed at me for reporting him and comes straight down here? He was clearly irate.'

'Oh, I hardly think he will do that. I've known David for years and I can assure you . . .'

'Did you think he would come and pay me a visit this morning?' she interrupted.

'No, but I don't think we could have envisaged that he

would have . . .' He was searching for the right phrase now, so Sarah completed his sentence.

'. . . been the kind of person who stalks and harasses women?'

'I think perhaps you are being a little unkind there. David didn't stalk you. He simply turned up, admittedly uninvited, in order to assist you with your research.'

'Then, when I told him to leave, he refused and became incensed.'

'Because he was upset at being accused of a murder he did not commit. That's a natural enough reaction from a man who has spent a large portion of his adult life in prison.'

'Firstly, we only have his word that he did not commit that murder; secondly, he did commit a different murder on his own admission around the same time; and thirdly, having an irate killer turn up on my doorstep like that was an alarming event.'

'I do hear you,' he said soothingly, 'and I can assure you we will take this seriously.'

'Good, because I am making a record of this call and if he shows up here again, I will hold you responsible.'

He clearly didn't like the idea of taking any future blame for David's actions. 'There are certain protocols we can enact,' he offered, 'if it will make you feel more secure.'

'Go on.'

'David currently lives in unsupervised accommodation. I could treat this incident as a violation of the terms of his conditional release and bring him out of there. He would then be made to reside in a more secure environment.'

'Do you mean prison?'

'I mean living amongst others in supervised accommodation.'

'I would prefer that to his current arrangement, where he can just hop on a bus and visit me.'

'Regrettably, I can think of no better course of action than that, so, with your agreement, I will enact the protocol.'

'I agree,' she told him. 'Absolutely.'

By that afternoon, Sarah had a splitting headache, which she put down to the stress of having to deal with David Young on her doorstep. Because she could no longer focus on writing her book, she took some aspirin and went upstairs to lie down for a bit. She had just managed to drop off when she was woken by sounds coming from the room below hers. Patrick was sanding and repainting the window frames in the guest room, she remembered now. When the scraping sound from the sanding ceased, it was replaced by another. He must have started the painting now because his voice came up through the vent. Was he talking to himself, she wondered at first, but no, it was better than that; Patrick was singing.

As the words to 'Jolene' drifted up towards her, Sarah couldn't help but smile then laugh at Patrick's terrible rendition of the Dolly Parton classic. There's a man happy in his work, she thought, but his singing didn't last long. He was soon interrupted by a second voice. Mrs Jenkins must have appeared at the doorway and Sarah could hear her clearly as she cross-examined Patrick about how long he was going to be in there and whether he was doing other rooms that day, so she knew where to dust and hoover. Their exchange wasn't particularly loud nor was it heated, but it struck Sarah that thanks to the vent in the wall, she could make out every word.

Mrs Jenkins was cleaning downstairs when Sarah caught up with her.

'Was the room beneath mine always a guest room?' she asked the housekeeper.

'When your aunt owned it? Yes, it was. It's one of the nicer rooms,' she explained, 'with a view of the grounds.'

'Before that, though? Did the family use it as a guest room or did someone occupy it permanently?'

'No, it wasn't a guest room then. It was a family room. Now . . .' Mrs Jenkins stood in thought for a moment.

Please remember.

'It was . . .'

Come on, come on . . .

'. . . Persephone's room,' she remembered at last.

'You're certain about that?'

'Yes, of course.' The older woman sounded like she was about to take offence at having her memory questioned.

'And my aunt Evelyn had the room I'm in,' Sarah checked, 'and before that it was Lucy Woodfell's?'

'Yes,' confirmed Mrs Jenkins. 'Why?'

I know things, I've heard things I wish I hadn't, but I cannot unknow them.

'Just curious,' said Sarah and she left the woman to her cleaning.

Sarah remembered the words in Lucy's letter to Evie. If she had been lying in the same bed Sarah slept in now, she could have heard everything going on beneath her in Sephy's room.

The more she contemplated it, the more convinced Sarah became that this might be the source of Lucy's forbidden knowledge.

The big question remained, however. If Lucy had heard something from Sephy's room, what was it and why was it so important? Sex? An affair? An argument, a fight or a confession of some kind?

Did it perhaps have something to do with the parenthood of Britain's next prime minister? Would anyone even care now if his real father wasn't Captain Alex Ramsay but one of a number of possible lovers Sephy might have entertained in her room? Toby Ramsay was thirteen years old by the time Lucy disappeared. This seemed to be a long time after the fact, if he really was someone else's?

Even after she had made what felt like a significant breakthrough, Sarah still felt none the wiser.

She was dragged from her thoughts by the sound of her phone ringing. It was Doctor Phillips.

'I'm calling you back because I wanted to put you at ease about David,' he told her. 'I had a long session with him today and he came to the realization that what he did was entirely inappropriate.'

'He does accept that?'

'Indeed he does.'

'But you are still bringing him into supervised accommodation.'

'Yes,' he said a little more tersely.

'How did he take that?'

'Initially, he was upset but he has accepted it. He knows he has to take responsibility for his actions, if he wants to return to unsupervised living.'

'When will that be? Not days, I hope?'

'Well, I can't say exactly, but not days, no. Months at the earliest.'

'Thank you.' At least that was one less thing for Sarah to worry about.

'That's all right,' he said. 'I just wanted to put your mind at rest.'

'Well, I appreciate it.' Maybe he wasn't a complete arsehole after all.

Chapter Forty-One

November

Sarah didn't scream. She almost never screamed. Women always screamed in films. That's how you knew something awful had happened, but in real life not so much.

The fox was lying on the kitchen table and no less frightening for being dead. Someone had killed it then taken the trouble to bring it up to the manor, break in somehow, then position it on the table, so that Sarah would see it as soon as she walked in. Its sightless eyes seemed to stare back at her, its orange fur was muddy and stained with blood and it looked as if it had been shot. Blood had seeped on to the kitchen table. The stricken animal was meant to frighten Sarah and it did, but she also felt a great sadness that someone would want to harm such a beautiful animal in this way.

'What kind of person would do something like that?' she asked Patrick once he had returned from burying the fox in some corner of the estate. He had taken the table outside too and promised to burn it. He had been the first person she thought to call and she was grateful for his prompt appearance. 'And how did he get in?' she wondered.

'I can't see any sign of forced entry.'

'What do you think I should do?'

'I think you should let me get a locksmith out, to change every lock, put bolts on the doors and new locks on each window to properly secure this place. It will cost a few quid but . . .'

'The estate can pay for it.' She was adamant about that and ready for a fight with Dickie if he protested, but she was pretty sure that a dead fox left to rot on her kitchen table would be sufficient justification.

The visit of the locksmith immediately improved Sarah's state of mind. He was there for hours, changing locks and adding them to windows, putting two sets of bolts on the inside of every external door. If someone had been using an extra set of keys to gain access to the house, that option would no longer be available to them. They would have to break in and at least she would probably hear them.

That night, Sarah felt calmer in the house than she had in months. Her sleep was almost undisturbed and when she did wake, it was from the sound of a sharp north-east wind buffeting Cragsmoor Manor, not someone prowling around downstairs, so she instantly went back to sleep.

The clock had been ticking in the back of Sarah's mind for almost six months now and there was precious little time left. The end-of-year deadline to complete her book was fast approaching and the ending still eluded her, but the pressure of that felt like nothing compared to the rigid cut-off point for her investigation into the disappearance of Lucy Woodfell. Sarah would soon be evicted from the manor house, making her homeless. She would have some money in her bank account, at least, but where would she go? She felt rootless.

When Dickie pulled the plug on the investigation, it would probably feel like a mercy killing. Like her aunt before her, Sarah had succeeded only in tying herself up in knots. She had gone over the same facts, rumours, lies and half-truths surrounding Lucy but failed to come to any concrete conclusions about what had happened to her. It was even more frustrating to know that, despite her initial fears, she hadn't been entirely dreadful at this and had actually uncovered some new information the police didn't have, just not enough of it to make a difference or prove anything.

She was determined not to give up until the very end of her time at Cragsmoor, though, and there was still one more person left to question.

Sarah drove up to Berwick, on the edge of the Scottish border, to visit the retired nanny. It was good to get away from the house for a pleasant drive in autumn sunshine, which took a little under an hour, because she didn't want to flog the old Triumph Sunbeam too hard.

Margaret had taken a while to reply to Sarah's letter, apologizing that she did not get out very often these days, even to post a letter, but she seemed genuinely interested in meeting her. When Sarah arrived, the old lady appeared pleased to see her and more than happy to discuss her life at Cragsmoor. Margaret shuffled off to make a pot of tea and slice some fruit cake. Her home was small but cosy enough for one.

'Would you like to see some photos?' Margaret asked when she returned with the tea and cake.

'I'd love to.'

The old lady came back with two old shoeboxes, filled almost to overflowing with photos of 'the children'. Most were in colour but some were in black and white. She had taken them herself 'with my old box Brownie' and spent some time showing them to Sarah, while providing commentary on each one, including who was in it, where it was taken and what year it must have been, though she sometimes struggled to recall the actual sequence of events. Sarah could tell the old woman was enjoying herself and did not feel she could interrupt her. She probably received few visitors and must have given up her own chance of a family years ago to look after other people's children.

Her time at Cragsmoor had begun with Olly, Freddie and Sephy from the first marriage, then she stayed on to look after Lucy, from the second, before eventually being lured back to help Sephy and the captain with their son Toby. Sarah endured countless snaps of picnics on lawns and trips to the seaside, of the children riding little ponies in the grounds of the house or playing on a rope swing there. Margaret was still a young woman back then and clearly thought a lot of them, which was why she had recorded so many of their childhood adventures. The children looked quite alike, especially the boys, Oliver and Freddie. You could tell that Toby Ramsay came from this family too. The girls were less similar. Lucy was a pretty girl but Sephy was striking even from a young age.

'Freddie and Sephy were close,' said Margaret, 'but oh Lord, they argued all the time and I had to referee their disputes.'

'What about Oliver?'

'Olly was a law unto himself,' she said. 'Never needed anyone else's company. Always involved in mischief and pranks but terribly bright. And boys will be boys,' she smiled indulgently. Sarah couldn't help wondering if men might not turn out better if people stopped using that excuse at every stage of their lives.

'He was fine until he went off to that college,' Margaret said, and she folded her arms defensively.

Her tone indicated the situation was the fault of the institution he attended and not Oliver himself. 'He got in with a bad crowd.'

Sarah didn't need to hear any more about Oliver's drug taking, so instead she asked, 'Was it Sephy's idea to bring you back to Cragsmoor?'

'Yes, it was.'

'Did you look after Toby from the start?'

'Not when he was a baby, no.'

'You were working elsewhere?'

'I was.' But she didn't add any detail. Sarah got the feeling of something being concealed by omission.

'Yet they did tempt you back in the end. With a big pay rise, I suspect.' Sarah forced herself to chuckle at that.

'Oh no, it wasn't about the money.' The old woman was indignant and, just as Sarah had hoped, she walked into revealing the truth by defending herself, 'They just needed help with Toby. He was a little challenging.'

'Bit of a handful, eh?' and Sarah plastered the smile across her face, as if making light of her enquiries. 'They all are, aren't they? Boys.'

'There was a bit more . . .' She could tell the old woman

was cautiously picking her way through sentences in her mind before she spoke them aloud, '. . . work to be done there,' she finally offered. 'On understanding the word "no". His parents didn't have the time to . . . but they knew I could . . . and he was such a bright boy. So clever with the Latin and the Greek and whatnot. Anyway, it all worked out in the end. I mean, it must have, because he is the prime minister.' And she beamed at that notion.

'Being so young, it must have been quite a blow for him when his aunt Lucy disappeared.'

The former nanny's face immediately darkened. 'Lucy going missing was terrible for us all, but Toby was only thirteen and he bottled it up inside. The young are better at accepting things.' Was this her way of rationalizing an apparent lack of grief from the boy?

Sarah described the impact that disappearance had had on her aunt Evelyn. 'She never stopped searching for the truth,' she explained. 'She even asked me to keep digging for her.'

'So that's why you're here?' If Margaret was aggrieved by Sarah's deception, she didn't show it. Perhaps she was simply glad of some company.

'Can I ask what you remember about that day?' asked Sarah.

'It wasn't very eventful, until that point. I spent time with Toby. Just like any other day.'

'He was a bit old for a nanny by then, wasn't he?' Sarah was hoping to persuade the nanny to reveal the reason why Toby was home-schooled.

Margaret looked pained. 'He didn't fit in at school, so they took him out and he had tutors at home for a while.

I stayed on to get him to do his homework and whatnot. I helped round the house too.'

'Was Toby expelled, Margaret? Is that what you are saying?'

'There was an incident with another boy,' she clarified carefully, 'a fight. It was suggested that he might be happier at another school.'

'Must have been quite a fight. Was the other boy injured?'

'He had to go to the hospital but he made a full recovery.' Then she added, 'in the end.'

'I'm glad to hear it.' So our new prime minister was a violent teenager, thought Sarah. It seemed almost all the Woodfells were volatile. 'You were sitting in the kitchen with Toby when Lucy was last seen. And you saw her walking away from the house, correct?'

'That's right, she was.'

There was something about the way Margaret said that, or perhaps it was what she didn't say, that made Sarah pause. What she hadn't said was 'Yes, I saw her.' Instead, she said, 'That's right, she was.'

'Her brother and sister both saw her,' said Sarah, 'and you saw her too.' The nanny gave Sarah a tight little smile and nodded her head quickly in affirmation. 'Didn't you?' Sarah probed.

'That is . . . erm . . . yes.'

'You don't seem very sure about that.'

'Well, it was a very long time ago.'

'But you told the police you saw her leave?'

'Then I must have done,' confirmed the nanny.

'Sorry, but I have to ask you this. Did you really see her go?'

'I was in the kitchen when Lucy walked by, but Sephy got a better look at her than I did. She saw her quite clearly.'

'And how clearly did you see her?'

'Well, I was sitting at the kitchen table with Toby while he did his homework, so I couldn't see quite as well.'

'I assume the kitchen table was close to that old range oven?'

'Yes, that's right.'

'And you were sitting there, facing the oven or the opposite wall?'

'The opposite wall.'

'So, you had Sephy and Freddie off to your side and Sephy was standing by the big window and she looked out and saw Lucy go by?'

'Yes.'

'There is no way you could have seen the path from there through that window, Margaret.'

'I said we saw Lucy because Sephy and Freddie looked out of the window and saw her go by and I confirmed that's what happened.'

'So you didn't actually see Lucy yourself but Sephy and Freddie saw her and told you about it.'

'Well, yes, but it was true.'

'How do you know?'

'Because neither Freddie nor Sephy had any reason to lie about it.'

They might have had every reason, thought Sarah, but she kept that to herself.

Chapter Forty-Two

It had been worth the drive to speak to the old lady. The more she thought about Margaret's testimony on the drive back, the surer Sarah became that she had been manipulated by Sephy and Freddie. Perhaps they really had seen Lucy walking away towards the beach and felt the need to comment on it to one another while the nanny was in the background, but this seemed a little contrived to Sarah. Margaret Malloy's admission that she was not an actual eyewitness to Lucy's departure towards the beach would explain why Warren Evans hadn't seen Lucy arrive there too and why he had stuck to that story for so many years. Oliver's testimony was at best unreliable due to his drinking and the vagueness of the timing of his sighting of Lucy heading to the rear of the house, and she could have gone back in. But if she did not leave the house again, then what exactly happened to Lucy? The truth remained frustratingly out of Sarah's reach. She thought of confronting Sephy and Freddie about Margaret's recollections, but what would that achieve? She knew they could just blame the faulty memory of an old woman.

Sarah didn't have much time left and yet she had so far failed to discover why Lucy was killed and who by, or what had happened to her body. If it had been driven away from the house by a family member, then everyone there that day would have had to have been in on it, since no car was reported leaving the manor. That would mean a conspiracy involving Oliver, Freddie and Sephy, the nanny and young Toby Ramsay, as well as anyone else who might have been working in the house or grounds. It seemed highly implausible that they would all maintain a wall of silence for decades, when they fought like cats and dogs over everything else. What then could have happened to Lucy? With each passing day, Sarah's frustrations grew. She wondered how her aunt, who had been so close to Lucy, could possibly have endured this for so many years.

There was a letter waiting for her in the mailbox. It was from Julian Hastings, author of the regimental history book that had featured Captain Alex Ramsay. Sarah had almost forgotten she had written to him and he apologized for the delay in replying. His publisher had taken some time to pass her message on to him, he said. If Sarah would like to meet then that would be fine by him. He lived some distance from the north-east but was heading for Edinburgh at the weekend for a military reunion and could meet her there, if she chose. Why not? The more she thought about it, the more convinced Sarah had become that the captain's apparent suicide involved Lucy in some way. Either their friendship had turned sour or he was grief-stricken by the manner of her disappearance, but had he himself caused it by killing her? Sarah had little more than a couple of weeks to go before she would be unceremoniously evicted from Cragsmoor, but she refused to give up until the very end. Edinburgh was only ninety minutes from Newcastle by train and she was cheered by the thought of an excursion to a big city some distance from Cragsmoor.

Sarah's good mood did not last long. It ended when her mobile phone rang an hour later.

'Miss Hollis? It's Doctor Phillips.' She wondered what on earth he could want with her this time. 'I'm afraid there has been a tiny development with David.'

'Go on.'

'I don't wish to cause you any unnecessary alarm, but it's best practice to inform you that David disengaged himself from his supervised living.'

'Disengaged himself?' As always with Doctor Phillips, it took her a moment to understand what he was getting at.

'He was alone in his bedroom and absconded through a window.'

Oh God, was he coming to get her? 'Where is he now? Have you any idea? Is he on his way here?'

'He may simply return to us of his own volition. You'd be surprised how many of them do that, once they've had time to reflect and cool off.'

'When did he disappear?'

'About an hour and a half ago.'

Sarah hung up without another word and ran to check the doors were all locked and bolted. David Young did not strike her as the kind of man who would allow the small matter of new locks to keep him from her, though, and she would have to leave the house occasionally. Each time she did, she knew she would be looking over her shoulder.

She decided to live as cautiously as possible until David was apprehended, especially after dark, when he might try to break in under cover of night. That meant double-checking that every door and window in the house was locked before retreating to her room and holing up there. It was doubly frustrating to her to be on her guard like this. Since the locksmith had worked on the house, she had no longer been plagued by intrusions she couldn't explain and there were no more alarming things left on the kitchen table to scare her.

She drew all the curtains and left the lights on in every room, to give the illusion that she might not be alone. She was almost done and was just checking the last of the doors when a sudden noise from within the house made her start. It came from behind her, from the kitchen in fact, and it took a second for Sarah to realize it was the sound of her mobile phone ringing and vibrating loudly on the worktop where she had left it. She ran back to the kitchen and grabbed it.

It was Patrick calling to ask how she was. He had been watching the local television news when they ran a story about David Young absconding.

'Fine,' she said, 'I think.'

Patrick calmly explained that he would drive up to the house, have a look round outside then call her from her front door when he wanted her to unlock it and let him in. He didn't have to explain that this was so she did not acci-dentally open her door to a man intent on killing her.

Chapter Forty-Three

Patrick arrived quickly and he was carrying a holdall. 'It's just a change of clothes. I thought you might feel safer if I crashed here tonight?'

'I would, yes, thanks, Patrick. You can have the room below mine.'

'Nice one.'

'And Patrick? Thanks for getting here so quickly and for, you know, taking it seriously.'

'No problem.'

With the kitchen table gone, they ate their evening meal together in the dining room, which felt too formal, so afterwards Sarah suggested they open a bottle of Evie's very good wine in the drawing room.

'Then I'll get the wine,' he said. Patrick went to the kitchen while Sarah lingered in the hall, taking a moment to take in the grand staircase, the fireplace and the carved Latin motto above it.

Patrick emerged carrying a bottle of Pinot Noir, two glasses and a corkscrew. 'What?' he asked, when he realized she was scrutinizing the Latin phrase.

'*Respice ut ante videas*,' she recited, 'maybe that's where they went wrong.'

'How do you mean?'

'It translates as "look back to see ahead", more or less. Marcus thought it showed the family's fixation with the past.

That's why it was placed so prominently above the great fireplace so that everyone could see it, but times change and the past is not always the best guide for the future.'

Patrick handed her the glasses then he opened the wine. 'Shouldn't it be, examine the past to find the way forward? That would make more sense.'

'Marcus reckoned the guy who wrote it wasn't educated. He was a craftsman who built amazing priest holes but he might not have been that well read.'

'He was well read enough to carve Latin phrases in the house,' he said, as he poured them both a glass and handed her one.

'But some of them might have been mistranslated. *Respice* can translate as "look behind" too, and that's what I thought it meant, but Marcus said it was most probably "look back" instead. That's what he thought, anyway.'

Patrick looked doubtful and Sarah realized she hadn't even questioned Marcus's opinion on the matter, since he was a proclaimed expert and had said it with such certainty. 'It's strange to think of Freddie growing up here, coming down these stairs every morning and seeing that motto hanging over the fireplace,' she said. 'He probably thought it was the only advice he would ever need and then he lost it all.'

'Well, no, actually,' he said and when she gave him a questioning look, he explained. 'That wasn't there back then.'

'Wasn't it? How do you know?'

'My mum used to bring me up here in the summer holidays, remember? There was a big stag's head hanging above the fireplace at the time.'

'I've seen it in the loft,' she told him. 'Minus an antler.'

'They replaced it with the motto.'

'You mean it was moved,' she asked, 'to fill the gap where the stag used to be? Where was it originally?'

'I don't know.'

'Patrick,' she said with a sense of urgency, 'how can we find out where it was moved from?'

The coffee-table book that Freddie had commissioned was still in the library. It contained photographs of every room in the manor and was a useful snapshot into the past that would show them what the house had looked like forty years ago. Sarah had to deliberately force herself to stay calm as she began to leaf through it with Patrick by her side. She knew that if they could find the spot where the Latin motto had once hung, they might have a clue to the whereabouts of the remaining priest hole. She didn't want to miss anything vital by going through it too hastily.

'There,' she said excitedly, pointing to a photo of the great fireplace. 'Your stag.'

'That's the fella.' It was a fine and noble beast, or had been, until one of the family's ancestors had butchered it and stuck it on the wall.

'Now we just need to hope we find a photograph that shows the Latin motto in its original position.'

She carried on flicking through the book and scanning every page, but she drew a blank. Had she gone through the book too quickly? She tried again. Sarah so wanted to find an important clue which would lead to a great reveal and tie it into her admittedly half-baked theory but, as she flicked more slowly through the book, she found no sign of the Latin motto. 'It's not there.' She couldn't hide her disappointment. 'I so hoped it would be.'

'Why do you think it matters?'

'I thought the Latin phrase might be telling me there was another priest hole behind the wall – the fourth one that everyone has been wondering about for centuries – but the plaque was mounted above the fireplace and the only thing behind it was the chimney. Marcus told me the guy had mistranslated and he was so bloody sure of himself that I put the thought out of my mind. It was only when I was explaining it to you that I suddenly started to question whether he had got this right. Marcus was sure the sign meant to look into the past.'

'But you think it literally means to look behind?'

'Yes.' Then she modified her statement, 'I mean, it might.'

'It might,' he agreed, 'but unless we can find out where it used to hang, we won't know what to look behind.'

'I know,' she said glumly.

'And also . . .'

'What?'

'Well, if we can't find the fourth priest hole and nobody else has ever found it, how can anyone have kept a secret hidden there?'

'Someone else *could* have found it,' she said. 'How else can a body completely disappear inside a house? Maybe they moved the motto to make it impossible for someone else to find it.'

'You can't just put a body in a priest hole and forget about it,' he argued.

'I know.'

'I mean, it would smell, for one thing.'

'There is that,' she conceded.

'Well then.'

'Okay, I don't know how it could be done, but I've run out of alternatives. Every inch of this house and its grounds was searched, including the three priest holes. Police scoured the trail running down to the beach and the land surrounding it. They even went into the tunnel, as far as possible. They used sniffer dogs and came up with nothing.'

'Could she have gone for a swim and drowned?' asked Patrick. 'I know you would normally expect to find a body, but if the tide took her out to sea . . .' He didn't need to explain the grim realities of a dead body in deep water with sea creatures.

'It crossed my mind,' she admitted. 'But there would be something left on the beach,' she insisted. 'A bag, a towel, some trace of the clothing Lucy wore to walk down there; even if she was wearing her swimsuit under it, she would have taken the rest of her clothes off and left them in a pile. She would have had a towel to dry herself afterwards. No one saw her on the beach that day or found any trace of her belongings. I don't think she went down to the beach for a swim. I question whether she went to the beach at all, in fact.'

'But weren't there witnesses that saw her go down there?'

'Freddie and his sister said they saw her go, but the nanny only said she did because they told her Lucy went by.' And she explained the conversation she'd had with Margaret.

'If someone did catch up with Lucy and kill her,

couldn't they have disposed of the body in some way?' he asked.

'Bury it and the dogs would find it,' she said. 'You can't burn it out in the open and you couldn't just hide a body somewhere because it would decompose and smell, like you said.'

'So, you move the body,' he suggested. 'Get it off the estate.'

'How?' she countered. 'You can't just throw her over your shoulders, carry her to your car, chuck her in the boot and drive off without anyone seeing or hearing you.'

'You leave her and come back in the night,' he offered. 'You wrap her up in something – tarpaulin, old carpet, a bloody big sack – I don't know, but under cover of darkness, you carry her back to your car, pop her in the boot and drive away.'

'Aside from the fact that you still have the problem of disposing of a body somewhere else, that couldn't have happened. Crucially, no one left the estate. Cars were always parked out front and no one was seen or heard moving their car. Nobody left the house.' She thought for a moment. 'That might be where the killer could have gone wrong.'

'How do you mean?'

'Because, if even one car had left the estate that day, we could not rule out the idea that Lucy's body might have been moved, but they all stayed put, which makes me believe that poor Lucy stayed put too. She is here, somewhere on the estate. I'm almost sure of it.'

Chapter Forty-Four

Sarah told Patrick she needed supplies, which was partially true, but what she needed most was to get out of the house for a while. She hadn't slept well the previous night, waking often, her unconscious mind turning almost every sound into an image of David Young slipping into the house to kill her, even though she had the reassurance of Patrick sleeping downstairs in the room below hers. David was on the run and could decide to come after her, but he wasn't the only threat Sarah faced. Whoever was behind the anonymous phone call and break-ins at the manor had already caused her distress. She felt besieged now and fearful for her safety.

Because she was so tired, Sarah asked Patrick to drive, and they left the estate and set off towards the village. Sarah was going to suggest they went further afield. A drive just about anywhere would be preferable to staying cooped up in Cragsmoor all day, going through the details of the case over and over again and worrying about David Young. She desperately needed a break.

Sarah was surprised to see activity down by the Dule tree on the corner. Judging by the way that two cars had pulled up and were blocking the road, something dramatic must have happened, but it didn't look like an accident and there was no wreckage in the road. Patrick slowed the car to a halt and they climbed out, continuing on foot. As they drew nearer, they saw that several people were staring at the tree, while three men were in the process of doing something beside it. As Sarah and Patrick reached the side of the road where the onlookers were standing, it was apparent from the looks on their faces that they had just witnessed something disturbing.

As they drew nearer, they saw that a man was hanging by his neck from a thick rope attached to a branch of the Dule tree. Three other men were trying to put a ladder against the tree trunk and keep it in place, so that one of them could climb up and get to him, though it was obvious it was far too late to help the lifeless figure. He was way past that.

David Young was dead. He had chosen to hang himself rather than risk losing his freedom again, and he had done it right by the manor house.

The press went crazy over it, of course. Luckily, they didn't know about Sarah's interview with David and she hoped Doctor Phillips would have the good sense to keep that a secret from them, unless he also wanted to be dragged into the media reports. As soon as word reached reporters that a convicted murderer had hanged himself, on the Gallows Tree, no less, close to the estate where Lucy Woodfell had gone missing, they put it down to guilt and openly speculated he must have been her killer.

Sarah knew it was a possibility but she wasn't convinced. If he really had felt guilty about killing Lucy then surely he would have killed himself years ago. She suspected that David Young had committed suicide because he didn't want to go back to prison and had persuaded himself this was going to happen, because of her. Sarah didn't believe he chose the Dule tree close to Cragsmoor because he had murdered Lucy Woodfell. She was certain he had done it to send a message to *her*. This is all your fault, he was telling her, and maybe it was.

Patrick reminded her that David Young was a disturbed man who had already killed at least one woman. She had been absolutely right not to let him in when he had tried to plead his innocence. Perhaps he *had* murdered Lucy. They would probably never know for sure, but Sarah was not the one who had killed him. He alone had chosen to take his own life. It was his decision to turn his death into a public gesture, and who knew what he meant by it or what was going through his mind at the time? None of this was her fault.

Sarah heard Patrick out but only half believed him.

Chapter Forty-Five

Sarah met the military historian, Julian Hastings, a couple of days later in the bar of a grand hotel, just around the corner from Edinburgh's Waverley station. The former paratrooper seemed sprightly for a man who must have been in his seventies and looked and sounded every inch the officer class, in blazer and tie.

'I thought we might have a couple of pink gins,' and he ordered for them both then ushered her to a table where they made small talk until the drinks arrived. Sarah wasn't used to drinking gin in the middle of the afternoon but Julian acted as if it was the most natural thing. 'Isn't it incredible that old Alex Ramsay's son is prime minister?' he said.

'How well did you know him?'

'Never served with him, obviously. I'm not that old, but I met him through the regiment and knew Alex for a number of years. What do you want to know about him?'

'Primarily, why would he want to kill himself?' she asked. 'The crash he died in was ruled an accident but I have good reason to believe it was actually suicide. The poor man survived the war then came home, only to drive into a wall forty years later. I don't suppose you know why he might have done it?'

Sarah expected Julian to be shocked by her suicide theory or that he might give her a non-committal answer and perhaps even a lecture about the effect combat can have on a man, even years after the event. Instead, she got a straight answer.

'Absolutely,' he said. 'He was dying anyway,' then he sat back and took another sip of his pink gin. 'Didn't you know?'

'No.' She was shocked to hear this. No one had mentioned it before, and now Julian had slipped it casually into their conversation as if it was common knowledge.

'Well, people never talked about stuff like that back then,' he explained. 'If you had something bad – really bad, I mean – you didn't mention it usually, even if it was the Big C. That's just how most people were. You kept your own counsel, went home and prepared for the end. With some people you only found out about it when their family announced the funeral. I rather think there's more dignity in that way, don't you? These days everybody bangs on about everything that's wrong with them. Why burden everyone else? Everybody pops their clogs eventually. Talking about it isn't going to alter that. Do you agree?'

'Erm, I don't know,' she admitted. 'But back to the captain; if you didn't know what was wrong with him then how did you know it was serious enough to make him take his life?'

'He was seen,' then he lowered his voice until it was a confiding whisper, 'in Devonshire Place. Our old friend Jerry Hammond bumped into him on his way to Baker Street. Alex was shocked to see him. Jerry said he looked like he'd just bumped into his wife on the way out of a knocking shop. Definitely wasn't happy about bumping into him. Jerry asked him what he was up to and Alex mumbled something about an appointment then wandered off in the direction of Harley Street.' She knew Harley Street housed the expensive private doctors beloved of the rich. 'Anyway,' he continued, 'Jerry thought it all seemed a bit rum, so he followed at a discreet distance, nosey bugger. He watched the captain go into a little clinic there. Don't ask me its name, can't remember. Jerry might. I suppose I could give him a ring, if you really want to know?'

'Please. Did Jerry have any idea what the clinic might have been specializing in?'

'Not exactly, but he did say it looked like a place of last resort. I remember that,' and he repeated it for emphasis, 'a place of last resort.'

'Did he think it might be . . .'

'The Big C? Yes, that's exactly the impression he came away with. He said it was the kind of place you go to when the chips are all piled up in the middle of the table and you are in desperate need of a couple of aces. Poor chap. The captain, I mean, not Jerry.'

'And this was how long before the accident?'

'A week, two perhaps, I think. Hard to be sure, such a long time ago.'

'I suppose if he received bad news there then . . .'

'He'd rather go out with a bang than a whimper? I think Alex was the kind of man who would prefer to die with his boots on.'

Mercifully, there were no members of the press outside the manor house when Sarah returned from Edinburgh.

Moments earlier, she had driven past the corner where the Dule tree stood and there was no sign that anything sinister had taken place there, which lent David Young's last act at such a peaceful spot an almost dreamlike quality. You could have been forgiven for questioning whether it had happened at all.

She hadn't been back in the manor house long when her phone rang and an already familiar voice assailed her.

'Yes, hello,' Julian Hastings was bellowing down the phone at her as if to bridge the distance between them, 'I got that name you wanted.'

'Name?' she asked doubtfully.

'Of that bloody clinic the captain went to,' then before she could answer, 'in bloody Harley Street.'

'Thank you, that's much appreciated.'

'No problem at all. Just had to give old Jerry a bell. He was in, doesn't get about much any more. You know, he has a dog and I'll never know why when he can't exercise it. Why take on a dog in the first place, especially when you live in an apartment? It's not fair on the old brute – the dog, I mean, not Jerry.'

She made sympathetic noises about poor Jerry and poor Jerry's poor dog, but he continued. 'Countryside is the place for them. Got to let them roam. No use keeping them cooped up all day on the fifth floor. Drives them mad in the end and that's why they bite children.'

'You mentioned the clinic,' she managed to cut across him. 'The name of it?'

'Oh yes, now . . .' there was hesitation in his voice and he fell silent for a moment. Oh God, he's forgotten it already. 'I've written it down on a scrap of paper for you ... which I just have to find ... not that pocket ... the other one ... argh ... here it is!' He sounded triumphant.

'Freyr Baal,' he said. 'Odd sort of a name. Do you want me to spell that?'

And he did.

'Freyr Baal? Does that mean anything?' she asked.

'Not to me. Maybe give them a bell and find out. Got to be in the phone book, eh?'

Sarah put Freyr Baal clinic into an internet search and nothing came up. She tried several variations and added the words private and cancer to different searches, hoping someone might have made a reference to them in a blog or an old article, but she drew a blank. She'd hoped they might still be going. She knew she wouldn't have been able to get private medical information from them about the captain, even after his death, but at least she would have been able to ask them what they specialized in treating. Of course, it was never going to be that simple, was it? Nothing ever is.

Perhaps Freyr Baal would remain a mystery. It sounded Scandinavian, though, so Sarah wondered if running it through an online translator might yield something. It did, but not what she was hoping for. The words were recognized as Icelandic but they didn't translate into English. Why not? Why would Icelandic words not be translatable? What words could not be translated? Names of people or places, perhaps? She decided to separate the words and key them in one at a time.

Freyr came up as an ancient Norse lord. Baal was

actually a Middle Eastern god. But what did these two deities have in common and why had they been placed together to form the name of a clinic in Harley Street? She checked Freyr first, expecting to see some reference to health or healing, and learned that instead he was associated with peace, virility and a good harvest. When she read the entries about Baal there was a similar connotation. He was the god of fertility.

'Oh my God,' she told the screen. 'It wasn't a cancer clinic, it was a fertility clinic.'

They were trying to give themselves a lucky blessing, from two ancient gods from different cultures, who would bestow good fortune on clients hoping to start a family.

Within a week or so of his attendance at the clinic, Captain Alex Ramsay died in the wreckage of a car crash he himself had caused. But it wasn't guilt about the death of Lucy that sent him over the edge. He didn't kill her. It was the news he received from the clinic that did it. Alex Ramsay did not receive a terminal cancer diagnosis; he must have been told he couldn't have children. But, crucially, Captain Ramsay already had a son. Toby Ramsay was around fourteen or fifteen at that point. Only then would the captain have realized that Toby was not his son after all, but another man's.

The captain must have wondered why it took so long to have one child and why they weren't able to have more. If his wife was fertile, he must have been baffled, so he went to the clinic to have himself checked out. Sarah could imagine the captain's shock and devastation if he was told he was sterile, which might very well explain his suicide within a matter of days.

But if Alex Ramsay wasn't the father of Sephy's child then who was?

Was this the family secret Lucy had learned? No one would have thanked her for exposing it back then. Was she about to tell the captain about the real parenthood of the boy when she was killed? The boy in question was now a man and the country's prime minister.

Sarah realized that one person must have known that secret even before Captain Ramsay, aside from Sephy herself. Whoever had actually fathered her child was in on it, surely, unless Sephy kept it from him. This secret was the one thing that might have been big enough to tear the family apart. Did Lucy walk in on Sephy and her lover or just hear them talking from the room above, while their words carried through the vent? If she had confirmed Sephy was having an affair and confronted her with the proof, then this might have been a sufficient motive for murder.

Could Sephy have actually killed her half-sister over it? Or did she get her lover to do it for her? Did he perhaps murder Lucy without Sephy knowing? It was possible, of course, but who was *he*? That was the next question Sarah had to answer, and since she was about to pry into the mystery of the true parentage of the prime minister, Sarah knew she would have to tread very carefully indeed, unless she wanted to disappear too, just like Lucy.

Chapter Forty-Six

That night, Sarah was restless. She kept churning over everything she had recently learned in her mind and her list of suspects had begun to narrow. David Young was dead by his own hand but, unlike the tabloids, Sarah did not consider his suicide proof of guilt. Warren Evans had disappeared, which was suspicious, but she was more inclined now to view him as a man trying to escape the torments of his past, rather than one trying to evade justice. Now that she had discovered the most likely reason for the captain's suicide, Sarah was convinced the guilty party was closer to home. Lucy had known the truth long before he did, Sarah was sure of this, and, since no cars had left the estate on the day she disappeared, Sarah also believed that Cragsmoor itself might still be holding the secret of what had happened to her body somehow. She kept coming back to the same thing. If you wanted to hide a room so that it would never be discovered, where would you put it?

No one had ever found the legendary fourth priest hole, not even the super confident Marcus, so perhaps it didn't actually exist, but knowing the Latin motto had been moved to the fireplace had convinced Sarah that it did. She went back to the library and went through the book again with little expectation of success. Photos had been taken of every corner of the house, but none revealed the original whereabouts of the Latin plaque in its almost two hundred pages.

Then a thought suddenly struck her. Hadn't the photographer taken hundreds of photos and Freddie then had to select the ones he needed for the book? There were so many, she recalled from her aunt's memoir, that they had littered the library. There must have been many more that didn't make it into the finished book. If only she could find them. Perhaps Freddie had kept them all, but where would he have stored them?

Sarah searched every drawer in the library then she rummaged in drawers all around the house, hoping for a miraculous find. She even went into the attic but baulked at searching its many nooks and crannies out of sheer tiredness and the general feeling of hopelessness caused by the size of the task.

She went back down to the kitchen and made a mug of tea, then took it into one of the cosier sitting rooms, together with the book about the house. Perhaps there would be some other clue within its pages if she looked closely enough. With that thought in mind, she sipped her tea and began to leaf slowly through its pages once more. She took her time and even read sections of the book on the history of the house, as well as scrutinizing its photographs even more closely than before.

By the time what was left of her tea had turned cold, she had filled in some of the gaps in her knowledge of the Woodfell family and Cragsmoor Manor, including its use during the Second World War and the turbulence it had withstood throughout centuries of its history.

She then reached the chapter on the priest holes. The

narrative was a familiar one, focusing on their creator and how he had built them in conditions of utmost secrecy but liked to use the Latin phrases placed by them to send a moral message or even a tiny clue to their whereabouts. The chapter was illustrated by images of the three known priest holes but it did not mention the unsubstantiated possibility that there might be a fourth somewhere. It was getting very late and Sarah was exhausted by now. She was about to put the book down to start getting ready for bed when her eyes fell upon the image of the priest hole at the bottom of the staircase. There, next to it, was a familiar plaque upon the wall. The one which said '*Ad caelum ire primum necesse est cadere*', which Marcus had translated as 'To ascend to heaven a man must first fall'. It was so small in the photo that Sarah couldn't make out all the Latin words but she knew them well enough by now. Nearby was that quote from Cicero, '*Vitam regit fortuna, non sapientia*', which, she recalled, translated as 'Fortune, not wisdom, rules lives.' This was the clue to the second priest hole nearby.

It was only as she peered closely at these plaques that she noticed something she had missed in her earlier haste to skip through the book. There was another plaque here in the photograph, directly underneath them. Surely this couldn't be it?

Sarah leaned forward excitedly and squinted at the page. She barely dared to breathe now, let alone hope. The words on that lower plaque were barely discernible and she couldn't make out all the letters, but she could see just enough to realize they spelt out *Respice ut ante videas*.

'Got you,' she said aloud.

Sarah went straight to the staircase. The light wasn't great here, the house a gloomy place even in daylight and it was long after midnight now. Even so, she was still able to clearly see the plaque that was mounted there.

'Vitam regit fortuna, non sapientia'

Those words had been directing true believers to escape their tormentors for centuries. Sarah's focus was now on the space that had previously been occupied by the other Latin motto. At first glance, it appeared no different to the rest of the brickwork and its vertical wooden beams, but as she peered closer, Sarah noticed a slight discolouration that tallied perfectly with the spot where the other plaque had hung, before it was moved to its current location above the fireplace. The wood here had been painted over with a dark varnish to make it blend in but, like any repair or restoration, it was not entirely perfect and could be seen close up.

Now all Sarah needed to do was decipher the true meaning of the words on the motto. *'Look behind to see forward'* – but look behind what and how?

Look behind the walls? She'd already done that and she knew there was a priest hole behind one of them. She recalled how Marcus had explained that when they first opened up this hole, the Queen's men would have been deceived by a false panel that was set over the entrance to the hiding place, leaving only a small gap that would have housed family jewels. They would have had to look beyond or behind this in order to find the hiding place of the priest. It struck her then that she had never actually gone inside to explore this one for herself and she had an idea. She pushed the vertical beam on the wall, just as Marcus had done, and it swung outwards to leave a gap large enough for a person to climb in. She wanted to make sure she wouldn't become trapped in it somehow, particularly as she was alone in the house, so she brought the tall table that she usually left her keys on from the other side of the hall and set the loose beam to rest on it, propping it open. Only then did she climb inside. It was a very small room but she could fit into it easily enough.

She turned on her phone torch and shone it on the walls around her.

Look behind to see forward

There was no sign of a hinge or join or even so much as a crack in the walls to her left or right. The back wall, however, had more of the vertical wooden beams and they looked a little out of place inside such a small room. Perhaps they were needed to support the structure but it seemed solid enough. The beams made the back wall look just like the outside wall she had already passed through. Sarah tapped on the far wall now. It didn't sound hollow but was perhaps not quite as solid as the other walls.

Look behind to see forward.

What if the maker of the priest hole had used the same principle he had employed when he built the cover for the first door and disguised it? It would have been something akin to genius to put a priest hole behind a priest hole. Who would have thought to look for one there?

Look behind to see forward

Could this be it? Sarah realized her palms were sweating as she pressed the top of the first of the two beams on the far wall, but nothing happened. Last chance, then. She placed her palm against the top of the second beam, pushed hard and it gave way easily, even after all these years, creating a gap like the first one she had just crawled into. 'Oh my God.'

She had found it. After hundreds of years, Sarah had found it!

Trying to suppress her excitement, Sarah aimed the torch into the gap she had uncovered, expecting to see another small priest hole, but she discovered far more than that.

Chapter Forty-Seven

Sarah called Patrick's mobile and when he answered groggily, she told him, 'I know it's late . . . but . . .'

'You found it?' he said.

'Yes.' Then she asked, 'How did you know?'

'Somehow, I knew you would.'

She felt buoyed by his faith in her. 'Sorry,' she said, in case he did not share her enthusiasm for the discovery at this hour.

'I'll be right over.'

No more than a quarter of an hour later, Patrick was kneeling in the first priest hole, shining a torch into the gap Sarah had found in its rear wall. She waited outside because it was too cramped for both of them.

Patrick turned round to face her now. 'Did you see how far back it goes?'

'Yes,' she said, barely able to comprehend it and feeling relieved that he shared her sense of wonder.

'It drops down to start with, but then it . . .' His voice trailed away and he immediately turned back to take another look and she waited impatiently until he came back with his findings. 'It goes down into about the same level as the cellar and I reckon it links up with . . .'

'The tunnel,' she interrupted. 'Most people thought the tunnel was dug for smuggling but it was created to help priests escape and only used for smuggling many years later.'

'It's amazing.' He beamed at her then and she realized she was grinning back at him.

'It makes perfect sense,' she said. 'The problem with priest holes is that once you are in one, you have nowhere to go, so if the Queen's men find it, they find you. This one was a work of genius and I'd be willing to bet the others are mostly designed to distract you from it. By the time his pursuers discovered the room's true purpose, the priest would have gone through it and out the other side. He would be straight down the tunnel and away.'

'As long as he put the beam back in place, they wouldn't even realize,' Patrick agreed. 'They'd be left staring at an empty little room.'

They were both elated. Finding the priest hole was an incredible achievement on its own, but it was only half the story.

'I should try and go down there,' he said.

'It could be dangerous,' she told him. 'Marcus thinks they blew up the exit with explosives and blocked the entrance in the cellar with a new stone wall. We don't know how unstable it could be.'

He considered this for a moment. 'Let me just take a look.'

'Are you sure about that?'

'Not entirely,' he admitted, 'but I think I'll be okay.'

'Do you want me to come too?'

'No,' he said quickly.

'Because I'm a woman?' she flared.

'Because I want you to get help if I end up trapped down there.'

318

'Fair enough,' she said. 'Can you even get down?'

'There are stone steps. I should be okay.'

He made to go and she said, 'Patrick . . .'

He turned back and smiled at her. 'You don't have to tell me to be careful. I will be.' And with that, he edged himself through the gap and dropped down. He turned back to give her the thumbs-up once he was through then he climbed down the steps and disappeared.

He could only have been gone for a few minutes, but it felt much longer. Sarah tried to blot out any fears for Patrick's safety but the tension was almost unbearable. What if he found nothing? What if the roof caved in on him and it was all her fault? She stood there silently waiting, listening intently for any sounds that might give her a clue to his progress, but she heard nothing.

Then, finally, Sarah heard a choking cough, which sounded like Patrick trying to clear dust from his airway, and seconds later he emerged. His head appeared first, through the gap in the opened beam, then he hauled himself back into the priest hole. Patrick seemed uninjured but he didn't say anything at first and she resisted the temptation to ask him what he had seen. Instead, she stood back as he crawled through the priest hole and climbed out of it, until he was standing next to her in the hall again. His clothes were dirty now.

She let him catch a breath then she asked, 'Did you see anything?'

Patrick nodded slowly. 'I found her,' he said simply, 'I found Lucy.'

Chapter Forty-Eight

They didn't call the police immediately. Lucy Woodfell's remains had been in the tunnel for thirty-six years, so another few minutes wouldn't make any difference and Sarah wanted to hear about it first. She felt she had earned that right.

'The tunnel seems fine, structurally, at least the bit under the house,' Patrick explained. 'It's solid rock and there are no cracks or loose boulders. You don't have to walk too far to find her, only a few yards. The body is sitting up, like someone placed her against the wall and got out of there in a hurry. It's decomposed, obviously, but you can still make out some of the clothing. Her jacket is made from synthetic material that doesn't fully rot. It looks like it matches what she wore that day.'

'I wonder how she died,' said Sarah. 'There'll have to be lots of tests on what's left of the body before we find out.'

'Actually, there's a pretty big clue down there,' he told her. 'It was blunt trauma, judging by what I found next to the body. A large metal poker from a fireplace.'

Sarah had to blot out the image of Lucy's face then in case she dwelt too long on the impact of that fatal blow from a blunt instrument.

'There's something else,' he told her. 'I checked for ID. It's an old habit from my army days. I didn't find any but . . .' he handed her an envelope, '. . . this was in her jacket pocket.'

Sarah took the envelope. She could just make out the faded words even after all these years. The letter was addressed to Evelyn Moore and it was the last one her friend, Lucy Woodfell, had ever written.

Sarah stared at it, contemplating its significance. Patrick had found the letter in Lucy's jacket. Either her killer hadn't bothered to look there or he'd thought there was no need to remove it, once he had entombed the body in the tunnel, presumably forever.

Sarah carefully opened the envelope and took out the letter. The ink had faded with time but she could still read it. She took it in slowly, a message from a dead woman that had waited thirty-six years for someone to read it.

Dear Evelyn

You are the only one I can turn to. Everything must come out now, and it will. Poor Alex. He does not deserve this and should never have become mixed up with my dreadful family. His only crime was to marry Sephy and this is all down to her and Freddie.

I knew they were disgusting. I knew they were selfish and only cared for themselves. I thought I knew exactly what they were capable of, but I never imagined they were fucking each other and have been for years.

I heard them. They were in Sephy's room and I heard them. It started as an argument and their raised voices woke me but then they calmed down and started laughing and joking. You know what they're like, always arguing over nothing then thick as thieves again moments later. I would have drifted off but then I heard quite different sounds coming from Sephy's room and I instantly knew what it was.

At first, I thought Freddie had gone and Sephy had smuggled James into her room afterwards or that he'd been hiding in the wardrobe all along, but no, I soon realized it was Freddie, not James, talking to my sister while he was screwing her. Both of them were calling out while they did it, until I couldn't bear to hear it any longer. My disgust was matched only by my fury.

I went downstairs and burst through the door to confront them – at least that way they couldn't deny it. They both screamed for me to get out, but even they were rattled this morning, though they tried to carry on as if nothing had happened.

I heard nothing. I saw nothing. That's what Freddie said to me, as if I could deny the evidence of my own eyes. He told me I had to keep quiet because it would ruin the family, especially Toby, and I knew what he meant then. He must be that poor boy's real father and he hopes to buy my silence with this knowledge, because he knows I would never hurt Toby, who is a complete innocent. Freddie said he would kill me if I told anyone.

I don't have to tell the world, though. Just the captain. Let's see how Freddie and Sephy bluster their way out of this when I tell Alex. They'll both get what they deserve then.

It's probably just as well that they have no shame because I am carrying enough of it for all of us.

Chapter Forty-Nine

Sephy greeted Sarah at her door. As she watched the younger woman walk up the path towards her cottage, she looked frail.

'I wondered when you'd come again.'

Sephy shuffled inside and Sarah followed her. They sat down in two stiff-backed armchairs facing one another and Sephy fixed her with an adversarial look. It already felt like a battle of wills.

'On the phone, you said you had news,' she said, 'and you have come here to ask me a bunch of bloody questions, right?'

'Wrong. Actually, I have come here with a bunch of bloody answers. Then yes, perhaps one or two questions.'

'For God's sake, what are you talking about?'

'I found Lucy,' Sarah said and the old woman's mouth fell open in shock.

Sarah spent an hour with Sephy before driving off to meet Freddie.

She had arranged to see him in advance and insisted they meet in a public place, dangling the truth about his sister's fate as a lure to get him there. The café was part of a chain that seemed to be in every high street these days, and the nearest town to Freddie's home was no different, though he looked out of place here.

'You said you know what happened to my sister?' They were sitting at a quiet table towards the back of the room. It was still public but quiet enough for them to talk in private. He sounded disbelieving but she could tell he was desperate to know what she had learned, which was why Sarah had teased him with this possibility.

'I'll come to that in a moment.' And there was a slight slackening of his posture, as if he didn't really believe she knew what had happened to Lucy. He clearly thought she was lying to get her foot in his door. 'You were the last person to see Lucy alive?' she recalled.

'Along with my sister, Sephy,' he agreed. 'The last time I saw Lucy, she was walking away from the house to the beach.'

'Not true. You were the last person to see her but she never left the house.'

He frowned, as if Sarah had misunderstood the situation. 'I wasn't the only one to see her leave. There were three other witnesses.'

'That's not true either. Oliver saw Lucy outside but she came back in. She must have done. By this stage he was drinking a lot. I doubt he knew what day it was, let alone the time. He was supposed to have a meeting with you, to avoid more ruinous legal fees, but you kept him waiting. Why?' Then she answered her own question. 'Because you were busy with Lucy.'

'Rubbish.'

'As for the other witnesses? Neither of them are credible, especially your sister Sephy. Your dear old nanny never actually saw Lucy; she just witnessed the charade the two of you put on while she was with Toby at the kitchen table.' Sarah mimicked them both. '"Look, there goes Lucy walking down to the beach." "Oh yes, must be going for a swim." A more suspicious soul than your old nanny might have worked out what was going on, but she never saw villainy in any of you, did she? That's why you chose her. She was the perfect person to back up your story.'

'I don't know what you think you've got here,' he told her, 'but it won't get you very far.'

'Well, let's see, shall we? What have we got? The body of your half-sister, for starters.'

That was like a punch in the guts judging by the look on his face, but he tried to recover his composure and act like a man who was surprised to learn of this stunning development. 'You found Lucy?' His voice was high, feigning incredulity, 'When? Where?'

'Yesterday, and you know where, Freddie. She was found in the house that you and your sister swore Lucy walked away from, in a spot hardly anyone could have known about. That rules out David Young or Warren Evans by the way. Only you, Sephy or Oliver could have possibly known about that spot.'

'Then Oliver killed her,' and he folded his arms as an act of defiance, but she noticed he didn't even ask her where that spot was, because he already knew. 'Prove otherwise. Go on.'

'Not Oliver. Poor, hopeless Olly wasn't up to it and Lucy wasn't the one he hated most. You and Sephy were top of that list, even though he had his doubts about Lucy. He thought she might be responsible for leaving the drugs in his bathroom, but that's not how she operated. It's far more your style to get him disinherited like that.'

'Oliver was destroying everything,' he explained. 'I never believed a few weeks in a clinic in Geneva would cure him. I thought leaving some drugs for him would give Oliver a choice. I didn't force him to take an overdose and I certainly didn't expect him to nearly die of it.'

'Whatever alibi you cooked up, it left Oliver distrusting Lucy because she was still around, but only because she still cared about him.'

'Not my fault she was so foolish, and Oliver was paranoid. He saw plots everywhere.'

'That's not surprising,' she said. 'There *were* plots against him and you devised them, but Oliver was a spent force by the time Lucy disappeared. He's not her killer.'

He didn't deny that. 'Sephy then?' he said lightly, as if he was giving up something that mattered little to him.

'I thought you would turn on each other in the end. Giving up your sister to save your own arse even this late in the day. That's shabby.'

'I didn't say she did it. I only answered your question about who might have done it.'

'She on the other hand said outright that it was you.'

'Bullshit.'

'I've just come from her. All I had to do was accuse her of being the killer and she crumpled. It didn't take much.'

Sarah played the recording she had made on her phone. Sephy's voice was clear and her words damning.

'Freddie did it. He told me he had to. She was going to tell Alex all about us. She threatened to tell him about Toby.'

'Toby wasn't his?'

'No.'

'He was your brother's?'

326

'Yes.'

'When did that begin?'

'A long time ago. I was still only a child. Freddie said it was a game. He was going to teach me. That first time was rape. It always was to begin with. Then, later, I decided I didn't deserve anyone else. I was already too damaged, too disgusting. Freddie degraded me. I was all he had and he was all I thought I deserved. I was a very good victim because I always came back to him. Then, when I needed a child . . .'

Freddie couldn't hear any more. 'Oh, dear God, Sephy, you stupid, stupid bitch!' He made a lunge across the table for the phone but Sarah was expecting this and she pulled it away from him.

'Sounds convincing, doesn't she? Well, she convinced me at any rate. I believed her and I think the police will too. I've already sent it to them. I expect they'll be popping round to see you later.'

'That does not constitute proof. It's just a mad old woman's word against mine. She always hated me. That's what I'll tell them. You have nothing.'

'I have a letter.'

'What letter?'

'The one in Lucy's pocket.' And she took a photocopy of Lucy's final letter from her bag and handed it to him. He read it while she continued to talk to him. 'The original is also with the police. You never thought to look in her jacket pocket. The letter was in there, ready to post to Evelyn. It was so nearly on its way to her.'

'This doesn't prove I killed her. It must have been Sephy. That's why she's so keen to frame me.'

'So, you say Sephy killed Lucy, and Sephy claims that

you killed her. Your word against hers. Interesting.' Sarah had expected this and was ready for it. 'I suppose we'll have to let the DNA evidence prove who's lying.'

'What DNA evidence?'

'Oh, there'll be lots of it.'

'From a body that's been down there decomposing for decades? I rather doubt that.'

'Down where, Freddie? I didn't say exactly.'

He looked more flustered. 'Down wherever. I assumed it was buried somewhere.'

'In the tunnel,' she said, 'as well you know. It was blocked at both ends, which kept it very dry. It was just like a tomb. The body decomposed but Lucy's jacket was made from a synthetic material. The police are confident they will still be able to lift fibres from it. When you carried her down there, you'll have been in very close contact with the body, and these days all it takes is a hair.' The expression on his face seemed to change slightly then. He no longer looked so sure of himself. 'Then there's the forensic vacuum. That's a new piece of kit, by the way, and the police can't wait to try it on this case. It uses a highly sophisticated wet-vacuum sampling device to retrieve DNA from surfaces that can't be taken to the lab, such as the walls of a narrow tunnel that I am sure you will have brushed against repeat-edly while carrying the body. Then there is the blunt instrument that was found next to Lucy. The poker from the fire. It must have seemed like a sensible idea to bury the murder weapon with the victim, but forensic science has improved markedly since then and it's going to lead to a conviction, Freddie. Unless you were wearing gloves. Were you?'

328

Freddie took a long time to answer. The grim expression on his face told her he was trying and failing to find a way out of this. She was proved correct when he suddenly said, 'No. I wasn't. I didn't plan it.' Then he added, 'I didn't plan any of this.'

Chapter Fifty

Sarah didn't speak for a while, letting the knowledge that he was finished waft over him, but she wasn't done yet. She wanted to hear every bit of the truth and get him to admit it all, but she knew she would have to move gently and carefully, taking him there step by careful step, or he'd clam up on her.

'You were my anonymous caller?' He gave her a puzzled look, creasing up his face in what he must have assumed was genuine bemusement. 'You'd make a terrible actor, Freddie.'

'I don't know what you're . . .'

'Talking about? You used a voice synthesizer.'

'I'm baffled, frankly.' He was dismissive.

'What you did to Lucy was far more serious than a threatening phone call to me. I'm not even going to bother to press charges but you could at least own it. I thought you'd be brave enough to do that and I'll admit, you were clever. I was genuinely frightened.' He couldn't help but smirk at that, which was an admission of sorts. Sarah had chosen the right tactic – flatter the man, tell him how clever he was, and he was more likely to own up.

'Then I changed the locks, the late-night prowling stopped and there were no more presents waiting for me on the kitchen table.'

He gave it up then, lightly and with a shrug. 'You can't blame a man for trying.'

'Did you turn the portrait around because you thought it would scare me or because you just couldn't bear to look at her?'

'Oh please,' he scoffed, as if that would have been weakness on his part, 'I did it to unnerve you.'

'And it did. So did that dead fox on my kitchen table.'

'Bloody vermin,' he muttered. 'Any country person will tell you that, but city dwellers like you love foxes for some reason.'

'However did you get it?'

'I still know people,' he told her. 'I have influence, if not power.'

'What about the photo of Warren in the newspaper?' She could visualize it now. Warren Evans staring at Lucy Woodfell like he wanted to own her.

'A private investigator dug that up years ago and sent it to me. I think he expected me to pay him for it or at least give it to the police so they could question Warren Evans again. But money was tight by then and the last thing I needed was to get the police involved. The PI thought Evans had done it, but I obviously knew he hadn't. He was just a randy teen staring at an older girl he couldn't have. The PI picked the wrong man to send it to. Now if he'd given it to your aunt, she'd have been after Warren.'

'Just as you assumed I would be, but I knew that who-ever left it there wanted me to think Warren was the killer, and breaking in like that rather dented their credibility.'

'I didn't break in,' he said. 'I simply used the keys to my ancestral home.'

'That's not normally how it works when you sell a house, but then the rules never applied to you, did they, Freddie?

You did what you wanted, whenever you wanted. You mostly got away with it too, because there was no one to stop you. You couldn't be fired or forced out. You didn't have a boss and even your father couldn't control you.

'You were free to run as wild as you liked. The trouble with having no pleasure denied to you is how soon it becomes boring. It's the forbidden fruit that tastes the sweetest and there was only one fruit that was forbidden to you. Your own sister. Even in your world that was the last taboo. Everyone would have turned against you, especially when they worked out that her son was your son. He *is* yours, isn't he?'

'I suppose so,' he said in a dead voice, 'yes.'

'And that's why you killed Lucy?'

'She found out about us. She threatened to tell everyone.'

'She wouldn't have done that.'

'Lucy told me to my face that she would,' he protested, 'and I believed her.'

'Of course she wouldn't. Imagine the shame for everyone, including Lucy.' The look he gave Sarah made it clear that he had never considered this before.

'And then there was Toby,' Sarah continued. 'Do you really think she would have destroyed her nephew's life like that, a boy of thirteen, no matter who his father was?'

'I didn't have time to think it all through,' he explained, as if even he recognized the folly of it all now.

'You could have denied you were the father. There were other candidates.'

'James Pond, you mean? Everyone knew he was really a queen.'

Sephy had already confirmed that the landscape gardener, her earliest boyfriend, was more interested in Freddie than her, which was why he was never a suitable candidate as a lover.

'You could have just stayed silent.'

'Lucy said she would tell the captain.'

'And that I do believe. It's clear he was already in the area when she disappeared.' Freddie looked as if he didn't comprehend. 'Didn't you realize? He got there implausibly quickly from London after she vanished – too quickly for him to have made the journey that night. I think she had arranged to meet him beforehand, maybe in the village pub they used to go to, or perhaps just in his car for a more private word. That would have been sensible. There was no telling how he would react to the news.'

'She took his side against us both,' said Freddie, as if this was entirely unreasonable. 'Lucy seemed enraged by the idea of him being deceived, as if he is the first man alive to have been cheated on by his wife.'

'Not many wives cheat on their husbands with their brother.'

'How do you know?' he said. 'I think Lucy was secretly in love with him or she wouldn't have been so bloody determined to tell him everything.' He had to assign selfish motives to the whistle-blower, as if being appalled by the deviant behaviour of her half-siblings wasn't enough. 'I had no choice,' he concluded.

'So says every man who has ever done a vile thing.'

'You don't understand. She was blackmailing me!'

'Why? What could she want from you?'

'She wanted me out. She wanted me gone. Lucy claimed I was running the estate into the ground.'

'And so you were,' said Sarah simply. 'Your ideas were costing a fortune: the golf course, the zoo, a book no one bought, buying shares in a gold mine. She was right. You were incompetent.'

'How dare you?'

'No. How dare you? You're a murderer. You killed your own sister.'

It took him some considerable time to come up with a response to that. She realized it was the first time he had ever been accused of the crime and he'd probably always been in denial about it, even to himself.

'What happened?' she asked.

'I lost my temper. She was goading me and I ...' He clenched his fists, as if recalling the moment. 'I hit her, a couple of times actually, quite hard, and knocked her to the ground. She didn't scream. I think she was shocked, but I knew if I stopped she'd cry blue murder, so I grabbed her and pinned her down.' He put his hands out in front of him and looked down at them, as if reliving the moment.

'You strangled her?'

Freddie looked as if he was vividly recalling the memory of that moment. His breathing became strained and, as he spoke, he seemed to be on the verge of hyperventilating. 'Yes,' he managed. 'I did it to stop her from screaming, then I realized I couldn't let go. If I did, she would tell everyone about me and Sephy, so I just kept squeezing. I thought it was done so I let go and stood up, then she sort of gasped and I realized I hadn't finished the job. I couldn't face doing that again.'

'So you reached for the poker and hit her with it.'

He closed his eyes and nodded slowly. Sarah didn't say anything for a moment. This was the first true account of Lucy's death and it demanded some respect. Freddie looked very weary now that he had concluded his version of events.

'And you dragged her body to the priest hole so you could put it in the one place where no one would find it,' she said eventually.

Freddie opened his eyes. 'I could still deny all of this.'

'You could,' she admitted, 'but that's going to be hard to believe. She was found in your house, in a room kept secret for hundreds of years. Who else could have known about it? I did wonder about that,' she told him. 'How did Freddie, foolish, drugged-up Freddie, find a secret room even scholars couldn't locate? Then I suddenly realized how. *You* didn't find it, did you?'

It looked as if all resistance had gone from him by now. He knew how this looked.

'No,' was all he offered in reply.

'Toby did.'

His silence was the confirmation she needed.

'The Latin prodigy,' she recalled. 'Even at that tender age.'

Freddie laughed bitterly. 'You should have seen him.' And he pointed as if the plaque was in front of them now, '"Uncle Freddie, I don't think that means what people think it means." It didn't take long. We found it together but he worked it out. I realized then that he was going to be someone. Such a clever little boy.'

She cut through his pride. 'Does he know?' And when

he did not understand, 'That his aunt was buried beneath that secret room?'

'No.' He was emphatic about that.

'Sephy knew, though. You had to tell her so she could help cover everything up for you. Between you, you cooked up that story about Lucy heading for the beach. You ruined Warren Evans' life with that, by the way.'

'Whatever,' he said loftily.

'Sephy told me she didn't want to see you go to jail. That you killing Lucy was as much her fault as yours. Even now, she still blames herself for the things you did.'

'Sephy was always the martyr.'

'Even for a bunch of inbred aristos, you really are a completely fucked-up family, aren't you?' His silence seemed to acknowledge that. 'I'm going to write about this,' she told him. 'I could perhaps keep Toby out of it but only if you admit everything to the police.'

'What difference would a confession make after all these years?'

'It would mean justice,' she said. 'That's what my aunt Evelyn wanted too, so yes, I want your confession.'

He thought for a while. 'All right then,' he said calmly, 'I killed Lucy.'

'Tell it to the police.'

'Perhaps,' he said. 'We'll see.'

This was neither agreement nor refusal, so Sarah pressed on. 'Were you always just planning to leave her there?' she asked.

He shook his head. 'I was going to wait till all the fuss had died down then move her, but it never did. Not for years. I thought they would assume Lucy had drowned or run off to start a new life abroad or something, but people stayed fascinated with her. It got to the stage where it was too risky to even contemplate moving her, much less find a new spot to bury her. Besides, after a while . . .' His voice tailed off but she knew he meant it would be too unpleasant to move a body in a bad condition. 'I thought it was better to leave her where she was.'

'You lived there for years, knowing that the body of the woman you killed, your own half-sister, was right under your feet. How did you sleep at night?'

'I don't believe in ghosts,' he said. 'The drugs and the booze helped. I don't sleep much anyway.'

'And when you finally had to sell the place, didn't you worry a new owner might find her?'

'Of course I did but I had no choice. The money was all gone.'

'So you sold up and hoped for the best, and when you learned who the new buyer was?'

'I bloody shit myself,' he said. 'I thought, of all the people to take on the place, why did it have to be her? I was told the buyer was anonymous. I assumed it was a foreigner with money, not fucking Evelyn. I admit for the first five years or so, I was worried. I kept thinking it was all over. Evelyn would find her and that would be that. If you think I escaped punishment you are wrong. Imagine going to bed every day for years and wondering if it will be your last night of freedom? Try and picture what it's like to hear a knock at the door and automatically assume that this time it really is the police coming to take you away. It drove me crazy. I seriously contemplated ending it all. I really did. I found no peace. None.' Then he sighed. 'But the years went by and nothing happened. I thought that if Evelyn was going to find her and work it all out, she would have done it by then, so maybe I'd got away with it.'

'You almost did but you made a mistake,' she told him. 'You didn't die before Evelyn.'

He let out a snort of a laugh at that. 'She handed it over to you and you found Lucy.' He mock applauded her. 'Clever girl.'

'Not clever,' she told him, 'just not too close to it all. Evelyn probably would have worked it out herself if she'd been a bit more detached, but she really cared about Lucy and knew you all too well to think of you objectively. Whereas I . . .'

'Don't give a fuck about any of us?' he asked.

'Correct.'

'What happens next? I'd offer to bribe you but I'm absolutely skint. I could threaten you, I suppose,' he said half-heartedly.

'It won't make any difference. You can't stop it now. I've already given everything to Evelyn's solicitor and the police. You're too late.'

'There are others who might harm you, you know, if this damages Toby.'

'Shady government people? Spooks? I don't think it really works like that. If this became fully public, a dozen equally entitled, venal men would fight each other to step into his shoes, though it's not Toby Ramsay's fault his father and mother are brother and sister. It's the first time I've felt sympathy for him.'

'So you don't want to destroy Toby?' he sounded surprised. 'Only me?'

'You destroyed yourself years ago, Freddie, without my help.'

He raised his mug in a mock toast. 'Touché.' Another sigh. 'I suppose I probably deserve it.'

'There's no probably about it. You killed Lucy and raped your own sister.'

She hoped her words might have some small impact on what remained of his conscience. Apparently not. 'Sephy is one of life's victims. She likes to do what she's told. I blame Father.'

'Why? Did he rape her too?'

'Don't be absurd.' He seemed strangely disgusted at that notion, while viewing his own abhorrent treatment of his sister as perfectly acceptable. 'He trained her to smile and say "yes" and "thank you very much, sir".' He mimicked Sephy: '"Marry the captain? Yes, of course, Daddy. Absolutely. Why not? I mean, it's only my life. Alex darling, you want me? No problem. You want a family too, well okay. There's just one little problem, you can't have children but don't worry, I'll do what I always do. I'll go and see my big brother and he will make it all better."'

Sarah was sickened by this. 'Did she tell you she wanted a child?'

He shook his head. 'God, no! I thought she had all that taken care of. On the pill, I assumed. She told me later she came off it, to give Alex the one thing he wanted: an heir.

'I hadn't seen her for ages. I actually thought she might have been serious about giving their marriage a try, but when she offered to come up and help me crisis-manage the estate I thought, I know what this is. It's a reconcili-ation and an admission. She can't live without me. I didn't realize she was a brood mare and I was her stallion. She only told me afterwards and by then it was too late. She was already showing.'

'How did you feel about it?'

'I wanted to throw her down the stairs.'

'Nice.'

'Well, I was worried, see. What if it looked nothing like him? What if he suspected who the real father was? Do you know how many men the captain slaughtered during the war? It might have been dozens. He was a killer.'

'Takes one to know one, Freddie,' she said. 'And when the baby came? Did he suspect anything?'

'He was too happy and stupid.'

'But you were still worried? That's why you lost your temper with Lucy when she brought those old photos of you as children to show everyone. The resemblance must have been uncanny.'

'I overreacted. He didn't suspect anything at that point. It only became messy when he wanted another. It wasn't the heir that finished him off, it was the quest for a spare.'

'You didn't fancy a repeat performance, then?'

'No, thanks.' He snorted. 'I made bloody sure precau-tions were taken after that.'

'By then the captain had sought medical advice,' she told him. 'He couldn't understand why he wasn't able to do what he had done before, when his wife was so healthy and fertile. Imagine that poor man's shock when the clinic informed him that he would never be able to have chil-dren and could never have *had* children.'

'Not my fault.' There was no sympathy or empathy from Freddie. 'I didn't force him to marry Sephy. I didn't deliberately get her up the duff. If you want to class one of us as a monster, it's her.'

'None of this would have happened if you had just kept your hands off your sister. Whatever strange and twisted bond you had, you were the one with all the power; you were older, stronger, and it all began because you raped her.'

'Have you really given the police everything?' he blurted. It seemed he hadn't quite abandoned hope.

'Yes.'

'Then why even come here? What do you actually want from me?'

'To hear it from you,' she said. 'To confirm what I already knew, to look you in the eye and tell you that it's finally over and that the next time you hear a knock at the door, it really will be the police.'

'I know it's over,' he said. 'Now, just go, will you, and leave me alone.'

'You know, it might even come as a bit of a relief. If you were to confess to them.'

'Get a good lawyer and shuffle into court on a Zimmer frame?' he asked. 'Concoct some story about it all being an accident and that I didn't really mean to kill her? Maybe get away with manslaughter and do ten years in prison, at my age? No chance.'

That probably left him with only one way out, but if he thought Sarah might have some sympathy for him, then he was very much mistaken. She'd finally nailed the murdering bastard and he'd admitted everything to her. Sarah had known it was never going to be easy and she'd been right to have a back-up plan, in case he denied everything or tried to blame Sephy, as she'd anticipated he might. Slipping in all that information about DNA and forensics had been the deciding factor in securing Freddie's confession. It was all the sweeter because Sarah knew something he didn't. She had made it up. Not all of it, of course. The science behind it was true and the equipment available to law enforcement agencies these days, but she had found that out on the internet. There was no guarantee that Northumbria police would be conducting those tests on the tunnel or the murder weapon, but Freddie didn't know that. Sarah just had to make him believe they would.

She turned off the recording she had just secretly made of his confession on her phone, slipped it into her jacket pocket and stood up. 'Goodbye, Freddie.'

Chapter Fifty-One

JUSTICE FOR LUCY AT LAST!

Crime author cracks cold case that left police baffled for
decades. Half-brother questioned for murder is PM's uncle!

Bestselling author, Sarah Hollis, proved she was a crime-writing
chip off the old block by solving a cold case that has stumped
everyone for almost four decades, including her late aunt,
million-selling novelist Evelyn Moore, and the police! Now
Sarah looks set to inherit the eccentric but much-loved mystery
writer's fortune, including the estate where the body of Evelyn's
closest chum, Lucy Woodfell, was finally discovered.

In an incredible twist, worthy of one of Evelyn's page-
turning books, the dead woman's half-brother has been arrested
and questioned by police in connection with her disappearance.
He is none other than new Prime Minister Toby Ramsay's
favourite uncle, Freddie, a man the PM once described as like
a surrogate father to him, following his own dad's fiery death,
in a car crash that might have been an accident but was believed
by many to have been suicide.

The journalist's enthusiasm for this story was obvious.
Strangely, it was the same reporter who had written the
derogatory piece about Sarah being a grasping failure and
Evelyn a mad old woman. Dickie explained the change of
angle: 'You're the hero now. They like you because you

solved the case and turned it into a great story for them. And they want to hear more. They'd like to buy the exclusive rights.'

'Would you mind giving them my response, Dickie?'

'I'd be happy to.'

'Using your best formal solicitor words, could you politely tell them to fuck off?'

He chuckled at that. 'It would be my pleasure, Sarah. I hope you won't take it the wrong way if I say there are times when you definitely remind me of your aunt, and I do mean that as a compliment.'

'I know you do,' she smiled, 'and I will take it as one.'

Freddie sounded like a hunted man when he called her early the next morning.

'They are after me,' he told Sarah. 'They're all after me now. The police and the press, everyone.'

'If you're looking for sympathy, Freddie, you've come to the wrong person.'

'No, I wasn't expecting that,' and even though he was obviously phoning her from a mobile with an imperfect signal, she still detected a sigh, 'but I thought you might want to know about my confession.'

'Oh.' She was surprised to hear this.

'You win, Sarah. I've admitted everything. Not in person, not yet, but I have written it all down. I even sent you a copy. Wasn't that nice of me?' She wondered if he was expecting her to thank him. 'It should be in your letter box by now. I've sent the same letter to the police and instructed my solicitor to release it to the press, so I can, what is it that they say these days, get ahead of the story.'

'So you've admitted to killing Lucy?'

'Yes.'

'Did you give the reason why?'

'You didn't think it would be that easy, did you? At least this way you have your culprit. Isn't that enough?' There was a pause. 'I . . . er . . . won't be calling you again.' And there was such finality to that statement that she became even more convinced he would never see the inside of a court room, much less a jail cell.

'Goodbye,' he told her brightly and then the line went dead.

Sarah wouldn't normally have checked the mailbox this early but a letter of confession from Freddie was an irresistible lure. She opened the door and padded across the gravel courtyard in her slippers and pyjamas, until she reached the far wall. There, she opened up the metal box and, sure enough, she found an envelope with her name on it.

Her first reaction to the absence of a postmark was confusion. Then she heard the unmistakeable sound of a car engine being turned on from the driveway. It was out of sight but not far away and emitting a loud, throaty noise, the kind you heard from an old petrol engine in a classic car.

Freddie still had the key to the gates and she hadn't bothered to change that lock. Sarah turned and started to run back to the house but she already knew it would be too late. She could hear the engine revving. It was roaring like a lion now and she wasn't even a third of the way there.

Nought to sixty in nine seconds?

And she had to run the entire length of the courtyard to reach the safety of the front door. No chance.

One of her slippers came off and she almost fell, so she kicked off the other one then ran as hard and as fast as she could in her bare feet, over the sharp, stony gravel, ignoring the pain, because she could hear the car behind her as it started to race down the driveway towards her. Sarah didn't dare look over her shoulder. Instead, she pumped her arms hard, powering her legs forward as fast as she could. The sound of the car's engine grew louder. Freddie was in that car and he was going to run her down. He had trapped her with the bait of that confession letter, and like a fool she had taken it. Now he would kill her, then himself, possibly in the same act, as he had to be heading towards the house at top speed if he wanted to make the crash fatal for her.

Sarah focused all her attention on the half-open door and prayed that it would not suddenly catch a gust of wind and close on her, because there would be no time to open it again. He would smash the car into her and she would die there, crushed between Freddie's precious Jaguar and the solid wooden door.

Behind her the car careered into the open gravel area between the postbox and the door, and she heard it slide as Freddie tried to correct its trajectory. It must have straightened and he pressed down hard on the accelerator once more, as it commenced its final, full-speed drive towards her.

Christ, it was going to be close, and she knew she had to gamble then. Sarah got as near as she dared, before

346

launching herself forward into a dive and throwing herself at the front door with as much force as she could muster. It was a counter-intuitive move and pain shot through her wrists, arms and body as she hit the door, forced it wide and was propelled through it, before landing heavily on the stone floor.

Just as she made it through the door, there was an almighty bang as the Jaguar tried to follow her. Its front end took the full force of the crash into the solid stone walls of the door frame. Sarah instinctively covered her face with her arms and buried herself as low as possible into the floor, fully expecting to be killed by flying debris. She did not open her eyes again until the terrible sounds of the crash, wrought metal smashing into unyielding rock as pieces flew from it, had fully died down.

Sarah was astonished to find she had escaped without further injury. She was too relieved to care about the cuts to her feet from the gravel or the bruises from her dive through the doorway. She turned and gingerly sat up. She was covered in small pieces of broken glass from the windscreen of the Jaguar. It was lodged in the doorway but mercifully it was not alight. She'd feared an explosion, but all that she saw was steam hissing out from beneath the mangled bonnet.

Cautiously, she got to her feet. Surely Freddie could not have survived that crash, but where was he? She walked to the car and peered inside but Freddie wasn't there. How could he have climbed from that twisted wreckage? He had to have been at least severely injured. How could he have walked away from this? It didn't seem possible.

She looked at the smashed windscreen, then she realized. He wouldn't have worn a seat belt for his last journey. Sarah slowly turned to look behind her and there he was.

Freddie had been catapulted through the windscreen at speed. While Sarah had covered her eyes and pressed her face into the floor, he had sailed right over her and his body now lay in a twisted, crumpled heap behind her. Freddie was a broken mess. There was a pool of blood around him and his limbs were horribly broken, with bare bone protruding through flesh and ripped clothing. One of his shoes had come off and it lay next to a head smothered in blood.

Justice for Lucy, she thought.

Chapter Fifty-Two

I, Frederick Woodfell, being of sound mind, more or less, and not at all coerced by anyone, hereby confess to the murder of my half-sister, Lucy Woodfell.

I will go to my grave with the guilt and regret I have carried with me for the last thirty-six years. I cannot and will not divulge the reason why I killed Lucy, but now that her body has been found at our ancestral home, Cragsmoor Manor, I know the finger of suspicion will forever point in my direction. In order to finally put an end to malicious gossip that has harmed others, I freely confess that I, and I alone, am responsible for this terrible act that has scarred my soul. Lucy witnessed a side of me that I have always been ashamed of and for that reason I felt the need to silence her, before she was able to reveal it to others.

I apologize for the distress this has caused those who loved her and for the many hours of wasted work from law enforcement officers, who searched fruitlessly for any trace of Lucy. I regret this but can at least put an end to further speculation. I take my motives to the grave but all else I confess openly now. Someone once told me it would come as a relief and in some small way it has.

Regretfully yours,
Frederick Woodfell

Chapter Fifty-Three

December

By the time Sarah had done a deal on the house, Toby Ramsay had already stepped down, making him one of the shortest serving prime ministers in British history. He cited 'an endless series of baseless accusations and salacious media interest in a family tragedy, distracting me from the business of government and rendering it impossible'. An anonymous friend of his told journalists that, though Toby had always coveted the job of prime minister, he never really wanted to do the actual work, so leaving Number Ten was probably something of a relief.

Sarah hoped her aunt Evie might have appreciated the fact that she didn't sell Cragsmoor Manor to a foreign investor or property dealer. Instead, she allowed Literary Heritage to take over the place for their permanent exhibition of twentieth-century authors. Where better than the house that had inspired Evelyn Moore's most famous work, *The Gallows Tree*? The fact that Cragsmoor was also the setting of a scandalous, true-life, recently solved murder was even better. They couldn't sign the contract quick enough.

Sarah had a few conditions, including a healthy annual budget for restoration and repairs to the minor structural damage caused by a Jaguar car slamming into the door frame. In return she charged them a tiny annual rent and benefitted from the knowledge that both the house and her aunt's legacy would be in safe hands.

Dickie seemed genuinely delighted that, against all odds, Sarah had secured her inheritance, and he took her through every aspect of it, even coming up to Cragsmoor himself to personally oversee the signing of the contract with Literary Heritage. He had already informed her there was a cottage in the village that went with the estate. 'Your aunt kept it empty when her last tenant moved on. She suspected you might prefer it to living in the manor but, as always, Sarah, the choice is yours.' That made the decision to let Cragsmoor go an even easier one. She decided to sell her aunt's London apartment but keep the cottage, which was a far nicer home than her old flat. Strangely, Sarah realized she no longer missed the capital. She had found a new home here, under the oddest of circumstances.

At her final meeting with Literary Heritage, the contract was signed and she left them to look around with Dickie, who handed Sarah an envelope on her way out. 'I almost forgot,' he told her. 'Remember I told you that your aunt wrote two letters? Because your investigation was a success, you get to open this one. Well done, Sarah.'

She thanked him and pocketed the envelope, deciding to read it later in a more private moment. Her walk down to the village took her to Patrick's cottage and he came out to meet her.

'How did it go?' he asked.

'I just gave the house away,' she told him. 'It wasn't practical to try and keep it on,' and she explained who the new leaseholders were. 'Don't worry, they want you too.

There's a long list of jobs to do and I suspect there always will be.'

'If they want me to help them out, I could,' he said easily, as if it wasn't of huge importance to him, either way. She had actually insisted he was kept on, along with Mrs Jenkins. 'Just keep her away from the visitors,' Sarah had advised them.

'I'm sorry it didn't work out.' He meant the house, or at least she hoped he did. They had only been seeing each other for a few weeks, after all, but it was going well. Then he asked, 'Will you be moving on?' She was struck by the worried look on his face.

'I'll be sticking around.' And she told him about the cottage.

He brightened at that. 'You'll be doing a bit of writing, then? Nice place for it.'

He was right. She would be doing a bit of writing. Sarah's latest book was finally finished and it had turned out darker than she had imagined. Her heroine had not only murdered her cheating, con artist of a boyfriend but run the police ragged afterwards, literally getting away with murder in the end. Polly, her editor, was almost as happy with the first draft as she had been about all the publicity Sarah had gained from solving the Lucy Woodfell case.

Soon she would have to start thinking about the next book. 'It is a good place for writing,' she agreed, 'but not today. I fancy a day off, for once.'

'Any plans?'

'No,' and it felt good to not have any.

'How about lunch? In the pub,' then he added, 'with

me, I mean?' as if that wasn't immediately clear. 'My treat, obviously.'

'How about you buy lunch today,' she offered, 'and I buy it tomorrow?'

'Tomorrow?' he smiled. 'I like the sound of that.'

They walked to the pub and Patrick went to the bar while Sarah sat at a table by a window. The bar staff were serving other customers while Patrick waited patiently for his turn, giving Sarah enough time to look at the last piece of correspondence she would ever receive from her aunt Evelyn. She opened the envelope and began to read.

Dearest Sarah

If Dickie has allowed you to open this letter, then well done. You did it! I thought you might. Clever Sarah.

I always felt you had twice my intellect and you are, of course, a far better writer than I ever was, though I know that kind of praise sits ill with you. It shouldn't, coming as it does from 'the great Evelyn Moore'. Ha, ha. My view? If you aren't suffering from imposter syndrome in this game then you probably have a monstrous ego already and that rarely ends well.

By the way, in case you are wondering, I wouldn't really have left all that money to the Tory party. I might be 'slightly right of Ghengis Khan', as you once told me, but I don't want Toby Ramsay and his pals squandering everything I've earned.

I prefer dogs. They don't screw each other over. I would have left it all to them if you hadn't stepped up and done what I asked of you. So, if you can spare some of your inheritance for a generous donation to the Battersea Dogs Home, in my memory, that would be nice. I'll leave the amount up to you.

You have it all now, of course, but I was going to leave you a bit more money anyway, even if you had come up with nothing, so you could write in peace, unhindered by the need to squander your time in some dreadful day job, overseen by a talentless boss you would only end up carrying.

I regret I won't be there to look Lucy's killer in the eye or to find out why they did it, but I'll admit I am also slightly relieved that I will never actually have to confront the bitter reality of what happened to my dear friend. I'm only sorry I had to inflict that on you.

Signing off now for good, with love and thanks. I hope you make great use of your inheritance, my girl. You've earned it!

Love
Evelyn

Acknowledgements

Huge thanks to the team at Penguin for helping me to bring this story to life. My editors, Joel Richardson and Grace Long, as well as Clare Bowron, all worked incredibly hard and showed great patience while I finally pulled this one together. We got there in the end and I am very proud of this book. Thanks also to Sarah Bance for her work, especially the tips on how to make the Latin sound right, but not quite perfect enough to fool her namesake in the book. Further thanks to Maxine Hitchcock, Sriya Varadharajan, Eloise Austin and Emma Henderson at Michael Joseph.

I am lucky enough to have the best literary agent in the business, Phil Patterson, at Marjacq. Thanks again for all of your support, Phil. I couldn't do it without you.

The following people have all helped me at crucial points along the way and I would like to thank them. Adam Pope, Andy Davis, Nikki Selden, Gareth Chennells, Andrew Local, Stuart Britton, David Shapiro, Peter Day, Tony Frobisher, Katie Charlton, Gemma Sealey, Susan Jackson, Ion Mills, Peter Hammans, Emad Akhtar and Keshini Naidoo.

Love and a very big thank you to my wife Alison, for putting up with an author in the house and never losing faith in me. I wouldn't have got this far without your unflagging belief.

Finally, huge thanks to my amazing daughter, Erin, who makes every day worthwhile and keeps me smiling, even when the words are refusing to cooperate. Love you always.

He just wanted a decent book to read ...

Not too much to ask, is it? It was in 1935 when Allen Lane, Managing Director of Bodley Head Publishers, stood on a platform at Exeter railway station looking for something good to read on his journey back to London. His choice was limited to popular magazines and poor-quality paperbacks – the same choice faced every day by the vast majority of readers, few of whom could afford hardbacks. Lane's disappointment and subsequent anger at the range of books generally available led him to found a company – and change the world.

'We believed in the existence in this country of a vast reading public for intelligent books at a low price, and staked everything on it'
Sir Allen Lane, 1902–1970, founder of Penguin Books

The quality paperback had arrived – and not just in bookshops. Lane was adamant that his Penguins should appear in chain stores and tobacconists, and should cost no more than a packet of cigarettes.

Reading habits (and cigarette prices) have changed since 1935, but Penguin still believes in publishing the best books for everybody to enjoy. We still believe that good design costs no more than bad design, and we still believe that quality books published passionately and responsibly make the world a better place.

So wherever you see the little bird – whether it's on a piece of prize-winning literary fiction or a celebrity autobiography, political tour de force or historical masterpiece, a serial-killer thriller, reference book, world classic or a piece of pure escapism – you can bet that it represents the very best that the genre has to offer.

Whatever you like to read – trust Penguin.